Keys to Your Heart

DanScribe Publishing

Keys To Your Heart

A Collection of Short Stories

ISBN 13:978-1517627324

www.danneyclark.com / www.danscribepublishing.com

The persons and events portrayed in this work of fiction are the creations of the author, and any resemblance to persons living or dead is purely coincidental.

Printed in the United States of America

Acknowledgements

To God our Creator, the Author and Finisher of our faith,
to family and friends, readers, supporters, vendors,
to all who put their trust in Jesus for their success,
and to my cover designer, editor and friend, Larry Patrick.

Introduction

While **Keys to Your Heart** is uniquely different than the original **Spoonfuls from Heaven** in content, they are very much alike in that they portray everyday life and showcase the result of our choices when dealing with life's challenges.

Each story has been specifically written for ages from late elementary through adult. The author suggests that parents of young children read these stories to determine in advance which stories they deem suitable for their own children.

These stories are written as they are given me by God with little outside influence from myself or the world. Some readers, I believe, may see themselves clearly as actors in these stories, and take heart if you do, because these words were meant for you. – dc

Table of Contents

Disappearing into the Pages

"Where is your sister?" Claire asked.

"I haven't any idea," I answered. "Probably in her room reading a book like she always is," I added sarcastically.

"Well, go find her and tell her that dinner is ready," Claire ordered.

I rolled my eyes and made sure my reaction to her order was noted, before standing to begin climbing the stairway which led to our rooms.

At the first landing I yelled, "dinner is ready," but of course received no reply.

She'd be wearing her headset and listening to music while reading some new book, I thought resentfully. She knew when dinner time was; but always, always rudely awaited a special invitation to join the family and... I was always the messenger sent with that invitation.

"Sar," I yelled at the top of my voice before entering her room without knocking, "dinner is ready, come on."

Sarah was twelve, the oldest of us girls, about to move on from the sixth grade into middle school. She'd been my hero until last year, but now she seemed to live in a bubble of her own making, a dream world where nothing but her books mattered.

The light was on, pillows were stacked against the headboard and I could see where her body had made its imprint in them, but there was no sign of Sarah. I could hear a song playing from her headphones lying on the bed. I moved to the bathroom which we shared, and pounded on the door.

"Dinner's ready," I screamed, but got no response.

The knob turned easily in my hand and I stuck my head in but was greeted with only darkness and empty space.

~ ~

"And who be ye?" a voice boomed from the surrounding darkness.

Sarah's eyes struggled to acclimate to the darkness in her new surroundings while trying to grasp where she was. Still clutched in her hand was her new book, *The Dragon Prince*.

"Why have you come?" the voice asked without waiting for an answer to the first question.

"I'm Sarah, Sarah Goodfellow," she answered, trying to sound self-assured, "I don't know where I am or why I've come."

"You don't know? Well, of course you know, Sarah Goodfellow," the voice stated loudly. "You've come to meet the Prince."

Sarah withered beneath the booming voice while becoming aware that she may not be dreaming as she had at first suspected.

"Why have I been brought here?" she asked

"Brought? You've not been brought," came the answer. "You invited yourself."

"Are you the Prince?" Sarah asked in a tiny frightened voice.

"Me, the Prince? Hardly so," came his laughing reply. "I'm but the gatekeeper."

A smallish form stepped from the blackness, it had a mushroom shaped head, two prominent elongated ears and stood a tad over three feet tall. Sarah could see its yellow, deep-set eyes even in the darkness; they were set closely beside his sharp protruding nose. They seemed to radiate a light of their own which winked off and on as his heavy lids opened and closed unnaturally. She wanted to laugh but held her tongue not knowing what sort of thing he really was.

He was dressed in a medieval manner with a short sword dangling uselessly from a wide belt around his more than ample midsection. A kind of chain-mail cap covered his nearly bald pate, allowing several errant red hairs to be seen hanging here and there. He continued toward her until he was back-lit by some sort of natural light emanating from the walls of the cavern where they stood. The light appeared to be a sort of luminescence like that of a lightening bug or firefly.

He stopped, sneering wickedly and exposed what few yellow teeth remained in his slit of a mouth. When he spoke this time, it was not the deep bellowing sound that had previously greeted her, but a guttural snarling nasal tone.

"Wye, ye be nothing but a child," he said depreciatingly, "a wee bit of a thing at that."

Sarah took offense at the little troll-looking man and replied, "I'm not a child, I am nearly thirteen years old, and as you can easily see, much taller than you."

Momentarily, a crafty smile slipped from his lips as they covered his rotting teeth, but he soon recovered and answered, "and I be the king of the castle by all accounts. I've served the Prince for a hundred years before you were more than a speck of dust."

~ ~

"She's not up there," I shouted as I descended the stairway, returning to the kitchen, "unless she's hiding."

Claire gave me a worried look before drying her hands on a towel and retracing my steps. All four of us followed like baby ducks behind their mother.

"See, I told you," I said, pointing out her obviously empty bed.

Claire turned to us and said, "Everyone spread out and look for her, no dinner until we find her."

Claire, as we all called her, was our step-mother; our natural mother had died of some rare disease which we could not pronounce. When our father had re-married he had chosen a younger woman, hardly a dozen years older than Sarah. She was a dutiful wife and a caring person who kept order in the house, which it had lacked without her. I think we all liked her but did not really see her in the role of a mother.

Just then, Father came through the front door, announcing his return.

"Up here," I yelled out first. "Sarah has disappeared and we are searching for her."

I got a sour look from Claire for my report. Dad made the landing in three or four giant steps, concern written all over his face. "Disappeared," he said, "how could she have disappeared?"

"She's not gone," Claire said reassuringly. "She's just not in her room and we haven't found where she's hiding yet."

"Hiding? Why would she be hiding?" Dad asked her simplistically.

Dad was really out of touch with the workings of a child's mind, I thought. It had been our mother who understood us, taught us, and had grown with us into her role. Father had always been either working or too tired from working to engage us and really get to know us. Claire, on the other hand, was not so far removed by age that she could still understand most of what we girls presented to her as normal. Luckily, we had no brothers.

~ ~

A hiss, followed by a burst of light issued from a sulfur match which had taken up residence in the creature's hand. Its flickering flame made his features seem all the more grotesque as he appraised his guest, before using it to light a nearby torch.

"Ye are strangely dressed," he observed as much to himself as to his guest.

Sarah looked down at herself recognizing that she still wore her school clothes. Make a note she thought, do not get them dirty or torn, or Claire will have my head. The family budget could not afford the burden of carelessness or waste. Odd, she thought, that she'd care about such things when seemingly having been transported to another place and time.

"Have ye no shoes?" was the question that refocused Sarah's attention on her present predicament.

To her chagrin she remembered that she had taken her shoes off before grabbing her book and lying on the bed while waiting for dinner. With the observation came notice that the floor of the cave was both rough and cold on her stocking feet.

"I've left them behind," Sarah admitted, then justified herself by saying, "I hadn't planned on taking a journey."

"It won't do, it won't do at all, we'll have to find a pair," he said as if to himself, "before you meet the Prince."

Sarah was trying hard to recall exactly what she'd been reading before finding herself here in this strange place. The book, as if in answer to her questions, began to feel strangely heavy in her grasp. As she took the weight of it in both hands, she raised it from the darkness and into the torchlight. The gatekeeper shrunk back at the sight of it as its cover came to life in the light.

~ ~

"Think back," Father said, "when did you last see Sarah?"

Beginning with Claire, each in turn verbalized their recollection of the events leading up to the present moment. It was Laura, the most outspoken of the twins, who made us aware that Sarah's shoes remained in the room. That fact gave us comfort, then as quickly took it away as we noted that if she was not in the house, she'd not have gone voluntarily without them. Thus, we began our frantic game of hide and seek.

~ ~

The black cover with the golden gilt outlining the form of a man-like creature with a dragon's head seemed to come alive in her hands, causing her to nearly drop it. The artist who had created it was both talented and proficient, seamlessly making the transition from the figure of a medieval knight to a fierce dragon. Sarah could sense the fear that this creature felt just looking at it... she felt it as well.

"Does this place have a name?" Sarah dared to inquire.

"Indeed it does," the gatekeeper answered. "And you'll soon know it," he added, smiling devilishly.

The light from the torch seemed to cause the walls of the corridor to come alive with moving figures, as the light ebbed and flowed with every step they took. Sarah's imagination painted pictures of writhing serpents and ghostly forms in her mind's eye. After several minutes, the floor of the cavern began a noticeable upward tilt, making it less easy to walk and harder for the barefooted Sarah to keep up the pace.

When at last they stopped, a steel-barred gate covered the expanse of the corridor, and behind it a large room became partially visible. The gatekeeper smiled smugly as he removed a key from the leather pouch hanging from his belt and applied it to the lock. Sarah felt his sense of pride and self-worth increase knowing that it'd been trusted to his care.

For the first time, Sarah could hear sounds, sounds not coming from either she nor her guide. They seemed to be coming from the very walls around them. Sounds like a far away moan or wind blowing through the barren winter trees late at night. She felt chilled, empty and alone, hopeless and afraid. The gatekeeper hesitated as he stepped through the opened gate and into the room, then resumed his course but at a much slower pace.

"Wait," Sarah said. "I need to rest, my feet hurt."

She watched as his form continued on without slowing and thought she heard, "there's time enough for rest when 'ere dead."

~ ~

They searched every nook and cranny of the house, from the basement to the attic and then back again, but found no clue. The back door remained locked and the front was visible from the kitchen where Claire and the children had been, making it unlikely she could have left without being noticed. Then there was the issue of the shoes, no one would leave without their shoes in the cold of the winter. Father checked and rechecked each window and found them all locked from the inside.

Finally, as darkness fell, Father went to the phone and dialed the number for the Sheriff. He explained what he knew and what he didn't know, answering questions in one or two word sentences. "No," (there is no trouble at home) "no," (she doesn't have a boyfriend) "no," (no one had an argument with her today) "yes," (she is doing well in school) "yes," (she seems happy and not depressed) and so on. Finally he hung up the phone and we all waited until a knock on the front door indicated the deputies had arrived.

Two men, both larger than our father, were invited in. Their grim faces indicated that they were taking Sarah's absence seriously. They talked first to Claire, then Father, before asking each of us to join them in the living room where we told them what little we knew. I had the impression that they suspected that she had not just walked away of her own accord. When we re-gathered in the kitchen, Laura reminded everyone present that the shoes were the key to the mystery and that she had been the first to notice them. The deputies smiled and nodded appreciatively.

~ ~

'Nearly numb,' Sarah thought to herself, 'my feet are nearly numb, I can hardly feel them anymore,' but still she followed. Her socks were worn through and bloody on the bottom where sharp stones had left their mark on her feet. At the foot of the long stone stairway she paused and looked upward. At the top, standing by the closed door, the little figure stood waiting.

At the landing, a pair of torches burned brightly enjoying the oxygen that the new elevation brought with it. Along a wall a stone bench beckoned to the tired girl, a pair of clean socks and shoes lying atop it.

"Do you have a name?" Sarah asked as she seated herself and put on the socks without asking permission.

"Gog," he answered in muffled tones, "of Magog."

The shoes fit perfectly but hurt her cut and bruised feet as she slipped them on. He did not mention and she did not question where they had come from. While she rested she noted that Gog seemed to be waiting for something to happen before opening the massive door.

~ ~

"Please come," Father was heard to say into the phone, there were both fear and tears in his eyes as he hung it up. He had called our pastor and explained what little he knew about Sarah's absence from the family. Within a few minutes there was a knock on the door and Pastor James and his wife Connie stood on our step waiting for entrance.

Connie rushed to Claire and took her in her arms while the pastor took Father's hand in both of his and led him to a seat nearby. We stood watching and wondering what we should be doing. I hadn't seen either of them since mother's funeral. We had stopped going to church when our prayers for God's healing had failed, but were now at the point of returning, not having any other place to turn. I'm ten, did I tell you that? I'm just a year and a half younger than Sarah, but three years older than the twins.

"Please come here," Pastor James said, holding out his hands.

The seven of us gathered together in the living room and joined hands in kind of a circle.

"Let's pray for Sarah," he said gently. "God knows where she has gone and God will protect and return her to us."

I closed my eyes and tried to pray while listening to him praying, but couldn't concentrate. I sneaked a peak at the twins who were trying to look serious in spite of the grins they were wearing on their faces. I frowned at them so they closed their eyes and moved their lips.

"...and in Jesus' name we pray for protection of our sister and daughter Sarah from the Evil One," Pastor James said, before closing with "Amen."

~ ~

Gog had just opened the doors and had motioned Sarah forward when a large gust of wind grabbed it and slammed it shut, shaking ancient dust from the surrounding walls. Gog, who had been flattened by the force of it, lay on the landing with a look of terror on his face. Somehow, the ridiculous scene struck Sarah as funny and she began to laugh. The more she laughed, the more she wanted to laugh until there were tears of joy running down both cheeks while she sat on the bench shaking uncontrollably.

The gilded brass doorknobs began to shake and turn of their own accord until finally falling away from the great doors and rolling down the steps. There remained no way to enter or exit the room which lay beyond.

~ ~

"Did I miss dinner?" Sarah asked while walking down the stairs, rubbing her sleep-filled eyes.

"I'm sorry, I must have fallen asleep," she apologized, before recognizing their guests.

"Pastor James, Connie," she said. "It has been so long, I'm so glad you've come to visit us."

When we all rushed to her, embraced her, and kissed her, Sarah had no idea what was going on, just that she was loved by both man and God... that was enough.

– The End –

Brown Dog

If he had a name no one seemed to know it. He was nothing special and seemed to more or less just blend into the background of the summer landscape. He was always nearby, always watching and waiting for a chance to play and frolic with the neighborhood children. They just called him "Brown Dog." The date was 1955, rock and roll was king, cars boasted V8 engines and automatic transmissions, radios and heaters. Jet planes were replacing propeller driven ones, and the sound barrier had long since been broken by the famous Chuck Yeager.

Laid out in 1854, Topeka, Kansas lies along the Kansas River and as a state capital is of very modest size, boasting just over a population of 127,000 in 2010. Originally it was founded as a "free city" by the anti-slavery groups, much the same I would suppose as those cities in Biblical times called "cities of refuge" where one would flee to avoid vengeance from their enemies. The name Topeka is thought to have been a combination of words from the Native American tribes who had lived nearby, but no one seems to know for sure.

"In the day" children found their own entertainment in the world which surrounded them, rather than depending upon electronic devices to fill their leisure time. Water has forever held an attraction to the young and old alike, and the Kansas River was no exception. Catching frogs, skipping rocks, cat fishing, and building all sorts of rafts and boats kept the local children busy. Seldom was there a drowning in spite of the association of children and water because they all had learned to swim at an early age, and to respect things they could not control. A lesson that possibly should have been shared with future generations.

No one claimed him or took him home with them at night after finishing their day's adventures. He just faded into the darkness, made his own way, and rested where God provided shelter. This too, possibly another lesson to be learned from our surroundings. Brown Dog was an obvious mixture of breeds but because of his slick coat and trim lines appeared to be some sort of pointer. He seemed fearless and wise as he watched and waited, learning from and teaching the children who appeared to be in his charge. Not one hesitated to accept his warm greetings or could resist his silent plea for a bite of their lunches. Rather, he ran at their heels or led the procession; he was always there among them, part of them.

His eyes were not those soulful eyes of the hound but rather the dark intelligent ones that seemed deep and mysterious as they bore into you. Often a raised ear or a cocked head communicated what he wanted to say to the children. He seldom barked but drew the attention of the children immediately to him when he did. He was the counselor, nanny, PE instructor, life guard, and security for the generation of children whom he raised.

Like a ghost he appeared as the winter's snows retreated away from the spring sunshine and again disappeared when the bite of winter forced the children inside. Had anyone wondered or cared they may have worried about him, but they were preoccupied with living life's grand adventure and had thoughts only for the day at hand.

My name is Timothy Timblestreet, my peers called me Timmy Tumblefeet because of my propensity to fall often. You see, when I was in the first grade I contracted polio as a result of the vaccine I was given. Although they called it a light case, it was sufficient to cause me to wear leg braces and move awkwardly about. When we moved to Topeka, I was repeating the first grade as a result of time lost to the illness and subsequent medical procedures and therapies that followed. The stigma that attached itself to those who repeated a grade was often life-changing enough without the added physical burden which my condition brought with it. By today's standards I was no doubt 'traumatized', but I didn't know it.

I had no close friends, make that few close friends, because there were those who were kind enough to tolerate me and include in their activities, whom I did consider as my friends. I now question if they would have considered me so had they been asked then. I only remember getting one invitation to a birthday party in my six years of elementary school.

By the third grade my ailment had become old news and those who had feared catching my condition had resolved themselves to either ignoring it or making fun of me. I became just part of the gang on the playground, lurching and pitching, in an effort to fit in. It was then that Brown Dog appeared out of nowhere and attached himself to me. To be accepted by our beloved friend was to be accepted by everyone. My life changed with his approval. Often I could feel him watching me as I moved about, seemingly trying to understand what caused my odd movements.

Midway through the fifth grade, while the braces stayed, my arm crutches were retired and stored away in some forgotten corner of our basement. I found that if I moved slowly and deliberately, that many would not even perceive the braces hidden under my trousers. My nickname was changed to 'Slo', nothing more, just Slo. I saw it as a vast improvement and a social victory. At some point, even my own family picked up on it and called me simply, Slo. By the end of the school year it seemed that the teachers had forgotten my name too and addressed me as Slo as well.

When May came, bringing with it spring and warmer weather, the gang began to hang out in the park down near the river. Brown Dog was beginning to show gray on his muzzle now and walked with a noticeable limp after long day of fun and frolic. I suppose in hindsight that the x-7 doggie year thing was catching up to him. I turned twelve that summer, five of eleven invitees came to our house for cake and ice cream. That may have been the finest day of my young life to that point. I saved a big piece of yellow cake topped with melted vanilla ice cream for Brown Dog. He smiled gratefully as he ate it without hesitation.

Even though school had been out for the summer nearly a month, July 4th was the unofficial beginning of summer in Topeka with parades and fireworks, and hot temperatures which raised the surface water in the river to a suitable level for swimming.

The Kansas river made a slow bend near the park before heading north and west, the slow current there and the tree lined bank made it an ideal place to swim. Rope swings placed by children long grown and with families of their own still hung from the branches of the ever present cottonwood and willow trees, as well as those added every year by some enterprising youth. Much like the construction of paper airplanes, someone always came up with a new and different way to do the same thing.

Elaine was a grade behind me, small and frail with beautiful brown eyes and long dark hair. She was perfect until she opened her mouth and tried to talk and began to stutter. The harder she tried the more difficult it always became until her eyes filled with tears and she ran away to hide her humiliation. I think we became friends because we understood what it meant to be different. Interestingly, when we were alone it seemed we could communicate with very little of the halting pauses and repetitions that caused her so much difficulty.

Often she and I, with Brown Dog following at our heels, would walk silently to the park, then sit beside the river watching the water on its way downstream. We'd stay until the sun began to touch the water, then walk home before darkness fell. Slowly, I think we fell in love, or in love with the idea of being in love. It was a magical time, a time of awakening and growing both physically and emotionally.

Elaine's father was the Baptist preacher at the little white church a block west and two south from where I lived. They lived in a little house on the lot beside it. Mr. Stinson was a burly man, both tall and wide, looking like someone who'd be more at home sawing down trees in the forest than standing behind the pulpit. His missus was hardly taller than her daughter and slim to the point of looking sickly. I liked them both and they seemed to like me as well. Pastor Stinson fed the souls of nearly fifty families each Sunday, who seemed grateful for his commitment.

My family considered themselves Christians and lived by the Golden Rule for the most part, but didn't spend a lot of time hanging around after the service ended to glad hand and pretend we were something we were not. That is the way my dad always put it. We prayed, tithed, and asked God regularly to forgive our sins. I can't remember ever being baptized or going through the ritual of accepting Jesus publically.

What I do remember is lying in my bed at night talking with Him and asking Him to heal me or at least help me understand why I had polio. He never spoke to me out loud but did help me to accept my malady and not focus on it. He also explained that someday I'd understand why it was necessary. I think I do, now that I have met Elaine, but I'm getting ahead of myself.

It was Labor Day weekend I believe, the last big hurrah of the summer when it happened. Families who had the money always traveled to some exotic and far away place, like Disneyland or Europe, while the rest of us picnicked and enjoyed camping out or celebrating with friends. The gang, now numbering a dozen, which included insiders and wannabees from the lower grades, all met at the 'pond'.

The pond is what we called the eddy where the water collected on the inside curve of the river where there was little current. It had a sandy shoreline and a short planked dock which stuck out into the water ten or fifteen feet. From the trees hung rope swings and on the sand, rock fire rings dotted the landscape.

I was seldom allowed to free myself from my leg braces, one of the few exceptions being when I was in or near water, bathing or swimming. Naturally, I tried to spend as much of the summer in the water as possible with my hardware piled with my towel at the water's edge. I was nearly helpless without them until the water buoyed me and helped to provide support, and then I could actually swim quite well. Often I just fell forward into the water from the dock into its cool refreshing arms, and then as I needed, I crawled out onto the sand or had help from friends to get back on the dock.

Several of the gang were already in the water when Elaine and I arrived. Others were doing acrobatics as they let go of the ropes and splashed far out into the pond. As always, Brown Dog trailed not far behind. In the distance, across the vast field of green, my parents with a throng of others enjoyed the warm afternoon, talking, throwing horseshoes, or playing cards on one of the picnic tables. Only an occasional concerned look from an anxious mother could be seen across the expanse of grass.

Several inner tubes supported resting teens as they sat back looking like an overturned turtle with a black shell. Elaine beckoned me in, while she treaded water and joined the crowd before then swimming out into the deeper water. I felt a cold nose on my back as Brown Dog added his encouragement. I went in, like a bag of concrete, and then bobbed up sputtering and blowing more like a whale. I used my legs in much the same way as a diver with fins would, from the hips rather than from the knees as I swam toward my friends. I always felt so liberated in the water, much the same I suppose as a bird does when he leaves the earth for his rightful place in the sky.

Someone had brought a beach ball so we broke up into teams and began a game of keep away with no rules or scores. With everyone intent on keeping the ball I suppose it was not unusual when Elaine ventured out farther than she had intended and was caught up in the fast moving current. I, of course, being the weakest swimmer had stayed closest to the bank while she and others had taken up positions farther out. When the ball had gone over her head, she had swam after it and found herself moving downstream and away from us at a rapid pace. The river curved out and away from the bank and within seconds she was a football field away and struggling to stay afloat.

Brown Dog was a blur as he leaped over my head and into the water, as I tried in vain to pull myself up and onto the dock. He swam straight out without hesitation as we screamed and yelled for help. A dozen sets of parents were seen running toward us, none in a position to offer effective aid as Elaine disappeared into the distance.

Only Pastor Stinson had the presence of mind to run to the parking lot and jump in their old sedan, following her struggling form downstream. Most of the crowd ran along the bank for a while before giving up and walking back, knowing they could not catch up in time to save her. Everyone except me had climbed out of the water and had gathered on the shore. As I looked I could see that Brown Dog was rapidly closing the distance between he and Elaine, then they both disappeared around the bend of the river.

I was told, but did not personally see, Elaine grasp the offered tail as Brown Dog swam around her and then focused on fighting the swift current that held them in the center of the wide river. It was her father in his car looking down from the bridge that crossed the river, who described the incident to all of us later.

As they neared the bank and the bottom came up to meet her feet she released her grip on his tail. Brown Dog turned back toward her, yelped once, swam by and disappeared into the water. His body has never been recovered.

Now, almost twenty years later, I seldom look at my wife Elaine without thinking of him, of the lessons he taught us of patience, unconditional love, commitment, and sacrifice. They still call me Slo, and now that I am approaching midlife with all the more reason, but many call me Pastor Slo with a smile on their faces.

I took Elaine's father's place when he retired. You see, after she and I were married, and after college and Bible school, after being blessed with two sons, I still hold the belief that Brown Dog was not just a dog but an Angel sent from God for a special reason and purpose, and was taken home when he completed his assignment.

– The End –

Far Beyond Redemption

The world is large and brutal and at the same time small and delicate and very personal. Perspective is the vantage point that provides the view, while experience is the tool that translates what we see into an opinion.

I was soft and pink, as are most babies, with stubby little ineffective fingers eager to grasp anything within reach. I spent most of my days lying and staring at the new world into which I had most recently burst. It seemed to be so new, so foreign, so hostile ...but interesting and entertaining beyond description. The liquid cocoon from which I'd just escaped had provided nourishment and safety but lacked the stimulus necessary to prompt my brain to develop. This new world was a constant source of that necessary stimulus. When I discovered my hands, feet, and mouth my world seemed complete.

Age three, my how time flies, I was already walking and talking, potty trained, and learning the meaning of "NO." Not that I paid any special attention to it until a penalty was exacted and the term was repeated. Looking back I see now that many never do really learn the meaning of "no."

I was the center of attention of my parents and grandparents. With the latter I could do no wrong, they did not know the word "no." I also had learned that 'original sin' had its mark, even upon babies; I became selfish and greedy and soon learned to lie. Yes, at this still young age I was an obvious sinner.

When Marlee was born I was devastated, I was no longer the center of the conversation in every family gathering, in fact, I felt ignored and persecuted. The only time I got attention was when I was being reprimanded. It took little time to learn I could easily regain what I had lost by breaking the "no-no" rules I'd so recently learned. She was crawling when I turned five, my parents seemed now to be playing the game with a different set of rules. They treated her much the same as our grandparents, "no" was only in the vocabulary for the older son. Nothing I had was sacred, everything had to be 'shared' and I hated the joint ownership thing.

I do not know that a child of five cannot really know hate, but I do know that I wished she'd just have gone away and let things return to the way they had been. I learned to be sneaky, to hide my things from her, and then to lie to Mom about where they were. To me, she had few redeeming qualities and was unworthy of the attention lavished upon her. Luckily, at age five I was able to escape each day for a few hours while spending time in kindergarten with my peers. There, too, I found that I disliked sharing time and attention with the other children. There, too, I found that breaking the rules got me special notice.

I'm now ten, a stout and sturdy fourth grader, tall for my age and self-assertive. Self-assertive, (who am I kidding – I am pushy and self-centered.) My parents waited for me to grow out of it, I did not. I became a bully and a thief, a force to be reckoned with even among the older children. If you had something I wanted, I took it, no excuse, no remorse, and received little if any recrimination. I played sports and was gifted at such but didn't like the rules. I soon found ways around them or chose to ignore them. I finally quit.

In middle school I found my stride with others just like myself, who were also angry and selfish. I also discovered that the bad boy persona attracted the girls so I played it to the hilt. At home I ignored my folks and they left me alone, no doubt wondering where they had failed or what could be done to undo it. I was nearly as tall as my dad and outweighed my mother by thirty pounds and found that I could intimidate them both, so I did. I came and went as I pleased, and felt no need to answer to anyone. I spent my first night in juvie in the ninth grade for stealing beer. I was the envy of my peers. The notoriety was worth the penalty for sure. My parents made arrangements for us to see a counselor, I deferred and they didn't press it.

Things didn't change much in high school except that I found myself a small fish in a big pond. I began to fight and soon I was revered and feared depending upon to whom you spoke. Once again I was notable among the crowd. Teachers passed me just to get rid of the problem and I was happy to move on without applying any effort. The SRO and I were on first name basis by my junior year and I found myself on probation for illegal consumption, big deal. Nothing changed except possibly that I learned to operate under the radar and get caught less. I smoked a little dope and crank but nothing really hard. My parents hadn't a clue; if they did, I didn't see it.

My grandparents said they were praying for me. I wondered why. I had everything I needed and took everything I wanted. I started selling drugs to afford more things and ignored my parents' questions as to where they came from. When I turned seventeen my Dad and I had a physical confrontation, he threw me out of the house but not before I broke his nose. It really didn't matter much as I had spent most of my time with my friends or at my girlfriend's house anyway. Her parents believed what I told them about being abused at home and let me move right in.

I dropped out of school and spent my time playing video games and hustling drugs to get by. They were well aware that we slept together but then they got all hot when she told them she thought she was pregnant, well duh. They asked me to leave.

I was on the street for a while until another do-gooder took me in. I let them play the game until finally their good sense over-rode their desire to fix the world and they too threw me out, but not before I took everything I could sell or pawn. I was busted by a snitch that I trusted and got thirty days and six months probation for possession. They dropped the 'with intent to deliver' charges. I made some good connections in county, some real shakers and movers, guys who could make it happen for you. It never occurred to me to ask why they were inside if they were so smart.

My parents never came to see me while I was inside, not that I cared or expected them to. No one from my crew either, only Marlee showed up to spend a few minutes trying hard to make the connection we had never had. I felt sorry for her, she was so naïve. She needed to toughen up or the world would walk right over her. She had tears in her blue eyes when she stood to leave and slid a 2x2 inch little blue booklet across the table that we shared. Apparently the guard missed it or he would have confiscated it. For that reason only I palmed it and slid it into my pocket, always nice to pull one over on the pigs.

Back in my cell with nothing to do, I took out my little piece of contraband and the first thing I did was get mad and throw it across the room. She's become a Jesus freak I thought. I slammed my hand into the wall and found its rough concrete surface unyielding and unforgiving. I may have broken my hand, time will tell, but the pain seems to be coming not from my hand but from somewhere inside, loneliness, and emptiness. The walls that I've built, the hard shell that

I've depended upon is starting to crumble. I'm nineteen and alone, all alone and no one cares. I have nothing, have accomplished nothing, and have no hope for the future.

I wished I was dead. No, I wished I was a baby again, sucking my fist, having my every need taken care of by someone who loved me. Tears filled my eyes and desolation filled my heart as I lay on the cot in the grayness of my cell. When I awakened the cell block was quiet and dark, with only the occasional snoring of another inmate to break the stillness. I reached out and retrieved the booklet and turned on the dim light in the corner by the commode. The cover read, "Would you like to know God personally?" Contrary to the familiar voice in my head which said "throw it away, it's crap, just more propaganda", I opened it and began to read. Yes, somewhere along the way I did learn to read in spite of my efforts to get through school without learning anything.

The little give-away was just over a dozen pages, simply written and easily understandable if one is trying to understand, even for me, even in my current condition and in my cell. It explained that God created us, that He loves us in spite of our mistakes and has created a way for those who trust in Jesus to be forgiven and saved from justice. I saw it as a pardon rather than a parole. There in my darkened cell, I whispered the words that set me free and changed my life for all eternity.

When I got out, I got my GED, then while working full-time, a BA from an online college, and finally a job leading my church's youth group. When asked if I felt that I had wasted over half of my life I said no. I think that God has put each of us right where He wants us. Ultimately, all we can do by making poor choices is to slow down His plan and get our education the hard way, but we can never change it.

– The End –

Debt and Debtor

Our chance encounters seem so impossible and so unplanned, but nothing could be further from the truth. God's plan is infinitely more complex and purposeful than we can ever understand and yet always happens just when and how He has determined they should.

"Thanks a lot, now I owe you my life," he said sarcastically.

"You owe me nothing," the young man replied, "I did it out of concern for you."

"Couldn't you see that I'd jumped from the bridge to commit suicide?" he asked accusingly. "Why did you feel the need to save me?"

The young man smiled sardonically then answered with a slight smile crossing his lips, "you were yelling 'help, help me', that didn't exactly sound like someone wanting to die."

The older man began to shiver, his lean frame shaking under his thin wet clothing, his new friend picked up his coat from the ground where he had thrown it and wrapped it around the man.

"I think I have a cup of coffee left in the thermos," he said as he walked the dozen steps back to where he had left his car. When he returned he had a massive stainless steel thermos in his hand and a throw blanket in the other.

Placing the blanket over the coat and wrapping it around the man who was sitting on the ground, he poured a steaming cup of black coffee and handed it to his new friend.

"Why are you doing this?" the old man asked sharply, "I can't repay you."

"I never expected that you could," was the younger man's reply. "I wouldn't have jumped in that cold river for any amount of money."

He sipped the coffee, holding the cup in both hands, enjoying the heat from the metal container and looking warily at the figure standing above him. "Why then?" he asked quietly.

"Because you needed what I had to give and there was no one else who could give it to you," he answered.

The old man did not answer but stood and held the cup toward his benefactor. "Here," he said, "you look like you could use something hot yourself."

Both men were smiling now as he took the offered cup and poured the last of the coffee into it. "Come on, it's getting mighty cold out here, let's go somewhere and have a bowl of soup and warm up," he said.

The old man followed him to the car and gingerly got into the passenger seat, then turned and said, "I'm dying, there's cancer all over inside my body."

The young man started the car then pulled into the evening traffic heading back toward the city. They rode in silence for several minutes before he responded to the news.

"We all are you know," he said finally. "Dying, I mean. This life is not supposed to last forever, it's just a stop over on our way to forever."

The old man looked at him as though he'd never considered what he'd just heard, though certainly he'd have had to have known that if not today, all die someday.

"This *forever* you are talking about, you mean heaven or hell don't you?" the rider asked. "How can you be so certain that we don't just die and that's all there is to it?"

As they pulled into the parking lot of a seedy diner with garish neon lights, most of which were either out or flickered as though they wanted to join them, the younger man replied. "I believe because I have faith, I have faith because without it life seems meaningless and impossible. A baby believes he will be fed but he neither knows nor cares where the food comes from. Faith begins with our first breath and is proven true with our last."

"So you're a Jesus junky!" the man challenged. "One of those who does good to earn a ticket to a heaven which does not exist."

A smile crossed the young man's lips. "I am indeed," he said. "I sold out to Him when I found I couldn't live without Him. I couldn't earn my way, buy my way, or find my way to heaven without Him."

"Everyone, I believe, was created to live forever, our only choice is where we want to spend our time," he said smiling. He added, "Jesus died for me because He was the only One who could take away my sin and make me pure enough to spend eternity with God in heaven."

When they opened their respective car doors and walked to the café, only a few patrons took the time to raise their heads to watch as they entered. The St. John's Bridge towered overhead as the lights of Portland reflected across the water to the east. As they seated themselves in a worn booth near the door, the old man began to shiver once again but his faded blue eyes seemed to be less cloudy and more alert.

"Coffee," a middle-aged black woman said as she turned over the cups and began to pour. "Is it raining again?" she asked, looking at the two wet men.

"Yes, thank you," the young man said to the first question, while ignoring the second. "What kind of soup do you have today?"

"Should have clam chowder and homemade chicken and noodles," she answered. "Can I bring you some?"

"Which one do you want to try first?" he asked his guest across the old worn formica table top.

The older man answered quietly, "maybe the chicken, does it come with bread?"

"I can cut you some, it just came out of the oven, still hot," she answered. "How 'bout you?" she said looking at the boy. "Chicken and hot bread be alright?"

"Yes please, two bowls," he answered. "And a refill before you leave if you don't mind," he added, pushing his empty cup forward.

She smiled and did as he had asked, then turned toward the kitchen.

The two men sat warming their hands on their cups looking at one another across the table, finally the homeless man spoke. "You really believe that stuff don't you?"

"I do," he answered simply.

"Where'd you get your faith, you witness a miracle or something?" he continued.

"Naw, nothing that you'd consider a miracle," the other answered. "But I gradually came to recognize that everything in life is a miracle of sorts, nothing happens without being part of God's plan."

"Even my cancer?" was the sarcastic question posed by the older of the two.

"Whoa, hold on there, I didn't say I understood how it all works," he said. "But yes, I believe that even the bad things can be used for our good and God does that."

The waitress brought two bowls of steaming soup and half a loaf of roughly sliced bread, still warm from the oven. "More coffee?" she asked pleasantly.

Both nodded and pushed their cups toward her. She returned with a pot and filled both, then left. The older man started to butter a slice of bread before looking up to notice his benefactor had bowed his head and was silently asking God's blessing on the food. He bowed his head also and closed his eyes with hopes of feeling something. He did not.

When he looked up the younger man caught his eye and smiled but said nothing. The contents of the bowls disappeared as if by magic as the two men ate in silence, as had the considerable pile of bread. They finally pushed back, their hunger temporarily satisfied, before looking toward the kitchen with renewed expectation on their faces.

"What'll it be?" she asked, pouring a third cup of coffee. "Another of the chicken or would you rather try the chowder this time?"

"I'll stay with the chicken," they both answered almost simultaneously.

The waitress smiled and took the empty bowls to the kitchen, then returned with them and another generous plate of bread. "Are you getting warmed up a bit?" she asked. "I might be able to rustle up some warm dry clothes if you need them."

Todd, he was the younger of the two, looked into her dark eyes and could see love and compassion, then down to her ample bosom where a small silver cross was contrasted against her dark skin. He instantly knew from where her compassion came.

"We'll be fine, but thank you," he said for them both. "We are going home from here and grab a hot shower and a dry change of clothes."

He caught the look of surprise on the face of his guest out of the corner of his eye but neither said anything as they began to consume their second bowl of chicken soup.

Finally the old man asked, "where's home?"

"I have a little house that my mother left me over on the east side nearly to Gresham", he answered. "Nothing fancy but cozy and warm.

How about you?"

The old man's voice seemed far away as though it was coming from another place or time when he said, "sometimes I get in the shelter, sometimes I just make do the best I can."

"No family?" Todd asked, fearing that he was asking too much too soon.

"Naw, they got tired of my smokin', drinkin', and carousing years ago. I haven't seen or heard from them in years," he said matter-of-factly, "got what I deserved I 'spect."

"You are welcome..." Todd said, letting his voice trail off. "I've plenty of room."

He half expected that the old man would refuse his offer and make some excuse but was surprised when he said, "that's kind of you, and if you are sure I won't be in the way."

He continued by saying, "I 'spect I'd know by now whether your faith is true or not if you hadn't jumped in the river and saved me."

The statement did not require a response and got none. Both could see the bottom of their bowls and buttered the shared last slice of bread and finished their coffee. Without ceremony Todd picked up the check that lay on the table, dropped a five as a tip and walked toward the cash register with his last twenty in his hand. From behind him a hand grabbed the ticket and a voice said, "Here, let me get that."

The old man walked past him, gave the waitress a twenty of his own, and said, "keep the change."

Todd started to object but remembered what an old priest had once said to him, "to reject the gift is to reject the giver," so he remained silent.

During the drive across the bridge neither spoke, each lost in their own thoughts, finally the old man said, "name's Ben, Ben Cross. I 'spect we should be on a first name basis if I am gonna accept your hospitality."

Todd smiled and offered his right hand, "Todd Smythe, pronounced Smith, glad to know you Ben."

They drove another forty-five minutes without speaking until Todd pulled the old car into the graveled driveway and shut off the ignition. "We're home," he announced as he got out of the car.

Ben sat in the car without speaking and made no attempt to get out.

"Come on in," Todd urged, having returned to the car to retrieve his new friend.

"Your mother was Alice?" Ben declared with a question in his voice. "Alice Smythe, wife of Thomas Smythe?"

"You knew them?" Todd said incredulously, "you knew my Mom and Dad?"

Ben seemed to be collecting his emotions before he answered, "I served with your Dad in Korea and built this house for your mother when I got home after the war."

"You're Uncle Ben?" Todd asked. "I was only seven when the news came that our father had been killed and remember the day that you showed up on our step with a hammer, saw, and a debt to repay, as you put it. You built this house."

Ben too was reliving the encounter of many years before, tears welled in his old eyes, but he did not speak.

"You said that Dad had saved your life and you wanted to do the best you could to repay him," Todd added.

Ben nodded.

Todd opened the passenger door and gestured to Ben. "Please come inside."

Both enjoyed a long hot shower and a dry change of clothes before settling onto the old worn couch in the living room, with still another cup of hot coffee. Todd had taken out the family picture album and had laid it opened on the coffee table. Staring back from the pages were pictures from decades before showing the smiling faces of Todd, his sisters, his mother, and Ben at someone's birthday party. Todd looked to be about eight and his twin sisters, with their front teeth missing, would have been six.

Ben touched the pages reverently, tears now tracing the lines of his cheeks while moving silently downward. "I remember," he said. "I never could quite get over it, maybe why I began drinking and ran my own family away."

They paged through the old album slowly and methodically, reliving the events portrayed in pictures and enjoyed many related stories which flooded to mind because of them. It was after 2:00 a.m. when the rigors of the day made it imperative that they should get some rest and retired to the two small bedrooms just off the kitchen.

Ben had showered, shaved, and combed his sparse locks of hair and had bacon frying in a pan when Todd joined him in the kitchen and poured himself a cup of coffee. Todd could hear the old man humming something as he moved gracefully about the small room.

"Sleep well?" Todd asked.

"Indeed I did," Ben answered in a deep resonate voice, seemingly out of place in his thin frail body. "Haven't slept that well in a while."

"Howju like your eggs?" he asked.

"Medium, or however they turn out," Todd answered. "Not too picky when someone else does the cooking."

He had scattered the hash browns and pressed them flat then had left them alone to crisp. When he turned them they turned like a pancake showing a rich dark brown on the top side. A memory of eating the same as a child came to mind. He wondered if his mother had taught Ben the secret to good fried potatoes or vice versa. He couldn't help wondering if they had been more than just friends but tried to dismiss the thought.

They enjoyed breakfast together and cleaned up the dishes before sitting at the old worn kitchen table where they finished up the pot of coffee.

"I loved your mom and your family you know," Ben volunteered. "That's probably why I couldn't be a good husband and father to my own. I couldn't help but to compare them to yours and they always came up short."

Todd had suspected as much but didn't respond.

Ben continued. "I'd have asked Alice to marry me but neither of us could put your father out of our minds. We honored his memory I guess by sacrificing our futures."

Ben stayed two more days; on the morning of the third he made excuse that he had an appointment at the VA medical center and asked for a ride downtown. It was on that final ride that Ben asked Todd, "How did you know when to ask Jesus into your heart?"

There it was, out in the open, the elephant in the room which had gone unnoticed until now.

Todd thought back trying to remember the exact circumstance surrounding his conversion and salvation, finally he answered truthfully, "I cannot truly say, there just came a time that seemed right and I was drawn to admit my failures and ask Jesus to forgive them. I felt a peace that I had never known, and wanted it to last forever so then I asked Him to forgive my sins and to be with me always."

Ben nodded then asked, "as simple as that?"

"As simple as that," Todd said. "He waits hoping that we will accept the gift of Himself that He gave as atonement for our sins and rejoices when some do."

A week to the day later, Todd received a call from the VA hospital advising him that Ben had died. They had been given Todd's name and number as next-of-kin and asked about his plans for the funeral.

Ben received a military funeral and was buried beside Tom and Alice at Todd's instruction, with only five guests standing at the grave-side. Todd now awaits the time when he will be reunited with his mother and father and to know for sure if Ben had made the personal decision to receive Christ as his Savior.

– The End –

Cardboard Cows

In a world where common sense is becoming more and more uncommon, and every plausible idea becomes a 'cause' with a following willing to protest and carry signs and banners, a few things from the past still ring true today. - dc

"What are those?" I asked incredulously, while looking across the wide expanse of green pastures that bordered the highway.

Our vehicle came to a halt as I pulled to the roadside of the meandering two-lane that split the farm fields in half. The morning had just begun, with the sun shining in a blue sky surrounded by wisps of lazy clouds. Out in the field at which we were looking was a man riding a residential-sized lawnmower back and forth across the acres and acres of pastureland. The task seemed daunting, impossible even, to groom such a vast expanse of green.

Apparently he had previously uprooted several dozen of the cows and had leaned them against the wire fence until he could return them to their places after the grass had been mown. It was obvious to us that the cows were just silhouettes of cows mounted on a frame that could easily be pushed into the ground. Those that remained in the far half of the field resembled realtor signs, but had been cut to shape with cows painted on them.

"They look like cows painted on cardboard," my wife answered my question. "I wonder if it is some kind of advertisement display or movie set."

I recognized that the silhouettes were commercially made and therefore would have cost some real money, that they would from time to time need repainted and maintained, and that their pastureland required constant care, without yielding a single marketable product.

I rationalized that it was someone from the city, new to the area who did not understand that God, not man, created his environment.

Our family is neither from the big city or a small farming village, we live in a modern city of nearly 200,000 but are surrounded with agriculture and open spaces. We however, as a family, do know that what we buy in the supermarket comes from God's creation, be it livestock, or crops from the fields. I have heard of some that are so disconnected from reality that a child would answer that milk comes from grocery stores and has no idea where they get it.

Across the highway, the mower made yet another pass, belching smoke and complaining loudly as it bore its burden steadily onward. Its rider seemed content and oblivious of our interest in his activities. We continued to sit and watch as gradually the groomed section widened to five passes, possibly twenty feet by several hundred yards long. Twice while we sat he stopped and refilled the fuel tank from a large can. My urge was to get out, cross the road, and interrupt his labor to satisfy my curiosity, but I did not.

By this time my family had lost interest and was grumbling that we had not had breakfast after checking out of our motel. My wife calmed them by suggesting that a town was shown on the GPS just up the road a few miles, where we would stop to eat.

As we approached the town, the speed limit dropped three times in the length of a ball field, finally down to 25 mph. I wondered fleetingly how many errant tourists had been slow to heed the warnings and had helped the local economy with their traffic fines. An attractive sign nearby said 'Welcome to Thomas, Drive Carefully'. I remember thinking how odd the name seemed for a town.

The street was built to accommodate four lanes but was striped for two and had 45 degree parking in front of the stores and shops on both sides. Our two girls were becoming vocal and obviously needed both a rest from the car and some nourishment. No sooner than the right front tire of the car came to a halt against the curb than their doors opened and they began a visual search of the surrounding area.

"Café," Stephanie heralded, pointing across and down the street. She was our Lewis and Clark, with very little ever escaping her sharp eyes.

Without waiting for my wife and me, both girls loped down the sidewalk as if starving, while talking to each other in some teenage language unknown but to themselves. They were already seated in a booth scrutinizing the menu when the bell over the door announced our presence to the other guests. As we seated ourselves and were handed menus, the girls began arguing over what they wanted to order. We accepted the offered cups of steaming black coffee and settled into the inviting soft, cushioned upholstery.

I perused the menu out of habit, already having made a decision to have the ham, eggs, and hash browned potatoes, then looked around the room at the other patrons. Had I been an artist I would have had the makings of a painting of sharp contrasts. At one table four 30-something's sat sipping their lattés, looking as if right out of a picture of a Fifth Avenue barista. Beside them, two old men dressed in overalls and beat-up ball caps sat with their aging wives. One of the men was tearing the tops off the sugar packets and dumping them into his cup like there was a shortage of cane somewhere and he wanted to secure his share. The husky young waitress sat plates laden with biscuits and gravy in front of the men, then followed it up with a side of link sausage. Their wives didn't stop their visit when she returned with their matching plates with poached eggs and toast.

A large man sat alone on a stool at the long bar drinking coffee and using his toast to clean up after his 'over easy' eggs. It was obvious to me by his manner and dress that he was a truck driver or route delivery man. A long sleeved western style shirt, jeans, heavy belt, and a chain anchoring his leather wallet in his back pocket was a more or less obvious mark of a working man. A John Deere ball cap and cowboy boots rounded out his attire.

A banker-pastor-or undertaker dressed in a three-piece and tie was in the corner booth talking with another dressed like him while nibbling on a club sandwich and chips. Our waitress returned, scooping up the menus without fanfare and began to take our orders. The girls began their ritual argument over what they had previously decided before being quieted by their mother.

"And you," she said to me looking down where I sat, "what can I bring you?"

I looked up, embarrassed to be staring at her extended abdomen only inches from my face. I felt my face redden as I raised it further and saw her smiling patiently.

"It's another boy," she said, no doubt referring to the object of my interest. "That'll be three for us. Have no idea what we're going to do with them," she added.

"I guess that's for God to say," I said glibly, before ordering my usual fare.

"I suppose you are right," she responded, "but the timing is bad, my husband just lost his job and with it our medical insurance."

After we ordered she said, "I'll be right back with your breakfasts," and turned to walk away. Somehow she and I had made a connection and I felt badly for her situation. Mentally I already doubled our tip as a way to try and help a bit.

"Poor girl," my wife said, echoing my thoughts. "I wish there was something we could do to help her."

Steph, our oldest, who knows more about life than anyone thirteen ever should said, "they should have thought of that before she got pregnant."

I felt like I had been slapped as I turned toward the girl I loved so much but didn't recognize at all. Audrey, aged eleven, looked at her too, then at me to see how I'd respond, so I took an extra minute to think.

Finally I jumped in hoping God was guiding my thoughts. "Steph, who's child will she be having?"

She gave me that 'well duh' look before answering. "Her husband's I should hope."

In for a penny, in for a pound I thought, as my wife looked at me sympathetically.

"Do you remember those cows we saw just outside of town?" I asked those at the table while directing my question at Steph.

"Ya, sure," she answered uncertainly, wondering what connection I was trying to make, "you mean the cardboard cows?"

"Yes," I answered. "Who do you think owns those cardboard cows?"

All three of my girls were beginning to think I had lost it when our meal was delivered and we stopped the discussion, blessed it, and began to eat. We ate like wolves, relishing the feel of our surroundings and the taste and texture of our breakfast. Finally, we pushed back as Bonnie, our waitress, returned with a refill for our coffee and began removing our dirty dishes.

"Thank you, Bonnie," I said, reading the name from her name tag, "that was a very good meal." My family joined me in declaring their satisfaction as well.

"What is your husband's line of work?" I asked, taking the liberty to inquire.

She looked at me quizzically before answering, "he's a minister, but with all of the old folks leaving and the new ones moving in with their strange new age ideas, the church can no longer afford to pay him."

I thought of the brief time we had been there and of what I had observed since we had arrived, including the cardboard cattle rancher just outside of town. "Have faith," I said. "A Father always takes care of his children. Someday soon all will realize that milk doesn't come from cardboard cows. Milk and honey and all good things come from God, Our father."

– The End –

Soul Thief

The Soul Thief does not wait for darkness or for occupants to leave their home to begin his larceny. Indeed, he openly attacks and overcomes his victims, many even while they know it is happening. He is cunning, intelligent and powerful, with many resources at his fingertips and many years of experience.

It begins when they are yet babies, newborns dependant upon their world to provide for their every need. They soon learn that a whimper or cry will get them what they desire, they become selfish and even needier as time progresses. They learn to covet, to want, to eat their fill at others' expense. "Mine," "mine" is their reoccurring call.

He endorses that, promotes it, tells them what they need, what they want is their due. Me, me, me becomes the center of their universe. As they grow and learn, they become more cunning and resourceful like their teacher. They reject the needs of others while focusing on themselves. He helps them reject and ignore the single voice which pleads with them to share, to love, to turn away from selfishness.

They eventually become carnal, lustful, greedy, and larcenous; all the while finding nothing wrong with their poor choices. And yet, with all they have, they have nothing; they are empty and hungry for more, always searching for what they lack.

He knows their time is short and that they belong to him if only he can shelter them from the light of understanding and reason which attempts to restore and save them from his thievery before their journey is complete. Some, a few, hear the Voice and turn away from him, others remain blind and self-absorbed until the curtain falls and the time of salvation is passed.

What does he offer? He offers that which the world values, those things which sinful man worships. Every sort of forbidden pleasure can be yours and all you must do is take it. At what cost you may ask, at the cost of eternal separation from God, called death.

Unlike others of his ilk, Damon was not tall and fair with blonde hair. He was dark haired and squat with wide shoulders and a thick powerfully muscled chest. His deep-set eyes were sheltered with thick black eye brows which nearly knit together at their center. Each of his hands sported six stubby but strong fingers with long broken yellow nails at their tips. Folded unseen down the length of his muscled back were two expansive black wings. He was certainly not what mortals picture when they think of angels.

Akin to the fables that drug users and problem drinkers tell themselves about having the ability to limit or quit, many tell themselves that they can control their passion for sin and say no to those things without help from anyone. Damon loved the arrogance of the stubborn mortals; he worked hard to build up their self esteem and stroked their egos until they felt a match for any challenge. He liked to think that he coined the phrase 'self-made man', which fit so very well into the mouths of those who enjoyed God's blessings, and loved it when they failed and lost everything. He was there to plant the question in their hearts, "why did God make this happen?" So of course it was they who took credit when they succeeded, but it was God they faulted when they failed.

Thomas, known as Tom by all but his grandparents and when he was in hot water with his mother or father, was a shade above average in most ways depending who was judging. He was gifted physically but not to a degree that he was outstanding in sports, and mentally only to the point that he had little trouble learning if he applied himself. If you could overlook his straight prominent nose and slightly too large ears, he was pleasant looking, if not handsome. Curly brown hair, twinkling blue eyes, and a ready smile behind his sense of humor made him fit well into most social circles his freshman year in high school.

Somewhat ashamed to volunteer the information, few knew that he was a virgin and assumed by his swagger and manner that he was among those who had scored. Tom and his family were regular attendees at their church where they were involved and welcomed into the many functions and activities that took the place of real Bible study. Campouts, potlucks, and a plethora of good DVD's about how to be a good Christian gave everyone a sense of belonging and following the right path, without anyone ever challenging them to pursue salvation. Even the pastors tip-toed around the awkward question of "are you saved?"

The battle for supremacy had begun for Tom during the summer after the sixth grade when he began to notice and appreciate the changes in the young women around him. It continued and increased in both frequency and urgency through his middle school years until it dominated both his waking and sleeping hours. Damon was there to plant a thought, to emphasize a touch, to give him a mental visual that could not be denied. At home he became reclusive, spending more time alone, opting out of youth group functions, filling his eyes with porn from the Internet, and his heart with lust. In his shame he knew he was losing the battle but ignored the Voice that called out to him to pursue righteousness. All around him the world paraded what he wanted most, taunting him, pushing him ever closer to the brink.

When a new family moved in halfway down the block from his

home he walked down and offered to help them unpack. Their U-Haul, which trailed behind an old battered Chevy pickup that had seen better days, was filled with worn but serviceable furniture, literally in every available space. That is where Tom first met Josh Stuart, his mother and father Ben and Laura, and their daughter Melissa. He learned that Ben was a minister who had moved to town to plant a church.

He and Josh hit it right off and began what was to become a life-long friendship. Laura was a beautiful woman, although on the heavy side, with a ready smile and a hug for everyone she met, while Melissa was slight built and shy, with large brown eyes and a quiet manner. Tom could feel his cheeks redden when Laura had pressed herself against him with a welcoming hug that left his imagination running wild. Ben offered him a firm handshake and a man slap on the back while he and Josh just smacked clenched fists. Tom froze like a deer in the headlights when Melissa moved toward him and finally shook his hand uncomfortably.

As the days became weeks, and the weeks months, Tom became a regular fixture at the Stuart's home. He and Josh studied, practiced shooting hoops, and enjoyed video games together. Melissa always seemed to be somewhere in the back ground quietly reading or studying, while Ben and Laura worked feverishly to make their new church a reality. Tom grew to like the common sense form of Christian life that Ben and his family practiced in their everyday lives and accepted their invitation to attend with them, while their young church struggled to become relevant among the many larger ones.

Tom continued to quietly wage his very personal war with sin as he was assailed from all sides by pictures, jokes, and women young and old who seemed to be doing their best to lead him astray by the way they dressed and acted. He was tempted to share his feelings with his new best friend Josh who seemed to be immune to the sexual barrage all around him, but did not.

One Sunday, Ben's sermon seemed to be speaking right to Tom's heart as he quoted Proverbs 23:7a, which said, "*That whatsoever a man thinketh in his heart, so is he*," and again Matthew 5:28, "*But I say to you whoever looks at a woman with lust for her has already committed adultery with her in his heart.*" Tom was convicted immediately of his lustful thoughts and dreams. The mere fact that he had not been able to act out his thoughts did not change the fact that he desired to.

He felt shame and then the fear that he was out of control and his lust seemed to have no boundaries. Then Satan cranked up the heat when he brought a girl into Tom's life that seemed too comfortable with her own sexuality and made it plain she was available. As they began to date it did not go unnoticed that Tom stopped going to church and became an infrequent visitor at the Stuart's home.

One day at school Josh came right out and asked, "I hardly see you anymore and our family misses you at church on Sundays and sitting around the dinner table, what gives?"

Tom first thought to make an excuse but knew anything he might say would be easily seen through, "I've been busy lately with Vicki," he said with a wink.

Josh frowned and asked honestly, "what's the attraction that's more important than God and your friends?"

Tom's face reddened and he felt anger at his friend's accusation, "If you don't know, there's nothing I could say that would convince you," he spat as he turned to leave.

"God loves you, we love you, but does she love you?" Josh asked. Tom continued to walk away and did not reply.

At home things became tense when Tom's grades began to slip and the school called to inquire why he had missed school two days this week. He had gotten into the habit of leaving right after the dinner meal with the excuse he needed to go to the library to study when in fact he'd been going to Vicki's house where her single parent mother worked nights. Things that night were unusually quiet at dinner, there was heaviness in the room as they ate. Tom caught the look which his father and mother exchanged when he excused himself to go to the library, but nothing was said.

Tom and Vicki had settled into a routine which began with kissing and touching but had not yet progressed to the point of no return when a firm knock on the door sent him scurrying from the room and she re-buttoning on her way to the door. On the step, illuminated by the porch light, stood Tom's father and mother.

"Please ask Tom to come to the door," he said firmly, leaving no room for her to deny Tom's presence.

She nodded and called, "Tom, there's someone here to see you."

He walked the few steps from the bedroom to the door as though he was walking to the gallows, his face red with shame, and his eyes cast down to the floor.

"Thomas," his mother said with an edge in her voice, "you are coming home."

They rode home in silence. From the back seat tears were evident on his mother's face, and a look of hopelessness that he'd never seen in his father's. Their darkened house evidenced that his brothers were already in bed as they pulled into the driveway. His father turned off the motor but made no attempt to open the car door. After several minutes he looked over the seat at his son and questioned, "what single thing do you think that your mother and I share that we value most?"

Tom was at a loss for words, trying to follow what his father meant. He said nothing.

"Integrity," came his answer to his own question. "Trust, honesty, and character."

"Son," he continued, "the path you are following will lead you to lose all of those and with it your self-respect and your reputation. It will divide your family, set a bad example for your brothers, separate you from God, and lessen the likelihood of a happy marriage sometime in your future."

With those words, both his mother and father left the car and entered the house, leaving him alone with his thoughts.

Tom sat, tears welling in his eyes, feeling empty and lost, alone and hopeless, knowing that he could not control his thoughts and desires. Finally he prayed, "Jesus help me, I cannot fight this alone, I need you, I want you to take this feeling away from me and give me your forgiveness."

Tom was not well-schooled in scripture but within seconds Ephesians 6:10 appeared from nowhere and filled his mind, "*put on the full armor of God....*"

– The End –

Left Behind for a Reason

And as it was in the beginning, so it shall be at the end, that a few will be called to stay and spread the good news of salvation among the unbelieving.

I took my position on the rooftop across the street from the church. There were three of us dressed in the black cordura uniforms of the metro SWAT and all with scoped sniper rifles with bipods on their forestocks. The sun seemed to rise that morning with a particular eagerness to announce the day. I remember now how it went from darkness to light with unusual rapidity and how the sunrise was particularly glorious and colorful.

The town had endured nearly a week of angry protests and civil unrest as a result of an unpopular mandate from the city council to crack down on gang-related urban crime. Ironic that the criminals were flaunting their right to protest the enforcement of criminal laws, I thought to myself. It was as if they felt they had the right to steal, sell drugs, and live off the earnings of others with impunity. While we in law enforcement knew that the less force used to control a situation the better, we also knew that they were armed and felt they had license to take to the streets and promote their lifestyle as they saw fit.

Let me say before I proceed to tell this story that my spiritual beliefs often put me at odds with the mandates of my job in law enforcement, as they did when serving in Iraq with the military. I have yet to find peace when trying to justify taking a human life, no matter what the circumstances. I have had this belief since age thirteen when I received my salvation by faith in Jesus' sacrifice on the cross. I felt comfortable and secure in that knowledge until this particular morning. This may be an appropriate time to tell you that a dozen years or more ago I read the captivating *Left Behind* book series. Like many Christians who believe that the Rapture is yet to come, I found them logical and comfortable guidebooks to the unknown future events described in our Bible.

I increased the magnification on my scope to twelve which allowed me to see the tiny earrings in the little girl's ears as she walked down the courthouse steps holding her mother's hand, and then backed it off to nine. Gathered in the street at the base of the expansive cement steps that led from the front of the building, several dozen youth dressed in black hoodies vocally made their presence known.

One of the two men at my side brought our attention to the fact that he had observed at least one with a knife and that another had pocketed a handgun. He reported his observation to HQ who immediately authorized the necessary use of lethal force as required to protect human life. I always choked on the wording of that phrase which literally meant take a life if it was necessary to protect a life. I remember thinking maybe I should ask for reassignment as an SRO in a local school.

I am thirty-nine, and have eight years on the force. I have never been required to discharge my weapon during that time, but have been shot at several times and stabbed once in the line of duty. Our small town numbers somewhere between 25-30,000, depending on who you ask and how much of the surrounding agricultural area you include. Until five years ago we had no gangs willing to declare themselves or challenge the authority of law enforcement, now we had three, all as a result of pushes in nearby larger cities to clean up their crime problems. They had simply moved their operations to the areas of least resistance.

The sun was now above the low mountain range that encircled our valley and the clouds that accompanied it were filled with rich tones of gold, purple, and red, which made it hard to focus my attention on the unfolding scene below. Well-wishers and supporters from the community had now gathered at the opposite side of the steps as the small entourage slowly descended toward them. On the ground, a dozen squad cars with lights flashing had delivered a contingent of officers in riot gear to the scene to try and thwart confrontation as much as possible. Our job was to watch, wait, report, and apply lethal force if necessary.

I should digress. Those exiting the courthouse were the witnesses and their families who had been instrumental in securing a guilty verdict of three members of the Bandoleros gang who had tortured and killed a shop owner and his wife after stealing drugs and money from his pharmacy. The witnesses had reported the crime from their own stores across the street, precipitating the arrests.

The press, leave it to the press, moved forward at just the wrong time with their cameras and mics, blocking our view as the *hooded* gang members moved toward the two families to confront them. The *citizens* in the opposition seemed to take their cue and moved in also. I estimate now over a hundred lined the street and sidewalks in front of the courthouse. On my left, Hank announced "knife", indicating that he had seen a weapon. Just as one of the gang members reached the woman and her children, the little girl on the right seemed to go out of focus momentarily then disappear completely, as what I can only describe as a small whirlwind enveloped her. If you are familiar with what in the southwest are called 'dust devils', you have an accurate picture of what appeared in my telescopic sight. Seconds later, the second child was consumed and spirited away in the same manner, then her mother and father, and finally many in the crowd randomly.

"Did you see...?" I began as I turned toward where my brother officers had taken up their positions, but stopped when I saw the butts of their weapons on the rooftop but no sign of either of them. Below me, the crowd was wailing and screaming, the gang was running away, and over half of those gathered including many of those of the police force were gone. I watched with an open mouth as the disappearances continued and the skies resounded with thunder. As I began to realize what I was witnessing I stood, confidently waiting for the wind to rapture me away to my waiting home as well... it did not.

I spoke into my shoulder mic, "Headquarters this is S1, repeat S1, we seem to have a situation here."

It was several seconds before a response came, "S1 this is HQ, we have a situation here as well, what do you observe?"

"HQ, both S2 and S3 have disappeared as well as what I estimate as over fifty civilian and law enforcement, including the witnesses and some of the press."

"Roger S1," dispatch answered. "We are observing the same here, I'll have to get back to you."

Man struggles to understand God, His Word, His purpose, and His design. Our best minds cannot conceive what He determined eons ago or the methodology He had determined to use to make His plans come to fruition. Across the world on that day, millions and millions of believers were taken home, where they walk in the presence of Jesus.

However, I believe myself and others were left behind to endure the Tribulation for a purpose. Try as you will to discount the lack of my salvation as the reason I remain, and use scripture to justify that *none* of the believers will suffer it, the fact remains that we who are here and subject to God's will shall remain until Jesus returns in the clouds.

– The End –

The Mayor

We had just moved from our longtime home to the small town of Buhl, Idaho, located in a very rural part of the state. I had semi-retired the previous year and with our children grown and living in other locations, the timing seemed right to slow down the pace and enjoy our remaining years.

We'd had little interaction with the locals with the exception of the grocer and the realtor who sold us our new home. While the residents seemed friendly enough, becoming part of the community was an earned privilege. If you weren't born there or married in, you'd likely always bear the stigma of your home of origin.

We were welcomed warmly into the local church but no one stepped forward with an offer of coffee or lunch and we were not ones to try and push our way in. We tried a Bible study group but found it uncomfortable also, as its members had been together for many years and knew the names and circumstances of three generations of each others' families. The study was enlightening but the fellowship seemed to exclude us, dwelling on past joys and sorrows, in which we were not participants.

I was kicking around the house one afternoon when my wife suggested I go into town and get a haircut. I'm sure she just wanted me out from under foot, but I did as she suggested and soon found a comfortable chair at the local barber shop. A half-dozen others like me were discussing the events of the day, the climate, the economy, and finally the upcoming city elections which were to be held the following month.

I listened attentively before joining in and adding my opinion to those of others around me.

When I finished speaking a bony, calloused hand was shoved toward me. "Brewster," the man said, announcing himself. "You are new here aren't you?"

"Bill," I answered. "We've just moved here from Boise, looking for a quieter place to retire."

Several others rose and made their way over and introduced themselves before returning to their chairs.

"Barber's Smitty," one said, hooking his thumb over his shoulder toward the only man in the room gainfully employed.

Smitty gave me a nod but didn't speak or stop his labors.

"What did you do in Boise?" a man with red hair and a mustache asked. "You hardly look old enough to be retired."

"I worked for the city, mostly in planning and zoning," I answered. "Towards the end, I was a supervisor and didn't do much, finally got bored just sitting around while others did the work."

That brought a laugh to the room and an observation from an older man with a walker parked in front of his chair. "Most of us don't feel that way, we jus' come down here to watch Smitty work, don't bother us a bit."

Another round of laughter circled the small room when Smitty threw a comb in his direction.

"You a Dem or 'publican?" one asked me point blank, bringing silence to the room, while everyone waited on my answer.

"Never thought much about it," I said honestly. "Mostly I vote for the man who represents what I believe is right, regardless of his side of the ticket."

I was proud to see several nods affirming their agreement with what I had said.

Brewster, I was not sure if that was a first or last name, took the floor again and asked, "you ever consider runnin' for office?"

Smitty had stopped cutting and had turned his attention to the discussion, as had his customer also.

Something inside of me urged me to listen and not take the usual way out. "Why?" I asked.

When I returned home without having gotten my hair cut, my wife looked at me quizzically and asked, "where have you been, I don't see a haircut."

"Well," I began. "I did make it to the barber shop but there was a bunch of fellas ahead of me so I just stayed on and visited with them. A couple of them think I should run for local office," I added.

"Why in the world..." she began. "Didn't you get enough of city politics over the last forty years?"

"This would be different," I tried to explain. "More slow paced and no big egos to feed."

"Ha," she quipped. "You don't think big egos exist only in big towns do you?"

Somehow I had known things would not go smoothly as I had driven home. She always did have a way of seeing through me.

Three days later I was sitting in the same chair in Smitty's shop, surrounded with the same six faces in their appointed seats but with a new face in the barber chair.

"How'd the missus take it?" Brewster asked, causing the gallery to laugh.

Of course I knew he was referring to my need to "tell all" regarding our conversation concerning the coming elections.

"You're next," Smitty interrupted, pointing at me as he took the barber's cape off the neck of the most recent customer.

Somehow, being confined to the chair and at Smitty's mercy, also gave me the feeling that I was also at the mercy of those gathered around me.

"Bill is it?" Smitty asked tersely, "how'd you want it cut?"

"Just shorten it up, taper the back and around the ears," I said, missing my barber back home who had cut it the same way for twenty years.

"You gonna run?" he asked, softening his tone a bit, "for Mayor."

I was surprised that he'd ask and told him so.

"Not surprised to hear," he said. "They were givin' 3-1 odds you'd back out."

"I never said...." I began. "Never told anyone I'd run for sure, said I'd consider it," I answered defensively.

"Well, you'd better get to 'considerin', the cut-off for filing is two days away. After that it'd take an act of Congress to get you on the ballot," he urged.

"Glad to hear you've made up your mind," Brewster said. "I been tellin' these guys you wuz a civic kind of guy and would make the right choice. I'll walk with you over to the City Hall and introduce you around soon as you're done here."

I could see I was being railroaded but was at a loss to stop the train. "Isn't there some kind of residency requirement?" I asked hopefully. "We've lived here less than two months."

"Resident of the state and homeowner is about all it takes," Smitty said. "They'll go over the details with you when you sign the papers and pay your registration fee."

My steering committee amounted to the six I had met in the barber shop, but soon included their friends and families as well. Over the next two weeks I can say that I enjoyed the looks, attention, and hearing snippets from their conversations that included words like *new* and *Mayor*, as my wife and I passed others on the street. I began to feel like a dignitary.

I had made it a part of my daily ritual to go into town and spend time with my new friends and supporters and was sitting in my usual chair when the *newsie* from our local paper stopped by with a camera and a request for an interview. The front page the very next morning had a not-so-flattering picture of me beneath the headline which read ***New Resident Challenges Incumbent Mayor for Top City Position.*** Below it, two columns recounted my credentials as a former city employee and my educational background.

It was at this moment that I had my first real misgivings, but also realized that the wheels were already in motion and only 20 days remained before the election. When the phone rang it was the TV station manager from Twin Falls, a larger nearby town, requesting that I participate in an on-air televised debate. I knew the whole thing was now totally out of control and that I had better get busy and do my homework.

I had yet to meet my opponent, who had already served one term as Mayor and had lived locally all of his life. I spent the next five days in the library and at City Hall in an attempt to gain some idea of who he was and what his job entailed. I could find nothing written about him that would give me anything to use against him. He was a family man with two children, married to a local woman, owned and ran the local Ace Hardware with the help of his wife and two part-time employees. Notably, he'd been class vice-president and had been a two-time state wrestling champion in high school.

He also belonged to the usual civic groups: Rotary, Chamber of Commerce, and Lions club. My new cronies at the barber shop filled in details outlining his service in the National Guard and time served in Iraq as a combatant. They offered no information about his rank or other accomplishments. Before we even met I stood in awe of him and wished I'd not have taken the bait when encouraged to run against him.

I was a mess the day of the debate, which was being held in the high school auditorium. Arlene was supportive and helped me dress for the viewers as I was at a loss of what attire would be appropriate. We settled on grey slacks, long sleeved white shirt and a tie. I suggested red like they do on television, she chose one of her favorites which had mauve and grey diagonal stripes. With Smitty's help I sported a fresh trim.

We arrived at the school an hour early and I tried my best to radiate the confidence I did not feel when I was greeted at the door and ushered backstage, where a makeup artist was waiting. It felt a little foolish when I took the offered chair and she began to apply various kinds of makeup and powder. I declined when she attempted to darken my lip color with a tube just like Arlene used at home. She coiffed my hair and commented that it would have looked better if it had two or three days new growth after being cut. Out of the corner of my eye I could see Arlene leaning against a wall, smiling and enjoying the whole ritual.

"You're the guy who wants to be the Mayor, aren't you?" a young voice asked, as a boy diverted my attention from her.

I hesitated for a moment and he continued. "My dad's the Mayor you know, and I think he does a real good job."

I guessed him to be about ten with red-blond hair and pale skin covered with a multitude of freckles. His dimpled chin was slightly extended as though what he had said held a challenge to it and his azure eyes were unblinking as he looked at me. Across the room a woman was speaking with Arlene.

"Let's take a couple of rolls on each sleeve," my make-up person suggested. "It always looks good to give the impression of a working man, and let's loosen the tie and unbutton the top button."

As she undid me, I felt more comfortable and more like myself, less like a city slicker moved to the small town to fix its ills.

"My name's Bill," I said, extending my hand to the young soon-to-be-a-man standing waiting for my answer. "From everything I've read about your father, I agree with you. He does a good job."

He gave me a puzzled look and said, "me too, but they call me Billy."

"Do you like to fish?" I asked him, obviously catching him off guard.

As he formulated an answer, I could tell I had asked the right question, a smile crept onto his youthful face.

"I love to fish," he answered. "Dad says I'm a natural, I caught a seven pound cat down on the Snake last summer," he added proudly. "Do you fish?"

"Yes, I love it too, but I have never caught a seven pounder," I admitted.

He was beaming now and snuck a glance at the woman standing beside Arlene, who I presumed was his mother and Chance Baker's wife.

"Do you and your dad fish a lot?" I asked my new young friend.

The question brought a worried look and sense of disappointment which replaced the grin. "Not as much as we used to," he admitted. "Seems like something always comes up and he has to put it off."

"Oh," I said. "I'm new around here, maybe he'd let me take you when he's busy and you could show me where the big ones are."

He looked questioningly at me, wondering I suppose what my intentions were. "I'd have to talk to him about that," he said. "Doesn't do to show everyone where your best holes are."

I nodded, showing that I understood just what he meant.

"Ten minutes, ten minutes," someone said as they ushered me toward the stage where the interviewer already sat waiting. From the opposite side a tall lean man in his mid thirties was duplicating my efforts. We arrived at our respective lecterns as though we had rehearsed it and gave each other a courteous nod.

"Thank you both for coming tonight," she began. "I'm sure our time here will be enlightening and well spent. I have a list of questions I'd like to cover and have been given others from the audience as well, if we have time to address them. Let me introduce each of you to our viewing audience. On my left is the incumbent Mayor, the Honorable Chauncey T. Baker, and on my right, his challenger William L. Sparks."

There was the usual applause and catcalls from the audience. When they subsided she resumed control of the debate.

"I will address the first question to our sitting Mayor and offer him time for an answer and then offer the same to our challenger. Each will have a moment to rebut as they feel the need, before we move to the next question. Then I'll address the next question to the challenger, Mr. Sparks and give Mr. Baker like opportunity to speak. Is that understood?"

We both nodded.

"Following the debate, both candidates will have two minutes to speak openly about why they feel they are the better choice to serve as Mayor," she said. "How would you prefer to be addressed?" she asked.

"Chance," was the immediate answer from across the room.

"Bill," I replied in turn.

"What will be your first priority as Mayor of the town of Buhl?" she asked my opponent.

"Quality of life," he answered without hesitation, then went on for a moment to explain what that meant to him personally.

"Now Bill, same question," she said. "What do you see as your first priority if you are elected to lead this town?"

"Same answer," I said. "The reason why we moved here from the bigger city was because of the quality of life that is apparent here. I'd hope to maintain what is already in place."

The more questions that were asked, the more I came to appreciate and admire my opponent and the less I wanted to occupy his office. Luckily for me, the remaining nine questions were questions for which I had prepared previously while doing my due diligence at City Hall and the library.

As the last question was answered, she thanked each of us and opened the floor first to Chance and then myself to give our closing statements. Chance stuck to the topics, naming the city's pending needs and his proposed plans to fill them. When he finished, a round of applause filled the room.

When it stopped all eyes turned to me. "I have little to offer," I said humbly, "which you do not already have in your current mayor. I personally stand in awe of him and his accomplishments, his dedication, and his commitment to his nation and family. If I were elected it would only be so that he could spend more time with his wife and children but with no thought to improve what he has given you."

Much to my surprise the audience began to stand and clap until none remained in their seats. I received a huge smile from my wife and a like one from Chance's wife, who remained standing beside mine.

As we crossed the room toward each other and shook hands, Chance leaned toward my ear and whispered, "let's have lunch."

In the diner, we were seated at a table rather than a booth, with our wives beside us and their children at the end, putting the Mayor and I directly across from one another. After our orders were taken and the waitress had gone, Chance broke the ice.

"I've lived here all of my life," he began, "and I believe this is the first time that a Mayor has not ran unopposed. Most often the incumbent has either died in office or just flat refused to take another term, forcing someone to step up and take the reins."

"Is that how you came to be Mayor?" I asked curiously.

"Yeah, Joe Talbot was Mayor when I got back from a tour in Iraq. He was somewhere between 80 and 100 I'd guess. He asked me if I'd be the Deputy Mayor while he got some of his medical problems worked out and I said yes. But he never did recover, died two months later."

"How long ago was that?" Arlene asked, inviting herself into the conversation.

His wife spoke up before Chance could answer. "Just over six years ago," she said.

We could tell by her tone that she hoped I'd win the election so she could have her husband back.

Chance had a twinkle in his eye when he said, "I've been hearing a lot about you from your lobby over at the barber shop, they think it's all *said and done* and that you've got the job. What do you think?"

"I think I'm voting for you," I answered. "I don't know how they ever talked me into running in the first place."

I got a sour look from his wife. My own wife was smiling now.

"Billy told me that you invited him to go fishing," Chance said.

I felt a little embarrassed that I had not talked to them first and said so.

"I was just making small talk with him and would never have invited him without talking to you first." I said.

"I know that," he answered with a smile, "and I know he'd never have taken you to the good holes anyway without checkin' with me first."

Of the 246 votes cast I received just over a dozen, the rest went to Chance. My best guess is that the six at the barber shop and their wives made it a point so that the vote would not to be unanimous.

We, my wife and I, are no longer outsiders looking to make friends and become part of the community. We get a nod or smile everywhere we go and everyone knows my name. With some urging I took the Deputy Mayor job that had been vacant since Chance moved up to Mayor, but not until receiving a promise that Chance would not leave me high and dry without ample warning.

A little over three months later, a drunken driver traveling through the area ran a stop sign and broadsided the Baker's car on their way to church. While his wife and the children survived with only minor injuries, the major impact was on the driver's side. Chance had serious trauma to his head and the internal organs on his left side, leaving him in a coma for nearly a week. It was during that time that I learned he was on dialysis. He had apparently lost a kidney while serving in Iraq and the remaining one had to be removed following the accident.

The prognosis was not good. They'd either find a suitable donor or he'd be relegated to dialysis for the rest of his life. When I learned that not only did treatment destroy the quality of life for the patient but also shortened that life as well, I approached Arlene with an idea.

"Honey, while they are searching for a kidney donor for Chance, what would you think if I was tested for compatibility?" I said as off-handedly as possible.

She looked at me with surprise registering on her face but controlled her initial reaction to tell me how stupid that sounded. Finally when she spoke, it was in a carefully measured tone.

"What if..." she began, then started again. "It's a big step, have you given it serious thought? Something could happen to you just like it did to him and you'd be in the same position."

"I know and I have," I answered. "And I'm sure it is unlikely that I'd be a match or that they'd need me. I may even be too old, I don't know."

"Let's talk with the pastor first and get his opinion," she suggested, with fear registering in her clear grey eyes.

Pastor Tom had become our friend as well as spiritual leader and made himself available later that same afternoon. After hearing a repeat of what I had said to Arlene, he grew quiet and simply said, "let's pray together now and ask God to guide you."

Sometime during the night, a verse came to mind and remained with me when I awoke. I recalled, "greater love has no man..." John 15:13 (KJV) *"Greater love hath no man than this, that a man lay down his life for his friends."*

After I showered, I was at peace with my decision and went right to scripture where I read and re-read the entire verse.

Over coffee I shared with Arlene what I believed was God's answer to our prayers. She said little. Later at the hospital we met with Chance's physician where I explained what I proposed. He pointed out, as had Arlene, the gravity of the decision and that because of my age, the first step would entail a comprehensive physical examination.

Chance was awake when we entered the room, his wife had left for a few minutes to run some errands. His thought processes had returned and he seemed vital and functional as I explained what we had just discussed with his physician.

His first reaction was, "who would run the Mayor's office with both of us out?"

How like him, I thought, to be worrying about others when it was he who needed the help, all the more reason to do what I was considering.

"What a giant ego," I said. "Arlene warned me that the size of the town had nothing to do with the size of the egos in it. They'll get by just fine and when it's over they'll appreciate us all the more."

It took a week to jump through all the hoops and over the hurdles required to consider me as a donor. During that time, my wife and family had more than a few discussions.

"You're a match," the doctor said into his phone, "but before we move forward, I'd want to meet with all of those concerned and clear the air and answer any questions anyone has."

Arlene took the news much better than I had expected, as a matter of fact she now seemed almost eager to proceed. On our way to the hospital she smiled at me and said, "I had a dream last night."

Of course when she didn't continue, she forced me to ask, "tell me about it."

"Well, not exactly a dream," she corrected, "more like a vision."

"So you had a vision?" I asked laughingly. "What did you see?"

"Okay," she said with a slight edge in her voice. "More like I heard Him."

"Him, God?" I asked, walking what I knew was a thin line.

"Maybe, maybe not, but someone like Him," she said. "He asked me questions."

I was having fun with her now and said, "so just maybe the God of the universe was asking you questions? What questions?"

There was no smile on her lips now as she looked me straight in the eyes and said, "He asked why I supposed we chose to settle in Buhl of all the possible places, and why I encouraged you to get a haircut, and how in the world you made up your mind to run for Mayor. He didn't have to say anything more; I knew what He was telling me."

And I knew what He was telling her too, that all of this and much more was part of His plan from the very beginning of time.

The surgery went well for both of us. I saw very little in the way of change regarding my everyday life after I healed. Chance however, even though the surgery was a success, would be on anti-rejection drugs for the rest of his life.

Chance, Billy and I spend a great deal of time down on the Snake trying to hook onto one of those big cats when not tending to the city's business, but Billy still holds the record.

– The End –

Lessons to be Learned

One could have found it humorous the way the graying old man with stooped shoulders and slow gate walked up to the young man who stood a half head taller and said, "I'm not gonna kill you son, just whip you so's you remember not to mess with my family again."

"Bring it on old man," the boy said for the sake of his friends who had now moved up to watch the encounter.

"I'm gonna take that cane away from you and stick it up your..." he began but finished with an "Ow!" as he found himself landing on his tailbone on the pavement.

As the youth had moved toward him, the older man had taken the crook of the cane and hooked the boy's leading foot, pulling it as he did. Before the boy could reach his feet, the cane came down making a sound like crushing ice on his extended forearm.

"That'd be the radius," the old man said quietly, identifying the broken bone in the arm. As he did, two of the young men in the crowd inched forward toward the old man.

"That'd be a real mistake boys," he cautioned, "three on one may give me cause to get angry and if'n I get angry, someone could get hurt bad or killed."

Meanwhile, the other boy had gained his feet and was opening and closing his hand to make sure it worked. There was hate in his green eyes as he began to circle the old man warily...

"I lose my temper more now that I used to," he said apologetically. "Came back with me from 'Nam I guess, when I saw the boys here complaining about their rights and all, and knowin' the ones over there died to give 'em those rights. I'm tryin' to work on it, losin' your temper doesn't do any one any good."

The crowd had gained a respect for the sage old man who stood at the center of the circle, but knew that the challenge could only end one way, the young strong football player could have easily bench pressed him with one hand.

"Put that thing down,' the boy ordered, referring to the cane, "and fight fair.'

The gray head seemed to shake itself in unbelief. "You must think stupid comes with age," he said. "I need my friend here to lean on, my good leg ain't all that good and the other's in a rice paddy somewhere in Asia." As he finished he tapped his right leg with the cane, producing a metallic sound.

With that revelation, the young athlete rushed him, head down like a lineman rushing to sack a quarterback.

At the last second a graceful sidestep put the old gentleman out of harms way, and once again the cane found flesh and bone, this time on the shin of the youth, who fell at once, grimacing in pain.

The old man was still smiling as he offered his hand to help the boy to his feet. At that second, two from the sidelines rushed him. He turned in time to put the end of the cane into the ribcage of one and before tripping the other, as he too went down among them. Had they the presence of mind he'd have been at their mercy, as he slowly used the cane to regain his feet.

"What is going on here?" the teacher asked as she walked from the school toward them, addressing her questions to the old man.

"Well," he answered smiling, "I'z jus' showin' these boys how to use a cane, ma'am. Looks like they'll be using one all too soon."

She eyed the three laying on the blacktop warily before smiling and answering, "well, it looks like they've learned all they can stand for one day Grandpa, why don't you come on inside and have a cup of coffee with me?"

The old man looked at his young, beautiful granddaughter, smiled and said, "you fellas 'bout tuckered me out, I'm goin' in and sit for a spell, you go ahead and keep practicing like I showed you."

As they walked he winked and said, "I heard you and your grandma talking last night about the hard time some of the students were givin' you, thought I'd come on down and meet them."

– The End –

Sustained

Albeit a part of every human life to die, Amanda had not considered her father and mother as candidates for an early demise. Bill had just last fall passed the half-century mark and Elaine was only forty-six when their little Cessna had disappeared without so much as a warning or mayday. The weather had been clear and warm, the blue skies promising an enjoyable and speedy trip from their ranch in Montana to Calgary, Alberta, where they had expected to enjoy a few days together while celebrating their anniversary.

It was not often that a working ranch could afford the luxury of having its owners spend an entire week away and leave the decision making to the hired help. Amanda had been away at college and in class when the first message had come but had remained hopeful and prayerful until the second arrived three hours later.

The little red and white plane had been spotted nearly at the snowy summit of a high mountain range slightly south of the Canadian border, lying upside down on the steep hillside with its wing light flashing but no sign of survivors. Rescue crews were enroute and were expected to arrive at the base camp by mid-morning the following day, barring possible additional inclement weather.

It was well known that in May, in the higher reaches of the Rockies, the weather was unpredictable and temperatures often fell to zero or below at night, making survival a challenge even for those prepared and uninjured. Amanda had only her faith and self-discipline to sustain her as she returned to the ranch to wait what she feared most in the world, being alone. She had no siblings; only aunts, uncles, and cousins with whom to share her burden, and then only by telephone, for none of them lived nearby.

Night had fallen and the majority of the hired help had come to the big house to share their concerns and give voice to their prayers, before leaving for their own homes. Only the foreman and one other made their beds in the two room bunkhouse a few hundred feet away, where they always were available to handle whatever nature or circumstance threw at the ranch.

Amanda had never felt more alone and in despair as the yellow glow of the lamps inside the house failed to give warmth and comfort or chase the darkness away from the corners of its rooms. She cried until tears no longer came, imagining those she loved alone and freezing to death in the darkness on a lonely, snow-covered peak somewhere far away. Her mind filled with a scene as if from a movie, of her father and mother holding each other, their broken bodies slipping into blackness as their lives ebbed slowly away.

She must have fallen asleep because she found herself awakening, but in a house that felt little like the home she had always known. It was still dark outside and so quiet that she imagined she could hear the beating of her own broken heart. In the adjacent room she could hear the tick-tock of the grandfather clock as the hands moved relentlessly in a circuit around its ornate face.

She felt empty, the first waves of fear and anguish had subsided but would return with the morning light and reports she feared to hear. Instinctively, she pulled the throw from the back of the couch and covered herself to her chin as she began to shiver. What would she do if they never returned home, how would she survive, could she keep the ranch or would she have to sell it?

Granted she was twenty-two, nearly finished with her senior year at the university, and reasonably intelligent, but was she ready to 'manage life', to address its challenges as they came, to make prudent decisions that would affect both her future and the future of others? She feared not.

When she awakened for a second time, her muscles were stiff and sore but she felt more rested and refreshed. For several moments she just looked out the window at the breaking dawn, not daring to think about what the day may hold for her. Lost in her thoughts, she jumped when the phone rang before running to answer it.

"Amanda?" said the soft, firm voice on the phone. "This is Tyke, Tyke Wilson, Sheriff of Valley County," it said, clarifying both who and why he was calling. "We got fresh snow during the night and it's snowing again now, but because of it the temperature has stayed above freezing, a rare thing at this altitude. Our best guess is that we are camped eight to ten miles down from the crash site and should be there before nightfall, God willing. The snow here on the south side is deep and the terrain too steep for snowmobiles, so we'll be forced to go it on foot and walk the ridgeline until we get closer."

Amanda was trying hard to absorb the considerable information she had just heard and to rationally apply it to the picture her mind painted for her.

"Thank you Sheriff," she said, her voice quavering, "Please thank everyone who is with you and keep in touch."

As she said it, "keep in touch" sounded so flippant and unemotional that she wished she had chosen her words more wisely. On the other hand, had she said what she felt, her tears would have muffled her words, making them impossible to understand.

"We will," he answered. "But I expect that we will lose cell service as soon as we move behind the mountain, that's why I'm calling now." "Keep praying," he added.

Amanda knew the Sheriff well and made it a point to always say hello if they met on the street in town. He and his wife were members of the local riding club that her parents had started a decade ago and continued to support. She remembered when she was a small child, he had often invited her to ride with him at the front of the parades when he had drawn duty as a color guard. She credited both he and her parents for her deep love of horses.

Montana has two things that are self-apparent, wide expanses of flat land and equally expansive high majestic mountains circling them. With the two came unusual and unpredictable weather patterns, with the bluest blue skies and the whitest white billowing clouds that turned black in an instant bringing hail, rain, or snow with them. An occasional tornado was often thrown in to keep the residents on their toes.

A knock on the door interrupted her thoughts – their foreman entered without waiting for her to respond.

"Mornin' Miss," he said. "I come hopin' to hear some good news."

Amanda quickly recounted her earlier conversation with the Sheriff and poured them each a cup of black coffee. As they sat at the large table, a hired man followed his boss in and took a seat and a cup without speaking, then another and another as the crew began to arrive for the work day.

With them today however, came their wives and children and copious amounts of breakfast foods, which they had prepared at their own homes. They visited with each other in muted tones which the children seemed also to pick up, thus keeping the revelry and noise to a minimum. Word was passed around quietly, just as was the food, that no new news had been presented which would bring with it either sadness or happiness. They got a late start that morning by ranching standards, seemingly wanting to stay and feel the strength of unity that numbers bring.

Lopez, the foreman, finally led the crew in a short prayer before shooing them outside to get started with the day's chores. Their wives stayed and cleaned up the breakfast dishes while some of the children crawled up on Amanda's lap and took her attention off the promised events of the day.

A few minutes after noon, Amanda's cell phone rang but was quickly disconnected without a message being received. She turned the television to the weather channel and noted that new storms were pressing down from Canada and would reach the mountains before nightfall. Tears welled up in her eyes as the enormity of the situation once again overcame her.

At 5:00 p.m. her cell rang again, this time it was one of the search and rescue crew who was relaying a message that he had received via walkie-talkie from those higher up the mountain. The crew had reached the wreckage and had found no sign of either of her parents, thus leaving hope that they were alive and mobile. There were however, signs of blood inside of the small plane. Amanda was both elated and afraid to assume too much, she knew that the Sheriff had told it straight and had not tried to make it seem more than it was.

Shortly after 6:00 the cell rang again, but the line was dead when she answered. A few minutes later it rang again, this time a familiar voice replied to her second hello.

"Amanda, this is Tyke," he said. "Keep praying. I've got a team out scouring the mountainside. It looks like Bill and Elaine survived the crash and left the site, presumably to find better shelter. Trouble is that the blowing snow has all but destroyed their trail."

"But... but you are sure they are alive?" Amanda asked, putting the Sheriff in a bad position.

"Hold on, I didn't say that," Tyke clarified. "What I said was that it appears that both were alive after the crash, and, I said to keep praying."

He softened his tone and continued. "If anyone could keep a level head and come out of this, it would be your Dad. He's no quitter and knows the mountains better than most."

"Thank you," she said in a halting voice, "thank all of them."

"Gotta get back to it," he answered. "We'll keep looking right up to dark and I will call you back either way."

Serena and Marie, the foreman's wife and sister, knocked on the door but came into the kitchen before Amanda could answer. In their arms were boxes of food enough to satisfy a Thanksgiving crowd. Everything had been wrapped in clean towels and had retained the heat on their short drive from home.

As the men and the rest of the families arrived, with them came more food and desserts. Two of the older children were dispatched to set the big table while the men sat and begin discussing the events of their day.

The subject that was on everyone's mind was not spoken of until Amanda said, "The Sheriff called and gave us hope, Mom and Dad have left the plane to find shelter. They are searching for them now."

"We should pray," Serena said, looking at her husband who then looked at Amanda questioningly.

"Yes," Amanda agreed. "We must depend upon God's mercy and love now more than ever before." She dropped her chin and began to pray.

"Over here," one of the crew called to Tyke Wilson. "They are holed up in a snow cave."

Tyke and the three others who just arrived on snow shoes hurried toward the mound where they stood waiting. The fresh snow had fallen and covered both footprints and other signs of human activity. Only the tall extendable pole with an orange plastic ribbon flying near the top made finding the location even possible.

"Bill, Elaine," Tyke yelled. "Are you in there, can you hear me?"

A muffled response testified to living, breathing humans safely buried several feet deep in the powdery snow.

"Sit tight," Tyke answered immediately, feeling foolish for saying it. "We'll have you dug out in a minute."

~ ~

A snow cave, if one is not an enlightened outdoor enthusiast, is simply the equivalent of an igloo which is hurriedly hollowed out and then sealed by means of a lighted candle on the inside. The heat from the candle melts the snow's surface just enough to turn it into ice and thus retain heat and add to the integrity of the structure. Skiers and other outdoor winter enthusiasts are usually quite aware of how to quickly fabricate such a safe harbor from chill of the wind and freezing temperatures.

When the plane had caught the updraft it couldn't have been at a worse time. They had just emerged from low lying clouds and were working their little plane hard to maintain the 9800 foot altitude necessary to fly over the snow covered saddle that lay between two high peaks. The wind coming up the north side of the pass, being pushed by the gathering storm, grabbed their leading wing, shoving the other straight downward toward the deep snow a hundred feet below. Bill did well to side-hill for the length of a football field before plunging that wing into the drifts and flipping over. They were fortunate that the snow absorbed most of the force of the crash and then held the plane tightly in its grasp. This prevented the plane from sliding down the steep hillside which continued a thousand feet before ending in a pile of large granite boulders.

Hanging upside down in their respective harnesses, Bill quickly accessed their situation but did not share the reality that he thought it unlikely that they'd survive. Elaine was bleeding badly from a large open wound near the scalp line above her left eye and did not have full use of her right arm. Unknown to Bill, until he freed himself from his harness and fell to the roof of the plane in a heap, his left leg was broken below the knee. He helped Elaine free herself from her harness and bandaged her head as she lowered herself to a place beside him. They quickly took off their light jackets and began layering themselves with the clothes in their luggage which was scattered inside the cabin. Out of habit, both had brought warm parkas and gloves and several sweaters and knit hats.

"We can't stay here," Bill finally said. "There's a storm on its way and we are too near the summit. I'm afraid the wind gusting against the plane will send it sliding down into the canyon with us inside."

Elaine concurred by nodding her head. "Where then?" she asked.

"I think if we drop down to the tree line we have a better chance of finding cover and fuel for a fire," he answered, trying to sound confident. "Will you look around and see what you can find in the way of food and water while I try and find something to splint my leg and improvise a crutch?"

Bill attempted to send a mayday without success, but did find that the battery remained intact and energized. He flipped a switch which lit the port and starboard lights located on the wing tips. Of course the one was buried under many feet of snow but the other was visible and would continue to flash until the battery was drained.

She did as she'd been asked, moving slowly and carefully in the cramped space, first emptying a large zippered canvas bag, then refilling it with what she deemed to be items more necessary for their survival. Bill took a large tube filled with flight maps and split it along its two foot length with his Leatherman, then wrapped several of the maps around his leg for insulation before covering them with the tube. The ever present roll of duct tape secured the two halves together. Elaine used their two woolen scarves to tie the makeshift splint securely in place and add protection from the elements.

"How long," she asked, "do you think they'll wait before they begin to search for us?"

"Probably a day," Bill answered. "Then it will take another or so to get a search party together and start ferrying them up from the flat-lands."

She actually laughed at his reply. "Well, it appears then that this is a good time to begin those diets we've been talking about. We've got a dozen bottles of water, some granola bars, part of a package of Fig Newtons, and the rest of that can of cashews you've been nibbling on."

"Check the pocket of my jacket," he said. "I think there's a few pieces of Jack Link's jerky left."

Elaine could sense Bill was trying to keep the conversation light and it worried her because she knew it was probably because he judged their situation more serious that he let on. "Think we'll make it?" she asked bluntly, while looking him straight in the eyes.

"God knows," he answered, "but we are better off so far than we deserve to be. We could be at the bottom of the canyon in a pile of rocks if that wing hadn't grabbed the snow and stopped our slide."

"How are we gonna do this?" Elaine asked. "The snow's probably waist deep or more. As quick as we get out we'll go down and you can't walk far on that leg."

As Bill considered what she had said, he nodded. "You are right, we'll need to stay as close to the plane as possible and conserve our energy, but far enough away that we don't get caught in a slide if it shifts."

He found two 4x6 foot plastic tarps still folded in a cargo pocket along the side of the fuselage, and she two army surplus woolen blankets. Together they began to assemble their larder of supplies and secure them with the remnants of their flight harnesses which had previously been cut loose from their fastenings. The wind had increased and was blowing stinging bits of frozen ice and snow through the broken windshield and door opening causing them to begin to shiver. Bill sensed that shock as well as the cold temperature was settling in.

"Look," Elaine said triumphantly, holding up Bill's little single burner butane pack stove. Then she laughed and added, "we'd probably have had power enough to make the summit if you'd stop squirreling away so much stuff."

"Less than a pound including the fuel," he objected, "and you'll be happy I did when we light it. There should be a 4 cup aluminum pot and some stale coffee too."

Now they were back on track, feeling confident and hopeful as they bantered back and forth, loading their gear, and preparing for the adventure ahead.

~ ~

Light poured into the compact little womb which had housed them through the previous day and night. Welcome voices seemed to caress their ears as both Bill and Elaine were carefully extracted from their little cave. Bill took the big hand of his friend eagerly as Tyke attempted to help him gently to his feet. But as his pain became apparent, Tyke abandoned the exercise and lowered him back onto the ground.

"Got a broken wing?" he questioned, referring to the leg rather than the arm.

"Yeah," Bill replied, "think so. Good to see a friendly face."

Tyke smiled, then turned to Elaine. "Hello pretty lady," he said. "Do you mind if we have a look under that fancy hat of yours?"

Traces of blood were apparent on her face and evidence of Bill's bandage job was not well hidden under her stocking cap.

"Sure Tyke," Elaine laughed. "Just don't muss up my makeup."

It was approaching 2:00 p.m. of the third day and the wind seemed to be on a late lunch break as the team made preparations to ferry the anniversary couple off the mountain. The five from search and rescue and the sheriff had brought two stretchers disguised as toboggans filled with food and medical supplies up the steep ridge from the staging camp several thousand feet below.

"You made good time," Bill observed to Tyke. "Good thing too, we were starting to run low on Champaign and caviar."

"You don't look like you suffered much," Tyke teased back. "I saw the stove and the coffee pot. Surprised you didn't bring your hibachi and grill steaks."

They'd just finished loading Bill and Elaine on the sleds when the weather returned right on cue, driving snow and chilling wind coming over the top and down the canyon walls.

"Let's get moving," Tyke said unnecessarily," as the two men in front pulled on the rope and started the sleds moving. The four in the rear of course had the more difficult job of slowing the descent to keep from plunging to the bottom. There was much more to the process than meets the eye. If you have ever tried to side hill you know what I mean, gravity fights you, wanting to go straight down to the bottom rather than taking the more gradual route.

~ ~

"Not much of a pilot, your Dad," Tyke said into the phone when he was finally able to get enough signal to call Amanda. "Landed it on its side in a snow bank. If I had the authority I'd write him a reckless flying ticket."

Amanda's face was warm with tears of joy, she looked upward and moved her lips in a simple gesture of thanks. "Are they alright?" she asked.

"Banged up a bit, a few scrapes here and there, but nothing serious," he answered. "We'll take a break in a few minutes and I'll let them call you back."

Ten minutes later the team had found a knob with scattered alpine spruce trees clinging valiantly to life on it and chose to take a short rest. Tyke tied his rope to one of them before walking forward and handing his cell to Elaine.

"Just hit redial," he said with a smile, "someone is waiting to talk with you."

Amanda and Elaine visited for several minutes before the Sheriff repeated the scene with Bill. The team was enjoying their rest, nibbling on energy bars and drinking Gatorade while lying in the snow nearby and talking. It was always a good day when they could call their work rescue rather than recovery.

They averaged only a mile or so per hour for the first several, but picked up the pace when the terrain began to flatten out and allow them to let nature pull the sleds toward their destination. The sun had long ago gone down behind the lofty peaks, but the waning light still remained as they entered camp. The camp itself lacked many of the comforts of home but did have tents with wood stoves and cots with warm sleeping bags, and a savory stew was cooking over an open fire.

Two big husky snow cats stood ready nearby to take the survivors, their rescuers, and their gear off the mountain to where others waited eagerly twenty miles and three thousand feet below them. Montana has an interesting geography, seemingly without variety, either mountains or plains pretty much sums it up.

When Amanda finished speaking with her parents, she began to spread the word, first to the crew remaining on the ranch, then to friends and relatives who had been notified earlier, and finally to their church whose members had been waiting for news and praying for them. Her father had mentioned in passing his broken leg and her mother's injures but had played them down, which by itself caused her worry. He was the kind of guy who'd wrap a dirty rag around a serious wound until he could finish what he was working on.

It was well past midnight when her brain finally tired of running scenarios through it and allowed her to sleep. The crew on the mountain, after enjoying a filling meal and passing around the celebration bottle, excused themselves one at a time and enjoyed a well-deserved rest in the shelter of the tent, with the silence of the night interrupted by nothing but the twinkling of the stars overhead.

~ ~

"Amazing," the doctor said while holding Bill's x-rays up to the light. "You have a serious compound fracture, and yet you were able to stabilize it to the point that it is already healing and needs no further adjustment."

Bill smiled. "God had it all *mapped* out for me," he said, knowing that it had been this doctor who had removed the *mapcase splint* from his swollen leg.

"Punny," the doctor replied. "Real punny."

They had gone to school together and had known each other and their families all of their lives which accounted for the light atmosphere in the examination room. They shared another laugh before the doctor gave Bill both oral and written instructions as to the care and rehab of the leg and asked his nurse to set a return appointment.

"Keep your leg elevated, stay off your horse and don't put weight on it until after our next visit," the doctor cautioned as Bill left the room.

As it turned out, Elaine had pinched a nerve in her neck which required several treatments before the numbness and pain left her arm, the scalp wound was superficial but required careful monitoring and cleaning to keep it from becoming infected.

During their recuperation, and with the inspiration of the Holy Spirit, both Bill and Elaine seemed to have a renewed interest in pursuing their first love, Jesus. Odd how sometimes it takes a gentle slap to awaken us to what is most important in life.

– The End –

The Morning

He arose from his chair and walked stiffly to the front door. The first few steps after sitting for a time were always the hardest, he was reminded, as his arthritis made itself known. His gnarled hand turned the door knob with some difficulty before it released and the door opened. There were three steps which equalized the elevation of the sidewalk to that of the front porch. The morning paper lay on the second, waiting to be harvested by its owner.

With care and deliberation, he made his way down all three steps, then turned and bent to pick up the paper. He'd found it much easier to reach it if it was a step higher than his slippered feet. The rising sun promised another beautiful spring day as it began its ascent in the blue of the cloudless sky. He noted it but did not vocalize his thankfulness to the God who made it so.

"Is it cold?' she asked, as he closed the door behind him and joined his wife in the living room.

"No, just a nip to remind us that winter is behind us and summer is still a comin'," he answered. She smiled and seemed to accept his appraisal of the early morning weather without comment.

As always, he took the front page and handed her the local section. After they had read their fill, they'd trade and then talk about what the editors had found interesting enough to print before having a second cup of coffee with their breakfast. And so it had gone for the last twenty years or so since they had officially retired for the final time. Each day had its beginning ritual which was looked forward to and enjoyed by both. Their children were raised and theirs as well with both immersed in their own lives, with little time to spare for their parents and grandparents.

"He's still at it," he said with disgust in his voice, referring to the sitting President. "This time he made a stand against Christianity at the Easter Prayer Breakfast. I still wonder how he ever got elected."

His wife nodded but knew better than encourage her husband in a political debate that served only to raise his blood pressure. She read the list of local upcoming events listed for their small community, then turned over the page to the obituaries. Somehow, as they had aged, they were drawn to read of familiar faces and names that appeared on earth for the final time. A few scant paragraphs attempted to describe the featured person's life but always failed to do them justice.

She read the names aloud, but the obituaries quietly to herself. He occasionally commented on a name he recognized and added his own memories. "Bill Jones, wasn't he the one who owned the Ace Hardware? Or Clara Schmidt, I think I went to school with a Clara, does it say if she was married?" He'd reread the obits later himself while she did the crossword puzzle and perused the not-so-funny funnies.

A small intake of breath in the quiet room made him lift his eyes toward his wife. She sat in her usual place beside him wide-eyed and pale.

"What is it?" he asked. "Are you alright?"

She paused another moment before reading their names aloud, "Paul William Smith and Wanda Lee Smith, husband and wife, were found today dead in their home, no cause of death has been determined."

– The End –

A Friend

It is not the number of friends that is significant – it is the quality of a friendship that counts. - dc

Blake was turning seven on Saturday and preparations were well underway to celebrate the event in grand style. Because of the timing of his birthday, he was the oldest in his first grade class. He was also the tallest at nearly three feet. One might find it interesting how at certain periods in our lives, age plays a major role.

The teacher was sitting at her desk when he entered the classroom early, several minutes before the bell would call the students in from their morning play in the school yard. She looked up, smiled knowingly, then asked innocently, "you are early this morning Blake, is there something you need to talk with me about?"

Blake hesitated a moment, running his tongue through the opening left by the four missing teeth in front of his mouth. "My birthday is Saturday," he answered smiling. "Mom told me to ask you if I could leave invitations for my party on the desks before class."

Mrs. Roseberry smiled as she seemed to consider his request, then answered, "do you have one with my name on it?"

Blake looked stricken, knowing full well that he had not included his teacher in the invitations he carried in his freckled hand. He'd carefully written inside and signed each invitation personally under his mother's watchful eye, as he mentally had pictured each student in each row in perfect order. His short fingers held twenty-one invitations, one for each of his peers, and not one more.

The teacher pretended to be checking her scheduling book before she asked, "what day is it again?"

"Saturday," he stammered. "At Chuck-E-Cheese at 3:00."

"Oh, I am so sorry, Blake," the smiling teacher said. "I already have the day planned. I wish I'd have know sooner. You can give my invitation to someone else if you'd like."

She watched as the worry left his eyes and a smile took its usual place on his lips. "Maybe next year," he answered, with relief plainly showing on his face.

She pretended to be writing herself a reminder for the next year then said, "you may go ahead and put the invitations on the desks, but you'll have to hurry before the bell."

Blake was one of her favorites this year, probably because he was polite and quiet in class and reminded her of her own son when he had been that age. Not that he wasn't as full of mischief as his peers, but he seemed to be able to restrain it so it did not disturb the other students. He had red hair and the pale white complexion and freckles that came with the package, and blue eyes that seemed too big for his face. Yes, she thought, definitely one of my favorites. Carolyn made herself a note to make a quick trip to the nearby store during her lunch hour and choose a special gift for her little charge.

The bell rang and with it the sound of a thousand conversations that filled the school with life and purpose. First grade, the petrie dish from which each individual life took its nourishment to grow and develop as God designed. Carolyn, now in her eleventh year as an elementary teacher, paused to wonder at how each life would change over the next dozen or so years.

It took several minutes for the din to gradually subside as each child took their assigned desks, put down their books, and opened Blake's invitation. Of course it immediately became necessary to discuss the invitation with everyone around them. She gave them several minutes before restoring order and beginning her lesson for the day. Blake sat quietly beaming a smile that revealed four missing front teeth, while relishing the special attention he was receiving.

Expectation seems to be an emotion brought on by our past experiences. The expectation of a joyous birthday was borne of Blake's birthday party the previous year, but of course the previous year he had lived in a nice upscale home in a prosperous neighborhood that was filled with friends with whom he had grown up.

His father had lost his job and with it their home. They had been forced to move into government subsidized housing where other families like themselves struggled just to make ends meet, but Blake had been able to continue at his old school. At his tender age, he knew nothing of the economy of life or about the driving force behind the desire for financial success.

Mankind, much like a child, wants everything and wants it now; it has no patience for waiting. Blake had not understood when his mother had patiently tried to explain the realities of their situation and the limitations that came with it. She had finally acquiesced to his demands that he should invite everyone in his class, while secretly hoping that most would not accept their invitation.

Money had come from a grandparent at the last minute allowing them the simple luxury of a *pizza night out* at the local Chuck-E-Cheese and the semblance of a grand party. They had been forced the previous month to delay the badly needed tires on their aging van, and with

God's help, hoped to do so for yet another month. In the past they would have simply gotten a new car.

Bill, Blake's father, was now working two jobs but bringing home slightly less than half of his former salary. His mother Lucinda, the care-giver of their infant daughter, hadn't the education to make any employment a viable option when considering a sitter would be needed for two young children. By necessity and by God's infinite plan they were forced into dependency. None of this, of course, was a burden that a seven-year-old could or should have to understand or share.

The morning went by slowly, with Blake checking the clock every few minutes until finally the bell announced lunch and with it freedom to spend a few minutes visiting with his friends. By the time the bell sounded again, calling an end to the lunch hour and the students back into their classroom, many of his classmates had returned his invitation while making excuses why they could not attend – several more lay on his desk with no explanation. As tears welled up in his eyes, he put his arms on his desk and his head on them to hide his pain from the class.

Mrs. Roseberry had watched with dismay as the children followed the cruel lead of the first few. She took note that these were the same friends who had enjoyed the pool and camped out in his big back yard earlier in the year when he had lived in finer surroundings. Luke 14:16-23 came into her mind as if by magic. She made a call to her husband.

"Tom," she said in her best business voice, "I need a favor."

Her husband was tempted to laugh at the way she presented her request. "Sure Hon, what can I do for you?" he asked.

"You know that guy who bowls with you, the one who manages the Holiday Inn?" she clarified. "How would you feel about spending the night with me there on Saturday?"

"Love to!" he answered enthusiastically. "Now what's the favor?"

This time her tone softened. "I have a student who needs the use of their pool for a few hours and a place to have a birthday party. I thought maybe he could cut us a deal if we had a room."

"I'm crushed," Tom replied while laughing. "I thought you wanted to be alone with me."

"That too," she said soothingly, "but the other thing is a very big deal. Will you call him?"

"I'll call you back," he answered before hanging up.

Her cell rang back twenty minutes later. "He gave me a deal and we can have up to ten guests plus family. No charge for the entertainment room."

"We'll take it!" Carolyn said, "and... I love you."

The end of class bell sounded a few minutes later and she watched as the students began to leave the room. She noted that José had walked over to where Blake was still sitting. Blake was a head taller than the diminutive Latino boy but seemed to be in animated conversation with him.

The teacher approached them with a smile and overheard their exchange.

"Thanks for the invitation," José said with enthusiasm. "I asked my mother and she said I could come but wondered if my sister Maria may come also. Her birthday was last week but we didn't have enough money to celebrate, she thought it would be almost like celebrating together."

Blake beamed. "Of course, I'd love to have her come, the more the merrier," he said. "I'm sure we'll have enough pizza for everyone."

"Blake," the teacher said, interrupting them. "I have some good news, it looks like I'll be able to come to your party after all if you still have an invitation."

Blake smiled as he took one off the top of the large pile still sitting on his desk. "I have yours right here," he said, and then added, "your husband is welcome too."

"I'm sure he would love to come," Carolyn said, "but I'd like to speak with your mother before I bring extra people along, will you give me your phone number?"

Blake wrote his number down and handed it to his teacher. "You can call but I'm sure she'll say yes," he said.

"Hello," Carolyn said, "this is Blake's teacher, may I have a word with you about Blake's birthday party?"

"Is something wrong?" Lucinda asked. "I told Blake to ask you before he passed out the invitations."

"No, nothing," she answered. "I just wondered if the location at Chuck-E-Cheese was written in stone. It seems that my husband and I have the use of the recreation room and the pool at the Holiday Inn on Saturday and wondered if maybe you'd consider having the party there."

If it was possible to feel joy through a telephone line, Carolyn was certain she had.

"Are you sure?" Blake's mother asked. "Do you know what they charge?"

"There's no charge," Carolyn answered honestly. "It comes with our room, and besides, I already told him I'd come wherever you have the party."

"We'll bring pizza and drinks," Lucinda promised.

"And we'll be hungry," the teacher answered.

"I'll need to let the parents know..." Lucinda said, half to herself.

"Why don't you wait until you talk with Blake and see who needs to be notified," she countered. "I just saw him inviting José and his sister but I did not mention the possibility of a change because I wanted to ask you. Why don't you discuss it with him and call me at home?"

Carolyn gave Lucinda her number and disconnected.

The party was a success, though not well attended, it was memorable in that it was where Blake met Maria who would become his wife nearly fifteen years later. José lived in the same complex as Blake and knew everyone there. He introduced Blake around and together they invited nearly everyone who showed any interest.

For the next five years Blake would smile and nod every time he saw Mrs. Roseberry on the playground or in the halls at school, she would nod and return the smile. Ten years went by quickly before one day when Carolyn, now nearing middle age, went to her mail box and retrieved her mail. Inside was an invitation for her and Tom to attend the wedding of Blake and Maria.

Bill and Lucinda had been fortunate to start a company which found success and now ran a small but prosperous manufacturing business. José had just returned after four years in the Marines and now stood a head taller beside his best friend and brother-in-law.

As the ceremony ended and the groom passed their table with his bride on his arm, he smiled and nodded at Carolyn and mouthed the words *thank you.*

– The End –

The Portrait

For as long as he could remember, the stern looking gray-haired old man with the scornful eyes had stared down at him from above the mantle of the fireplace with a menacing and reproving look. As a child, he'd ventured into the mahogany-paneled room lined with books and heavy wooden furniture, only to feel the eyes following him like a savage animal, waiting for opportunity to pounce. The portrait was encompassed in a heavy ornate frame that had withstood the rigors of several generations, measuring nearly four by six feet, making its subject nearly life-sized.

The grand old mansion, resplendent in its day, still stood resolute on the hill at the end of the long driveway, with an imposing cold presence emanating from its many heavily-draped windows. Never, or nearly never, had anyone ever seen light escape from within that may have signaled that it was inhabited. In early days, a buggy or an occasional horse-drawn surrey may have evidenced the presence of a visitor. In a more modern day, horseless carriages of all sorts and vintages disgorged their passengers before pulling to the rear and into enclosed parking garages.

Nathan Jacobson led a very solitary and uneventful life following the death of his parents and the failure of his single attempt at marriage. Claire, his bride of just a few weeks had died mysteriously, from causes unknown, as was widely speculated among the town's folk.

Claire was a local woman whom he had met at boarding school. She had been just nineteen and he twenty-one when the spark had lit the fire that burned so brightly within them for but such a short time. Unknown, of course, was if she had been attracted to the man or his money, possibly both. She had been an orphan, with little to offer beyond her sparkling smile, soft melodic voice, and twinkling eyes, which were full of life.

He, on the other hand, had been born into a large family, with its lineage tracing back to the founding fathers and beyond. Aristocracy was the name they preferred, bluebloods they were called by the less privileged. Possibly sometime before crossing the ocean and beginning their lives in America, they had indeed been of noble birth, but those stories had been lost as each subsequent generation produced fewer and fewer offspring until there was no one to carry on the family name. He was the last of the line able to perpetrate both the bloodline and name, and now he had grown old and remained without prospects for children.

Bitter, alone, and disillusioned; he was seldom seen and never outside of the walls of his home. Only those bringing necessary food and consumables, the housekeeper and manservant, now had access to the interior of the mansion. He was only forty-two but would have easily passed for seventy with unkempt, scraggly, long grey hair and eyebrows, a hawk-like patrician nose, and deep-set piercing eyes, much like those of his great-great grandfather whose portrait was previously mentioned. Indeed, a newcomer may have likely judged the portrait as Nathan's own.

"Grayson!" Nathan called to his servant, as he peered out between the heavy drapes on one of the many windows overlooking the front courtyard. "I think I just saw movement in the shrubbery along the front fence."

The tall stoop-shouldered man in a worn uniform nodded and joined him at the window. "Indeed sir," he agreed. "There seems to be two or three children hiding among the bushes. I'll go down and run them off."

"No, bring them to me," Nathan replied. "I want to hear their explanation before I call the authorities."

"As you wish," Grayson answered, as he left the second-story room.

Nathan continued to watch as Grayson hurriedly crossed the expansive yard from the circular driveway and confronted the three children. Two walked ahead toward the house while the third was helped along by the butler who had a firm grip on the back of his worn jacket. The young man tried frantically to break his hold but without success.

Nathan made a production of allowing them to stand for several minutes in the entry while he descended the grand looping stairway toward them. The two smaller boys stood looking down at their tattered jeans and their untied shoes while the third, the one whom Grayson had provided special incentive to come along, stood with his head up defiantly, silently watching Nathan's approach.

"What have we here?" Nathan asked the room, not expecting a response. "Trespassers to be sure," he answered his own question. Grayson said nothing. "Thieves and vandals up to no good, I suspect," he added.

The towhead with the attitude spoke up. "That is not true, we are neither thieves nor vandals, we are children without homes looking for protection from the cold and those who would harm us."

"You'll address me as 'Sir' or you'll hold your tongue," Nathan declared in a loud voice. "Tell us, who are these whom you say are looking to harm you?"

The shortest of them seemed to find a voice and declared, "the older ones and the *man in black*... Sir."

At most, the lad looked to be no more than six and possibly even younger, but he seemed to have a maturity far beyond his years. The boy standing beside him nodded in agreement but added nothing.

"The older ones, you mean older homeless children like yourselves?" Nathan questioned. "And who is this *man in black* to whom you refer?"

Again the towhead spoke. "There are gangs of runaways and orphans who live in the streets stealing from each other and preying on the young and innocent. They work for the *man in black* and do whatever he tells them."

Nathan had adopted a more reasoned look. "Grayson, please escort our visitors into the kitchen," he said, "and offer them something to eat if you would."

Grayson must have had a strange look on his face, he had never been *asked* to do anything in all of his years of service. He'd never even heard a please or thank you.

"Yes, certainly sir," he answered. "Come along lads and let me see what we have to offer you."

Thomas Paul Hardy, Tom to his few friends, was by his own count eleven when he ran away from his abusive stepfather, following his mother's death. Shirley, like her current husband, had become a drug addict and a thief, doing anything necessary to feed the animal that eventually devoured her. He'd been on the street only a few weeks when the gangs tried to recruit him, promising the security of numbers and the protection of their *Godfather, the man in black*, as they called him.

Tremain Washington Blackstone, known as 'Blackie' by his peers, was in his early twenties and already well connected in nearly all of the unsavory criminal activities of the small town. He pimped, dealt drugs, bought and sold stolen merchandise, and ruled with an iron hand. When Tom refused his generous offer, the gang was alerted to capture and bring him to Blackie for punishment and re-education.

Having been forced by circumstance from a young age to become self-sufficient, Tom, now twelve, was resourceful and crafty and had yet to be captured. He also had a compassionate side which drew him to those in need, thus the two younger boys he'd chosen to hide and protect. Their short-term association had been summarily interrupted when Nathan's sharp eyes had spied them hiding in his hedgerow and Grayson had been dispatched to capture them.

The boys were hungry and ate with great relish what leftovers Grayson could conjure up, but remained leery of what their captor's real intent might be.

"Grayson, do we have anything more suitable for these lads to wear?" Nathan asked.

"No sir," Grayson replied. "Nothing small enough for children. I could check with my Mrs. and ask if we have anything at home."

"Would it suit you to spend the afternoon shopping?" he asked his servant. "I'll provide the funds of course and keep you on salary."

Grayson nodded and smiled. "As you wish, Sir," he replied, wondering about the change in his employer's attitude.

"Would you ask Mrs. Fox to come in before you leave?" Nathan asked, "I have a request of her also."

Cathleen Fox, now nearly seventy years old, had been in the family's employ for three generations, first as a nanny and later a housekeeper after Nathan had grown. She came and went as she pleased with little direction from Nathan who allowed her, for the most part, to make any necessary decisions concerning the day to day operation of the mansion. She ordered and paid for food stuffs, handled the bills and payroll for she and Grayson, and only consulted Nathan when she felt the need for his approval. In fact, she was the manager of the house.

"Sir?" the gray-haired portly woman said as she entered the kitchen where the children remained eating.

Nathan smiled at her as one would have their own mother, and then answered. "Mrs. Fox, we have guests. May I ask that you draw them a hot bath and show them where the necessary items for personal hygiene are kept?"

The old woman gave the three a critical once over, then smiled a grandmotherly smile and answered, "I'd be pleased to, Master Nathan, they certainly are in need of such."

"Thank you," he replied. "Grayson has gone to purchase suitable clean clothing. Do we have adequate bedding?"

She smiled and answered, "certainly Sir, we have twelve beds already made up and several more which are not currently serviceable but can be made up if necessary."

Looking at the three children, a shadow of a smile crossed Nathan's face, replacing the stern look it had grown to know. Something inside the man seemed to be awakening and taking on a life of its own.

"Boys," he said, addressing the three, "if it pleases you, I'd like to offer the accommodations of the manor to you with only a single request, that you respect its furnishings, Mr. Grayson and Mrs. Fox, and abide by their rules. Will you do that?"

The two younger boys nodded eagerly, both with full mouths and unable to answer. Tom, however, raised his eyes and asked, "what's the catch? What do you expect us to do for you?"

"So cynical for one so young," Nathan observed smiling. "You must have been betrayed by those who you trusted. I expect you to treat us the way that you are treated; nothing more, nothing less."

Thomas said nothing more, but did not break off eye contact until Nathan lowered his eyes. An hour later, and their meal gone, they were shown up the stairway to the second floor bath.

"Rub-a-dub-dub, three boys in a tub..." Cathleen thought to herself smiling as she laid three fluffy towels on the stand nearby and cautioned the boys about splashing water on the floor. She had great-grandchildren their ages and greatly missed their once frequent visits to her home. Possibly these three ruffians may come to fill the hole in her heart if they stayed on.

Nearly two hours had passed when Grayson pulled his old car into the driveway and began unloading bags and packages into the foyer. To his great surprise, Nathan opened the door for him, then went to the car and picked up an armload of packages before joining him in the house.

"They are upstairs in the bath," Nathan said, anticipating Grayson's unasked question. "It is my hope that we may provide them food and shelter."

Grayson marveled as his employer followed him up the stairs, arms laden with new clothing, wondering at the change apparent.

Underwear, t-shirts, socks, jeans, and jackets for each were taken from their packaging, with a second set put aside for another day. Grayson had done well to guess their sizes but had forgotten pajamas, slippers, and shoes. It both felt and looked like Christmas as the three squealed and laughed, while the two men watched silently from the doorway.

"On the 'morrow," Nathan whispered, "we'll go into town and fit them for shoes."

"We?" Grayson questioned. "Will you be coming along, Sir?"

"I think I will, I believe it is the proper time to begin handling some of my own affairs," Nathan answered. "Dear Mrs. Fox has raised me from a child, it is past time for her to take a well-earned rest."

The old butler smiled but did not answer. He couldn't wait to see how Cathleen handled it.

Pleased, but still somewhat skeptical, Thomas let things progress while keeping a close watch on them. He cautioned the two younger boys to stay alert and let him know if they suspected any skullduggery. He half expected that an attempt would be made to turn them over to the county authorities or even possibly the *man in black* if the price was right. He couldn't however, figure why the old man had ponied up money to buy them new clothes if he intended to do them harm. Maybe he expected them to be sold as sex slaves that he had heard rumors about. His head was full of scenarios which pointed to the possibility that this stranger had a motive for his generosity.

After three days Nathan did contact the authorities and invited them to his home for a discussion. The three boys did not show themselves and stayed in hiding until the delegation left. Nearly a week went by uneventfully while the children began to feel comfortable in their new surroundings and began to explore the vast estate. Neither Nathan nor Grayson interfered or even made it obvious that they had noticed.

Three sedans pulled up in the circle driveway and parked as nearly a dozen men and women disembarked and made their way to the house. Grayson greeted them and seated them in the dining room around the large mahogany table. Mrs. Fox offered coffee, tea and a variety of freshly baked pastries to the guests as they became comfortable. Nathan entered after several minutes with a broad smile and several well-received compliments to the women in attendance.

"Thank you all for coming, please do enjoy Mrs. Fox's fresh pastries and partake of the hot beverages as you desire. Earlier I made my case to some of you for the need of a sanctuary for the young in our community. I expect that you have had time to consider my proposal and have returned with questions," Nathan said pleasantly, before taking his seat at the head of the table.

The Mayor stood. "Mr. Jacobson, your kind offer has been the subject of many discussions among both the city and county leaders and including several from the clergy. We, of course, are overwhelmed by the magnitude of your generosity and I may add that a few remain skeptical fearing that there may be an ulterior motive."

One of the county commissioners rose from his seat before Nathan had a chance to reply. "Sir, please do accept our apologies in advance for the skepticism that the Mayor has voiced, but try and understand that it is quite unusual that one would offer such a gift without requiring something in return," he said.

This time Nathan allowed the room to quiet and made certain that no one wished to speak before rising. "Ladies and gentlemen, your concerns are duly noted and I would have been disappointed if you had NOT felt the need to protect your citizenry from some plot to indebt or otherwise misuse their trust. I can assure you that I too have given this enterprise considerable thought and I too have questions and misgivings, but they are not about my offer to provide shelter and housing for indigent children, they are about my personal ability to do so.

As respects the financial dimension that would affect your taxpayers, I offer a completely funded perpetual trust to be overseen and managed by competent professionals. My reward, if you choose to be crass, has already been received. Those here representing the clergy and those with Christian values already understand, it is my hope that others among you will someday come to the same understanding."

A tall man clothed in black with a white collar sitting at the far end of the table smiled and nodded without speaking. Nathan had remained on his feet and looked intently around the table and into the eyes of each guest. Mrs. Fox was quietly making her way around the table filling and refilling their cups. Grayson followed a step behind her with a serving tray filled with pastries.

"As I was taught so many years ago in Sunday school, my debt has been paid in full by the sacrifice on Someone willing to give whatever was necessary that I may live," Nathan added. "What I require is professionals from the community able and willing to provide the education and training I lack concerning the raising of children. This will not only be their home, but the place where they may get education and love."

When Nathan was seated the pastor rose and began to clap. At first some hesitated, but within seconds all had risen and were joining in the applause, smiling, and nodding their heads in approval. When the applause had ran its course and the group reseated themselves, the Mayor remained standing.

"Sir, I think I speak for the majority here, we applaud not only your generosity but also your foresight and altruistic motives and am pleased to accept your offer," he said.

Nathan hesitated, then stood. "I'll ask my attorneys to prepare the necessary documents for your approval and inspection and then proceed to implement our agreement. Now, if you'll indulge me for another moment, I'd like to introduce my guests and friends to this body."

Of course Mrs. Fox and Grayson had explained in minute detail the purpose of the meeting to the boys before helping them groom themselves and dress appropriately. Grayson led them into the room and introduced them as he would have introduced royalty. All three stood uncomfortably, eyes on their new shoes.

Nathan arose, walked to them, wrapped his arms around them

and said, “these are my sons of whom I am well pleased.”

Thomas, Robert, and James were the first three, but many, many more followed over the successive years. The man who had never had progeny of his own raised and cared for hundreds of children in the mansion which was later known throughout the entire state as Jacob's-sons Home for Children. Upon his death, Nathan left a well-funded trust and a vast network of charities all committed to providing for the needs of the young and indigent.

Oh, and the portrait? It was replaced by another with Nathan standing behind the three boys and flanked by Grayson, his wife, and Mrs. Fox.

– The End –

The Dream

I feel compelled to relate a recent dream which I feel privileged to have enjoyed. Although I myself have a clear understanding of it's meaning, I will leave its message and interpretation for my readers. Unique to me in that it began, was interrupted by wakefulness, and then resumed seamlessly to its conclusion. It was very detailed and compete which leaves me challenged to properly describe it...

I had a sense that it took place at an unspecified location somewhere in Mexico, near a small village by the sea. It began with a young man walking alone on the white sandy beach. He walked a distance before coming upon the horribly sunburned forms of twin newborn babies discarded and lying in the bright midday sun in a coarsely woven cotton covering.

It became obvious to me as we neared that they had been abandoned to die, their umbilical cords beginning to wither under the heat of the scorching sun. Bodies partially covered, the features of their faces had nearly disappeared under the blisters and loose skin cooking from their skeleton-like faces.

The man gently lifted the pair in their would-be shrouds and carried them to the shade of a nearby shelter. Once there, he tied a thong from his sandal tightly around their cords before removing them and laying them carefully aside. With water from a nearby spring he cooled their bodies and lips while he spoke soothingly to them. He drained the remaining umbilical fluid into a bowl, then deftly used the blade of his knife to cut the cords into strips, much like those of a pasta noodle. Into the bowl he then added aloe from a plant nearby and several medicinal natural plants to form a thick balm.

As pieces of their delicate skin fell away, he covered the tissue with the balm before carefully positioning each strip. He moved quickly but efficiently in his labors, then covered each recreated face with the remaining balm.

I had a sense that some time had passed and that also the specter of death had passed them by, when I realized that he was feeding them goat's milk and honey. At this point I awakened for several minutes before returning to my bed and resuming the dream.

The scene now is in the village. The man, much older now, had entered the town and was approached by a much younger man who said, "I am Tomas, are you our father?"

The older man looked at him curiously and did not answer directly but said, "I am but a humble sculptor, why would you ask?"

"I know of you sir, you are quite famous," Tomas replied. "My brother Timothy and I are sculptors also, we are just now working inside this church to restore what age and misuse has destroyed."

The old sculptor smiled but said nothing.

Tomas continued, "how could it be that you are not our father, and yet both he and I look just like you?"

Finally the older man said, "I knew you when you were very young and I restored the tender skin of your faces that the sun had taken away. I had only my own image that I had seen in the water as a pattern for your faces.

...and then I awoke.

– The End –

The Advocate

The grey overcast of the morning, with a slight drizzle and light wind, should have told her that this Monday would not usher in a pleasant week. She was 57 years old and had worked steadily since high school. Both her body and vitality had taken quite a beating over the long years of hard work. Finally, just last year, she had been made supervisor and given a desk where she hoped she could get off her feet and manage the young and aspiring who arrived with hope in their eyes and a spring in their step, despite being up half of the previous night partying.

She'd been passed over many times, not because of her abilities but because of her lack of secondary education. She'd been pregnant at 18, again at 21, and their youngest had come just after her 31st birthday. Her husband was an on-again off-again truck driver who had never quite found whatever nitch that he was sure he was created for. Over their years together he'd started and quit over two dozen well-paying jobs for the right one, but never found it. At 60, with real health concerns, a poor track record, and lack of incentive to even try, he spent many hours a day watching daytime television or playing games on the computer.

Gaye wondered if her body would last another five years until she could take early retirement. She already had varicose veins from spending too many hours standing on cement floors and had been diagnosed as pre-diabetic. Thank God, she thought, for the health insurance that came with the package her employer offered. The $200 which they deducted from her check provided both of them outstanding coverage and benefits. They'd have been sitting well with their home free and clear if they had not been forced to refinance twice to make up the shortfall when his employment faltered and finally stopped after buying his new pickup and boat. The boat sat in the driveway covered with a tarp because he could not find anyone who was not working to fish with.

She mused at how the key seemed to always offer one last bit of independence before finally yielding to her and turning in the lock and allowing her into the warehouse at the back of the store. Her cubbyhole office was in one corner, with a single window facing outward. She turned on the lights and unlocked a second less-challenging door knob lock before entering and sitting down her purse, lunch bag, and coat.

Her desk, as it had been the previous Friday when she had left, was still stacked with orders waiting to be shipped and others on the floor waiting to be inventoried and put into stock. It seemed never ending, with delivery drivers ignoring the hours plainly shown on the loading dock and showing up just at quitting time with some lame excuse why they were hours late. Of course that meant her meager budget would pay overtime to unload them so the delivery drivers could go home and spend the weekend with their families.

Her manager would then try and hold her feet to the fire for the increased labor costs of her department. Twice she'd refused to accept the freight, telling the drivers to come back Monday, only then to be called by that same manager who'd himself been called at home by an angry freight company dispatcher. She'd been required to leave home, open up the warehouse while a smirking driver stood idly by, and operate the forklift herself without the compensation that any hourly employee would have received.

The sheer volume of paperwork had forced her to become orderly and organized, she was glad now that it had. Her predecessor had been as unorganized as a yard full of chickens, with a booming voice to keep his crew in line and a box overflowing with paperwork which was sorted each time something needed to be found.

With their small home, three children, and a husband away or 'relaxing', she had needed to learn the art of organization at an early age. She had implemented the same when she had taken over the warehouse manager job.

The coffee maker had just finished dripping when the first of her employees entered through the back door. "Mornin' Marge," he said smiling as he walked by her open door. He'd called her Marge from the first morning he'd arrived. It remained their own little private joke. "The coffee smells good," he added.

"Help yourself," she offered, knowing well that the young man did not drink coffee.

She liked Tom. Unlike several of the others, he checked in on time, and did a day's work without forcing her to find and dispatch him to each individual task. Many of the others would, like small children, wait for her to instruct them in detail, then do only the minimum which she had described. They'd step over work waiting to be done, and then ask what they should do next.

Her full crew of six finally arrived, one right after Tom, three at straight up eight, and one at ten after. She'd long ago given up on trying to impart a proper work ethic on the late comer. When she'd tried they'd always wasted a second ten minutes debating why traffic had been unreasonably slow, or why she'd been forced to stop and fuel her car on the way rather than the night before. Gaye had just begun the ritual of subtracting an hour a week from the 40 which always magically appeared on the time card.

Just a few minutes before ten o'clock the manager entered her office and closed the door behind him, which was always a bad sign. For the first few minutes he talked about the economy, the declining profit margin in the store, while never really looking her in the eye. He finally handed her a sealed envelope and said simply, "I'm sorry but we are going to have to let you go," before quickly adding, "you of course will have your 401k, vacation and sick pay, and will be eligible for unemployment."

"When?" she asked. "When it is effective?"

"Friday," he answered, sounding relieved that she had apparently not felt the need to argue or had broken down in tears. "I was hoping you'd bring Tom in and show him the ropes."

Gaye smiled sardonically and replied, "No, you show him the ropes. I'm taking vacation beginning tomorrow morning and will expect to pick up my final check on Friday."

The surprised look that immediately came over his face was quickly replaced by one of bitterness and distain as he left without another word.

"Tom," Gaye said while standing in the doorway of her office, "may I have a minute with you?"

Tom lowered the forks of the Hyster to the floor and jumped agilely from it. "Sure," he said in his usual manner, "what's up?"

It was evident to her that he had not been contacted or briefed on his upcoming career move. She felt a little sad that it was she who would announce his promotion and her retirement at the same time, and that she'd leave and throw him to the wolves by not schooling him on the job.

"Looks like you are due for a promotion," she said, while trying to keep her voice light. "As of tomorrow morning you get to move up to the big office." As she said it she indicated the cubby that had been her home for so many years.

He looked puzzled and concerned as he seated himself across the desk from his friend and supervisor. "What about you?" he asked, registering the concern that had made him her favorite.

"Movin' on to greener pastures," Gaye answered glibly, "time for you to try your hand at it."

"But... but..." he began before noticing that Gaye's eyes were rimmed with tears. "I'm not ready, I don't know the job and you know it."

"I'm sorry Tom, I really am, but they left me no choice and already had you earmarked for the job," she answered. "Let's take the rest of the day and I'll show you what I can. But keep it between us and you always have my phone number if you have questions. You'll grow into it just like I did."

Gaye grabbed a legal pad and handed it and a pen to Tom, smiled and said, "start taking notes."

The day seemed to go by quickly as she tried to cover the details of the job that were not written down on anyone's job description, things that were expected but never appreciated.

"Remember," she said quietly, "for a while you'll have them over a barrel, they don't have anyone but you who can make it happen, take advantage of that. You can call the shots and start off with the clean slate I never had. Same with your crew, tell them what you expect of them and don't let them take advantage of your good nature. It might be a good time to tell Earlene that if she shows up late again, you'll find someone who can be here on time."

They laughed at the shared the joke.

Tom asked, "where are you going?"

"No clue," she answered, thinking about it for the first time. "I didn't know I was leaving until this morning."

"I'm not sure I want the job," Tom said, trying to sound supportive, "if that's the way they reward you after all of these years."

"You know better than that, Tom. You need the job and it will not change their decision if you leave," she replied. "They'll just find someone else who needs work."

He nodded knowing that she was right – he had a young wife at home and a baby on the way.

"Let me suggest that you don't let them put you on salary, tell them you want a raise in your hourly wage," she said smiling. "That way you'll be paid for what you do and have time at home with your family."

"Will they do that?" he asked.

"Stand firm and tell them that's the only way you'll accept the job," she answered.

They spent the last few hours going over the paper flow portion of the job, the administrative duties regarding the crew, before she walked to the floor and told the crew what to expect the following day. Most wished her well and expressed surprise at the announcement. She handed Tom the two keys and left the same way she'd come in that morning, without fan fare or further notice.

Rejection, she thought as she drove home, it was more the rejection than the loss of the job that bothered her. As she pulled numbly into the driveway she took notice that the pickup and the boat were gone but gave it little thought. Finally he got off the sofa and went fishing she thought to herself, and about time too. They'd been paying for both the truck and the boat for over a year and neither seldom left the curb. He'd always had some excuse not to go.

She put down the small box which contained her personal things which had been in her office and poured herself a tall glass of iced tea before noticing a single sheet of paper on the kitchen counter. She recognized her husband's handwriting and was interested to read what he had written as an excuse for being absent. It read: "As you already know it has been a while since I have been happy and have felt fulfilled in our marriage. I've met someone online and am taking my pickup and boat and leaving to find happiness with her. You can keep the house and furniture and we'll call it even. Doug."

Gaye read the note twice before realizing that this was not some cruel joke but a good-bye from the husband whom she had cared for and supported for thirty-five years. Remarkably, she felt little loss but some amazement that he'd thought of her only as a meal ticket. She couldn't help feeling resentment in that he had forced her to get a second mortgage on the house so he could walk away with the titles to both the boat and truck and leave her to pay off the house a second time and "call it even," as he put it.

She read the note a second time as though reading it would somehow change what was written on it, then laughed out loud as she said, "I wonder if his girlfriend has good medical insurance?" She kicked off her shoes and traded her tea for a "Long Island" in a rare moment to dull the pain and apprehension she was beginning to feel.

Five years minimum, eight if I want full benefits, she thought to herself while trying to guess what her financial future held. Doug had been right about one thing, it had been months and maybe years since their marriage had been anything but a convenience for either of them. She may miss having someone to talk to but the freedom to make good decisions without having to explain them to him may well be worth the loss.

He'd become like a selfish child and she for the most part had enabled him by her hard work. She resolved to get the papers filed and the divorce over before the newness began to wear off for Doug and his new meal ticket. She didn't want to find herself supporting him with what was left of her retirement fund. Tomorrow she would file and hope that he did not contest the divorce. Life is always easier when you can leave the past behind and not drag it around with you.

It was not long before the Long Island iced tea brought about its desired effect. Since she seldom drank the liquor, it first relaxed her and then made her drowsy. When she awoke she was still on the couch, the television still flickered but had been muted, and now her bed beckoned. She awoke at her usual time, assessed the situation and rolled over and went back to sleep. At 9:00 a.m., when she opened her eyes for the second time, guilt forced her to put on the coffee and crawl into the waiting shower. The house was quiet, unusually so… or maybe just empty she thought, as she turned on the radio.

Gaye finished dressing, enjoyed second and third cups of coffee, and burned her last piece of bread while trying to make toast. Good start for the day, she said to herself. She had always been one to stay organized with the aid of scraps of paper laughably called lists that she carried with her often long after they had fulfilled their original purpose.

Attorney, bank, bread, check in with the unemployment office and find out the details about how the system worked, gas the car, take his name off the credit cards, contact friends and family and give them a heads up… the list seemed endless but provided the direction she needed. CYA, she thought, as she wondered why she felt the urgency to make a clean break with Doug. He'd proved untrustworthy and self-serving and she could not afford to let him bury her in debt after he was gone.

As she began making calls, she found that taking him off the cards while still married was not possible, she was forced to cancel them and reapply in her own name, which she did. Likewise at the bank, she closed out the joint account and opened another only in her name that required picture ID for transactions, as per advice from her friend and banker who had been married and divorced more than once. She also got a recommendation for a good divorce attorney before leaving the bank on her way to her next stop.

While she was in the grocery store her phone rang. It was a merchant calling to question why their credit card had been declined. She took special satisfaction that she had moved quickly enough to prevent her debt load from increasing at the whim of her soon to be ex. She was in her car pulling out when her cell rang again, it was Tom.

He apologized for disturbing her then asked a quick assortment of questions of what, when, and how. Gaye was pleased that their friendship had allowed him to ask and told him as much. Tom related that the manager had done exactly as she'd told him to expect and was grateful for the advice she had given him about standing up for himself. She promised to meet with him when she came by Friday for her final check. A second merchant called while she was fueling her car, a second card had been presented and declined. She hurried to her appointment with Claiborne J. Stevens Jr. at his law office, feeling smug and secure.

"You cannot divest yourself from him without due process," he told her when they had settled in and began to discuss the measures she had taken to protect herself. "You live in a community property state and as such share both the benefits and responsibilities that come with it."

She must have looked tearful because he climbed down off his soap box long enough to change his tone of voice and add, "we'll get you through this and protect you from his poor spending habits and schemes as best the law will allow. Be advised however, that regardless of his contribution to it, he is entitled to a portion of your 401k and other assets as well as being responsible for half of your joint indebtedness."

Gaye was learning fast that the law could not force people to play fairly and act justly.

"We will ask the court to freeze both your assets and liabilities which will prevent either of you from sharing future debts. I'd ask you to present as complete a list to my staff as you can as quickly as possible so we may get them into the records," he said.

"I hope to have the 401k information by Friday and will work on others between now and then. What about day to day expenses?" she inquired.

"Pay them as usual but keep track of where the money goes, some of it is out of your joint pocket, but personal expenses for example will be out of yours. Just keep good records for the Judge," he added as they concluded.

"How long..." she asked, letting her voice trail off.

"A month or two, if he doesn't contest it, longer if he does," came his answer.

"How much..." she asked again, not wanting to hear his answer.

"For the most part that depends on him, how badly he wants to leave and what kind of advice he gets along the way," Clay answered. "Hold onto that letter which states he just wants the truck and boat and we'll try to use that in our settlement offer. Do you know how to contact him?"

"I have his cell number," Gaye replied. "I'm still paying the bill for it."

"Give that number to my secretary," he instructed. "We'll notify him that we need a mailing address and that he needs to get his own cellular plan."

She climbed into her old car and rested her head against her hands which gripped the wheel, while tears ran down her cheeks. Although she hadn't been inside of a church for years, she had been brought up in one and had given herself to Jesus while still in grade school. It sounded more like a moan when she entreated the Lord to take away her pain.

"I cannot do this alone," she admitted, "please help me Lord."

As hard as it had been, she had always muddled along and found her way in life in spite of life's obstacles, but now she seemed overcome and without hope. She had finally come to the end of herself and pictured herself circling the bowl on her way to oblivion.

When she finally returned home, nearly all of the things on her list of to-dos had been crossed off. All that remained was to make some calls and file her claim for unemployment, oh, and to make the list of assets and liabilities for the attorney. She called a realtor friend and asked if she could help her get an inexpensive appraisal and a payoff on the mortgage. The realtor offered to do a market appraisal for free and called her back in fifteen minutes with the payoff figures from her mortgage company.

A call to her credit union provided the remaining balance that had been borrowed against her 401k and its approximate current value, exclusive of taxes. Her old car was free and clear but needed tires and maintenance that they had been putting off, and their credit card balances were small and had been paid current every month. She vowed to cut the cable television and computer servers to a minimum now that there was no one to utilize them all hours of the day.

It also seemed like a good time to pay attention to what kind of foods she was bringing home from the grocery. Doug had lived on snack foods and anything that could be microwaved and she had been drawn into the practice a little at a time also, because she often did not feel like preparing a full meal after working all day.

Gaye finally took a seat in the lounger and opened the newspaper. The headlines held little interest and likewise the local events section. Eventually she worked her way to the comics, which seemed anything but funny, and then finally to the obituaries. She paid special interest to the ages and causes of death of those featured. Many were older than she but several were much younger.

Two of the younger ones strongly inferred that the cause may be self-inflicted but did not state the facts directly. Momentarily she wondered what would cause one so young to take their own life. Before putting the paper down, she spent several minutes reading the help-wanted section where she circled a couple of possible employment possibilities.

The 5 o'clock news and weather did little to lift her spirits with little but tragedy catching the spotlight. It seemed that circumstances worldwide were filled with famine, floods, and natural disaster, and with man's inhumanity to his fellow man nearly beyond comprehension. She shut off the television and made herself a green salad for dinner, then picked up a book and began to read. When she awoke it was nearly morning.

She arrived at the unemployment office promptly at 8:00 only to find they opened at 9:00. Rather than waiting an hour, she drove to a nearby IHOP and had breakfast. When she returned at a few minutes to 9:00 there was a long line already waiting for the doors to open. Lesson learned she thought. At 11:00 she took her place at the desk of a young man who promised to help her. What he did was to explain that all she could accomplish was to file and start the clock running.

Benefits, if any, would come after the customary waiting period *if investigation* showed that she was eligible. Meanwhile, he encouraged her to get out and look for work. When she left she felt as though it was his money that she may or may not get someday, if found worthy. He seemed to forget that for forty years she had worked without interruption, and unemployment insurance had been paid on her income for just such a time as this.

On her return home, an invisible hand gripped the steering wheel and guided her into the parking lot of a small non-denominational church. Hers was one of only three cars in the lot. Gaye had no idea why she was there but found herself leaving the car and walking up the steps and into the building. A portly woman, looking to be in her early sixties, looked up and smiled as the door closed.

"Hello, may I help you?" she asked.

"I'm not sure," Gay answered honestly, "I am not sure why I'm here."

Again the older woman smiled then said, "perhaps you are right where God wants you to be. Can I offer you something to drink?"

The room was unusually quiet Gaye thought to herself as she sat and waited for the woman to return with two bottles of water. She wondered if they were all alone in the building. During the short visit that ensued, Gaye found out that the woman, Marlene, was the pastor's wife who had taken over duties as church secretary after the previous one had left. The church was one of many with declining membership causing its leaders to look for ways to balance the budget. Eliminating a paid clerical position had seemed a practical way to cut costs.

"Oh, I don't mind," Marlene replied to Gaye's question. "I just mostly answer the phone, take messages, and catch up on my knitting as time permits. I expect as God increases our membership again, I'll be at home doing much the same."

They shared a laugh.

"I've been laid off," Gaye offered, surprising herself, "and my husband has left me," she added without thinking.

To her surprise, Marlene smiled without offering comment.

"I'm not sure what the future holds," she continued, soliciting advice from her new-found friend.

Marlene looked her directly in her eyes for several seconds before answering simply, "none of us do, Dear. None of us do."

A door opened from a side office and an elderly man with thin grey hair entered. When he saw Gaye, he smiled then looked at Marlene. "You should have told me we had a guest."

Marlene returned his smile then answered, "I was about to, but we were sharing a little *woman time* first. Tim, this is Gaye. Gaye, this is my husband Tim, our pastor."

Gay stood and took his hand and felt a genuine connection.

"Would you like a tour?" he asked, continuing to smile. "It won't take long."

Gaye guessed the whole structure only slightly larger than her own home but with very little wasted space. The offices were small and austere, the sanctuary was well maintained and functional but looked a little worn and dated. She guessed it could have squeezed in no more than a hundred at most when Easter, Christmas, weddings, or funerals required it. Tim walked beside her chattering like a proud parent showing off pictures of his children.

"Perhaps we could invite you to join us this Sunday," Tim said as he concluded the ten minute tour and returned to the office where his wife sat.

Gaye, like most who are called upon to make a decision without previous consideration, began to think of all the reasons she could not.

To her surprise she heard herself answer, "yes, I think I'd like that."

Marlene stood, gave her hand a little squeeze, and then said, "I'll save you a seat next to me, I nearly always have to sit alone while Tom is at the pulpit."

On the return trip to her home Gaye mused at the depth of the connection she had felt for both Tim and Marlene in the short time she had known them and also how they had seemed to help lift the weight of despair from her shoulders. She was looking forward to the upcoming Sunday.

Friday finally came and with it the apprehension of facing her former employer and co-workers. Tom of course was glad to see her and walked right up and gave her a warm greeting and a hug, most of the others nodded but pretended they were too hard at work to stop and say hello. She was slightly disappointed to find that Tom had organized the office and adopted his own paper flow system that seemed to be working. Secretly she had hoped the whole thing would fall apart and they'd have to close the doors without her. Of course she knew that was foolish and that she'd not been as indispensable but her ego had hoped they'd come begging to have her back. From the looks of things that would never happen.

She walked through the swinging doors which separated the warehouse from the retail floor and made her way to the office in the front. Inside she could see the manager sitting at his desk trying to look busy in spite of his head nodding and his chin occasionally dropping to his chest.

"Morning Norm," she said a little too loudly as she entered and shut the door with a bang behind her.

His head jerked upward and for a moment his eyes expressed a mixture of panic and fear. Gaye nearly laughed and wondered what dream she had interrupted with her audacious entry as she took a seat without invitation across from him. After the look of bewilderment left his eyes it was replaced by one of near hate before he took control and gave her his best kiss-ass smile.

"Why, good morning Gaye," he said a little too cheerfully. "I had expected to see you earlier."

It was only a few minutes after 9:00. She thought to herself, 'I'll bet he got up early just to make sure he was in his office before I came.' She couldn't remember ever seeing him before nine in all the years they had worked together.

"I saw no reason to beat you here and have to wait," she said, "so I just enjoyed a leisurely breakfast before coming down. Do you have my check?"

He took out a folder with her name legibly written across the top and made a production of opening it slowly and pretending to read it through for accuracy before answering.

"Our senior management has asked me to go over this with you in detail and have you initial each page after you have read and approved it," he said, with satisfaction apparent in his voice.

"I'll not be signing anything without first having my attorney look it over," Gaye answered. "Give me copies of everything and after he has given his approval, I'll sign and return them."

He had not expected to be rebuffed but recovered his composure and replied, "I cannot give you your severance pay or retirement until they are signed."

"I'm in no hurry," she lied, knowing she needed the money badly, "copy everything including the checks and disbursement voucher and I'll be out of your way."

Fifteen minutes later she was leaving with a handful of paper, $20 in her purse and another $150 in her checking account, on her way to the law offices of C.J. Stevens Jr. and hoping he'd take time to expedite her paperwork. After talking to the receptionist she seated herself and was told they'd try and work her in to Mr. Stevens' busy schedule. She felt a little chastised by the tone of the woman's voice but wasn't surprised that the attorney wasn't just sitting at his desk waiting for her to drop in.

Clay followed an elderly couple from his office talking as they left, thanked them for coming in and said his good-byes before noticing Gaye sitting quietly waiting. He checked his watch, recovered his composure and said, "how nice to see you Gaye, I'm running a little late today, could we talk over lunch?" Then turning to the reception desk said, "I'm taking a client to lunch. Please don't expect me back for two hours."

The receptionist nodded woodenly, made some notes on the pad in front of her, then picked up the phone and began dialing. Gaye supposed she was rearranging his afternoon schedule.

Soon they were seated in a little bistro just down the block from his office and were looking over the scant menu. To his credit, if he felt pressed for time it never showed. Gaye stole a glance at him and secretly wondered why she had never found a guy like this when she was dating. Of course she immediately knew, she'd been drawn to the physical rather than the heart and the head. She'd never even dated someone who planned further than their next paycheck or vacation. That's how she'd ended up with Dan.

He'd been first string quarterback, big and strong, with lean chiseled features and a ready smile that made her and her girlfriends swoon. At the time she'd looked at him as a catch and had given herself willingly to him on prom night when he'd insisted. Just under a year later they were married and had a six month old baby. He'd gone to work for his father driving truck and was bringing in more than enough money to allow them to squander it. When their second was born they owned a mortgage, two nearly new cars, and payment books which took some of the fun out of making money. But still they lived well, enjoyed partying and all of those things young couples do to try and be grownup.

"May I see those," Clay asked, motioning to the bundle of papers Gaye had lying in a vacant chair. "I'll try and give them a glance while we enjoy our lunch."

Gaye found herself looking at his left hand where a well worn gold band encircled his finger. She watched as he read carefully through the paperwork and made a few notes on a small pad he'd had in his jacket pocket. Neither of them said anything until the waiter arrived with their sandwiches. He laid the papers aside, bowed his head and asked the Lord's blessing on the food without asking.

"Can't forget to thank the One who pays the bills," he said with a boyish grin. Gaye just nodded but her thoughts went back to the little church she'd visited and her short visit with Pastor Tim and Marlene.

"Mr. Claiborne," she began, before he held up his hand and interrupted her.

"Please call me Clay," he said smiling again. "My father was Mr. Claiborne and wanted everyone to pronounce every syllable of it too, he was a pompous man."

That makes it easy she thought, I've been calling him Clay in my mind from the moment we shook hands. "Well Clay," she began again, "as you can see they want everything tied up nice and tight, they wanted me to read and initial every page. It made me kind of jumpy. What do you think?"

"I think you are a smart woman," he said sincerely. "They've slipped a few things in there that are not standard and it may not be in your best interest to sign. I'll look it over at home tonight and have some suggestions for you in the morning. Are you available in the morning?"

Gaye felt a little tingle that she hadn't felt in years when she answered, "well let me see, I've no husband, the kids are grown and gone, haven't found a boyfriend, and no one seems to be calling to offer me a job, yeah... I can work you in."

They shared a laugh, then he checked his watch and apologized saying, "I really hate to eat and run but I promised to be back and our two hours have flown by. Maybe next time we can plan it and get to know each other better."

They stood and walked to the cashier where he paid the bill and pocketed the receipt before opening the door for her.

"Thank you, thank you for everything," Gaye said as they reached his office. "I am sorry to have dropped in on you like I did."

"I am glad you did," he answered. "I usually don't have anyone to have lunch with so I just eat at my desk. I really enjoyed it."

As Gaye walked across the parking lot a thousand thoughts fought each other for dominance in her mind, not the least of which was the receding figure of the tall spare man with the engaging smile. She reminded herself then and later again that night, when his face reappeared to her as she fought to find sleep, he was taken.

True to his word, Clay called just as she was getting out of the shower. She rushed to get the phone before it went to messages and smiled to herself at the picture she presented in the mirror as she greeted him. She blushed as though he could see her through their telephone connection; standing naked, dripping wet, holding a towel ineffectively in front of her.

"Good morning," he said with energy in his voice. "I hope I did not interrupt your breakfast."

"No, I'm just sitting here reading the paper and enjoying a cup of coffee," she lied.

"I read through your paperwork and have made some notes for discussion, do you have any time free today that we might visit?" he asked.

Gaye felt goose bumps forming which she doubted was from the temperature of the room. "Of course," she answered, trying to sound business like, "what time is good for you?"

"I'm afraid I have a full schedule already," he said sounding remorseful. "I was hoping that you might be available again at lunch time. I could have my secretary order something in, that would give us more time together. Do you like Thai food?"

"Love it!" Gaye answered enthusiastically, "what time?"

"11:30?" he answered with a question in his voice, "or is that too early for you?"

"I'll be there," she answered, "and thank you for making this so easy for me."

There was a pause before he answered, "my pleasure, see you then."

Gay felt, or thought she felt, that he was trying to make a connection with her that was more than an attorney-client one, then felt immediately guilty for her thoughts. She toweled her body dry, enjoying the feel of the plush cotton on her skin, then applied the necessary lotions and creams to various parts of it and began to blow her hair dry. For the first time in recent memory she felt alive, vital, and hopeful. The strain of the past few days was already showing, both in her figure where she had lost five pounds and on her face where worry and concern had also left their mark.

She pulled, then rejected, several items from her closet before choosing plain white slacks and a contrasting blue casual top. She'd been told that blue brought out the color of her eyes. As she thought about her choice she wondered why she cared if he noticed her eyes or not, after all he was her attorney and not an available suitor. She parked her car and walked into the law office at twenty after eleven and smiled at the receptionist ,then took a seat in the waiting area.

She had just settled in when Clay, sporting a broad smile, left his office, then personally escorted her to a seat at a small sitting area away from his desk. On the small table beside the plush chairs was a small stack of papers, a note pad, plates with napkins and silverware, two glasses with iced beverages in them, and several cartons of what she presumed was Thai cuisine.

After showing her to a seat he joined her and spoke. "I hope this is not too presumptuous of me," he said, motioning to the meal, "but I feel that it is to your advantage if we can reconcile matters regarding your dismissal right away."

Both urgency and sincerity were evident in the tone of his voice but in addition there was an inviting quality as though he was enjoying their short association as much as she.

To her surprise Clay bowed his head, hesitated a moment and asked the Lord to bless their food. "It's best when it is still hot," he explained, motioning to the various cartons which he began to open and offer to her. She needed no further invitation to fill her plate while he did the same.

"It's almost like a picnic," Gaye commented. "I'll bet your wife appreciates your creativity."

A look of loss and pain came over his face in spite of an obvious effort to hide it.

"I lost my wife five years ago in an automobile accident," he said quietly, "but yes, we both enjoyed the spontaneity of simple little things like a stolen moment at lunch."

"Oh, I am so sorry," Gaye said, feeling the pain which radiated out from him. "I just assumed....." she added, letting her voice trail off.

He dismissed her failed efforts to apologize, regained his smile, and then said, "in truth, you are the first one with whom I've felt comfortable to share lunch with since that time."

Gaye cautioned herself to move slow, respect his situation, and honor the memory of the wife that he had obviously loved very much. She could not deny, however, the ray of hope that made itself known deep in her heart. For several minutes they ate without speaking, enjoying the spicy food and the moment uninterrupted. Both took additional smaller portions from the remaining feast as they began to satiate their hunger.

Clay finally slid his plate aside, wiped his mouth and fingers on his napkin and became the attorney that he was. "While you finish," he said, "and with your permission, I'll read selected portions of your paperwork and explain those areas which I personally find in question."

Gaye nodded and directed her attention away from her plate to Clay as he began to speak. For the next twenty minutes he read and explained his logic and why he'd found some parts of the dismissal agreement objectionable. Then he went back over them and offered his suggestions as to revisions which he felt served her best interest. Gaye nodded agreement and asked questions when things did not seem clear to her. In the end they modified the agreement together before she authorized him to have it drafted for her signature.

"Doug called the office," Clay said, suddenly changing the subject, "or I should say he had his girlfriend call in response to our request. We told her that we could not deal with her, that we'd need to speak directly to him. I hope that is agreeable to you."

Gaye smiled and then answered, "I love it. He never did want to take responsibility for anything himself. I'm not surprised he'd try and get her to do his dirty work."

"I thought you'd like that," Clay said in an uncharacteristically informal manner. "Besides, we can legally only deal with him or his attorney."

"Oh," she replied. "Has he gotten an attorney?

"Not to my knowledge," Clay answered. "If he does, the attorney will certainly make us aware of his presence first thing."

"This is nice," Gaye offered without explanation, meaning to refer to the informal setting and their business lunch.

"It is," he replied. "When we get all of this behind us, maybe we can enjoy a real lunch together without the distractions of legal ethics or issues."

Gaye hoped that she not just misread his intentions, and that he found her company interesting and enjoyable. Her heart leaped at the strange connection that she was feeling for her attorney but swelled with hope that this was not just some rebound thing resulting from her recent rejections from her employer and husband.

Nearly two weeks had passed since that fateful Monday morning when it seemed her life was falling apart all around her, but Sunday morning dawned literally as a new day. When she had awoken the sun was already shining, and though still cold, the sky was cloudless and blue, holding no threat but rather a seeming hopefulness. She was looking forward to spending time again with Marlene and hearing what words God had given Tim for the ears of his small flock.

The previous Sunday the message had been from Job, it had most appropriately outlined the several calamities which seemingly struck him without cause. She, of course, related easily and wondered if perhaps there was a parallel in her life from which she could gain some comfort. She was looking forward to this week and hoping to receive peace or direction from it.

As she entered the church at a quarter to ten many of the regulars had already taken their seats and more were following her from the small parking lot. Instinctively, her eyes searched for the one face she knew, Marlene; but then stopped in disbelief when a second familiar face seemed to reach out toward her. Clay was sitting alone near the front just to the left of the podium with his head bent forward and his eyes trained intently on something lying in his lap. His Bible, she assumed. Instinctively she questioned if by chance she had spoken of her visit to the church in one of their conversations or if something else had drawn him to this particular church on this particular morning.

Across the room, to the right Marlene was watching the faithful as they entered, nodding and smiling appropriately as her eyes caught a familiar face. They locked eyes and with an unspoken invitation Marlene nodded to the empty seat beside her. Gaye took the offered seat and clasped Marlene's hand in hers and exchanged a quiet and brief greeting as Tim ushered himself up the two steps and stopped at the lectern.

"Good morning," he said in a sincere voice. "It is very good to see both familiar and new faces this morning. I pray that I may be worthy to speak from God's word this morning what each heart needs to hear. Shall we pray?"

Pastor Tim lead them in prayer, with several in the congregation feeling prompted to add their Amens and words of encouragement as they felt drawn by the Spirit. A man who was introduced simply as Brother Bill then took a few minutes to make announcements and read the short list of names of those asking for particular prayer needs.

Gaye looked to her left and could see Clay quizzically looking directly at her as though asking "what are you doing here?" She, of course, was wondering the same of him. It did not seem to Gaye that she absorbed as much of the sermon as she should have, instead her mind spent a great deal of time filling itself with impossible questions and inadequate answers of a more worldly nature.

When the service ended and the congregation stood to leave, most spent several minutes visiting with nearby friends. Before leaving, Clay walked directly toward her smiling. His graying hair neatly combed, a tasteful sport jacket and tie, and a confident stride belying his age gave him a most pleasing demeanor which was not lost on Gaye.

Marlene assumed that Clay was coming to greet her as he approached and said, "Mr. Stephens, you will never know how many times I've prayed to have you rejoin us, it's wonderful to see you."

"And God does answer our prayers, doesn't He?" Clay said before wrapping his long arms around Marlene, "and always at just the right time."

As Tim stepped down from the podium and had finally detached himself from his adoring flock, he made his way toward them, smiling broadly.

"Clay," he said as they clasped hands and then shared a man hug, which testified of their feelings for one another. "You are the answer to prayer. It is so good to see you again."

"And you," Clay returned, it has been too long."

As the conversation hit a lull Clay moved toward Gaye. "And you," he said with feeling. "I am so pleased to see you. Have you been coming here long?"

"My second week," Gaye answered. "I stopped in on my way home from our first visit and have been coming since. You?

Clay looked slightly uncomfortable when, after looking first at Tim and Marlene, admitted, "It's been nearly five years since I have been able to set foot into God's house. I spent the first year asking Him why and the last four blaming Him for letting it happen."

Everyone understood without explanation that he'd just referred to the accident which had taken his wife.

Gaye offered him a half-smile, then said, "kinda goes with the sermon, doesn't it? I gotta bet that Job felt much the same way."

The four of them nodded.

"What has changed?" the old pastor asked Clay point blank.

"A lot of things," Clay answered, avoiding the subject, then added, "not the least of which is my new client Gaye here."

Gaye felt herself redden as both Tim and Marlene turned their attention toward her.

"How so," Pastor Tim queried.

"Well, let's just say that after meeting Gaye, I finally realized that God does not take pleasure in exacting pain on His children and that He does nothing without a purpose," Clay admitted. "Maybe I just got tired of feeling angry and sorry for myself."

"Sounds like a reason to celebrate to me" Marlene said, changing the subject. "How about letting our pastor buy us lunch?"

"Yes," Tim agreed, "how about letting us buy you both lunch?"

Fifteen minutes later the lights were turned out, doors locked and the foursome were on their way to enjoy the midday meal together.

Monday morning Clay called, as Gaye was dressing with plans to spend some time looking for work.

"Good morning," he began. "Do you have time to stop by and sign a few papers this morning? If so, you could deliver copies to your former employer and we can see what kind of reception they get."

Gaye nodded, and then remembered he couldn't see her nod over the phone. "Of course," she answered. "I should be down there in about a half hour if that is alright."

"That's fine," Clay answered in his best business voice. "They are at the front desk with your name on them."

When she disconnected she couldn't help wondering at the change in his manner and if she may have misread his intentions in her desperation to find a permanent lasting relationship. Or maybe she had scared him off in her eagerness to make a more personal connection. After all, what could he possibly see in an out-of-work, aging warehouse supervisor with a high school education?

True to her promise, Gay walked into the law office twenty minutes later, through the open door she could see Clay sitting at his desk attempting to look busy but failing miserably. His hair was mussed, his face haggard and lined, and his eyes red-rimmed like he'd pulled an all-nighter preparing for school finals.

"I wonder if I could speak with Mr. Stevens," she found herself saying as she signed the papers where they were marked and returned them to the secretary.

"He's asked not to be disturbed," she replied, and then quietly added, "I think he is not feeling well."

The woman copied the signed forms, retained a copy for their records, and returned the originals to Gaye. Gay left and drove the short distance to her former place of employment and walked into the manager's office without waiting to be invited. He looked up in surprise as she laid the papers on the corner of his desk.

"Here are the signed forms with some corrections and deletions which my attorney and I have made," she said. "Please pass them on to the decision makers and tell them the clock is running. If we don't hear back from you in ten days we'll file a wrongful termination suit for age discrimination and see you in court."

She turned and left his office before he could respond, wondering if Clay really thought she had a case or if they'd try and starve her out knowing she had little to fall back on. It had all sounded so easy and predictable in his office with him assuring her of the outcome. Now she questioned the wisdom of taking on a multimillion-dollar corporation which had a legal machine already on retainer. Fear found its way into her mind, choking out the happiness that bolstered her hope for the future.

She could not force herself to spend the day job hunting and returned home to an empty house wishing desperately that she could turn back the clock and give life a second try. Twice she had to stop herself from dialing Doug's number before drifting off into a troubled sleep.

She awakened wondering if the noise she was hearing was real or part of some dream she was still experiencing. She had never quite gotten used to the variety of ring tone choices that her new smart phone had and was often surprised when a caller, text, or incoming email prompted her to respond. Add to that her smoke detectors, and the programmable doorbell her husband had purchased online, the choices of "audio alert" sounds seemed endless.

Her clock read 2:47 a.m. – forget the old days when the time would have been about a quarter to three – modern times are precise in terms of digital readouts. The sound was insistent and repeated itself after she was awake, thus eliminating the option that it was a dream. Her cell phone lay on the bedside table, her alarm clock remained silent, and she smelled no smoke. She climbed from her bed, put on a robe and pulled the curtain back which covered the glass beside the front door.

Under the dim glow cast by the porch light Clay stood looking wet and miserable. A heavy rain was falling behind him, evidenced by the wet sidewalk and gutters flowing like small mountain streams. Overhead lightening lit the night sky with thunder following close behind. She opened the door just as he pushed the doorbell one final time.

Unprepared to give some smart remark, she simply moved aside and said, "come in out of the rain."

He did so without further urging. As he passed by she noted that his shoulders were sagging and his whole posture cried out of defeat and hopelessness. She took his coat, turned on a light beside the sofa and looked into the wretched face of her friend and advocate.

"I'll make us some coffee," she volunteered, then hit the button which lighted the gas fireplace as she passed by it. She knew the minimal heat produced by the inefficient appliance would produce the illusion of heat more than raise the room temperature, but noted he had immediately been drawn to it anyway.

While she filled the reservoir and measured out the grounds she watched him as he attempted to find comfort in the flickering flames which promised what they were ill fit to deliver. The self-assured, independent man she had come to know over the past few weeks had disappeared, leaving behind a hollow shell of a man lost and desperate.

He stood, his back to the flames, eyes cast downward as though studying the carpet, his clothing dripping water on the floor around him. Without a word she handed him a steaming cup of black coffee before leaving the room. When she returned she was holding a bath towel, her husband's robe, and a change of dry clothes.

"Why don't you try these," she offered, handing them to him and turning on the light which illuminated the nearby bathroom, "then we can talk."

Clay left the room without a word and much like a child, did as he was told. It seemed to Gaye that he had lost direction and had no will of his own and had come to her as a place of safety in a storm of life over which he had no power. She drank her coffee slowly, trying to make sense of what she felt and what she saw. She prayed. As he returned to the room and joined her she'd been given direction and wisdom.

"Tell me," she said softly, "what you are feeling and why you have come here tonight."

Clay looked up from where he'd been staring at his feet and caught her gaze. His eyes were deep set and filled with sadness and despair, red rimmed and shiny with tears.

"I… I'm not sure," he answered. "I think I'm falling in love with you but I cannot forget my wife and put her behind me. I don't know what to do."

As she spoke, Gaye felt a rush of sympathy for him, a form of love as would a mother feel for her child. "Never try to forget her, love her for what she gave you, for what you shared, for the memories she left behind, but if you truly ever love me, never compare me to her memory. Time will make her more and more perfect in your eyes and me less and less so, I could never live up to that standard."

She thought she may have detected the birth of a sad smile on his lips as his mind struggled to assimilate what he had just heard.

The room remained quiet until finally he spoke in a weak, strained voice. "It hurts so badly, I feel so unfaithful when I consider the possibility of creating a new life without her.

"Perhaps the timing is not right, maybe you are trying to move too quickly," Gaye answered gently. "I feel something for you too, but I'm not divorced yet. Neither of us is going anywhere soon, let's just take life slow and easy, enjoy our friendship, and see where God leads us."

Clay exhaled as though he had been holding his breath but in fact was letting go of his frustrations, fears, and anxiety. "Maybe you are right," he answered in a quavering voice.

When he awakened, he was lying on her sofa with his head in her lap, she was gently running her fingers through his thinning hair. Outside, the rain had stopped and the sun risen in promise of a new day.

Later, it seemed strange to see Clay sitting across the table from her, garbed in Doug's robe. She wondered instinctively how it would feel had they been husband and wife, lovers and partners, but had no concept of it. They each picked at a plate of toasted Eggo waffles, topped with a poached egg and several strips of crisp bacon. A fresh pot of coffee was already half gone before they spoke.

"I'm sorry," Clay said in a voice that had more strength and resolve, "I was so overcome last night… and you were the only one I knew who could understand."

"I'm flattered," she answered sincerely. "Where do we go from here?"

"I'm not sure," he said, "but I do know that I crossed the line as your attorney."

"And friend…," she added.

"Did I tell you that Doug called just before I left the office and said he's willing to sign off on the divorce?" he asked. "I'm afraid that I was so caught up in my own misery that I forgot to call you."

Gaye didn't answer but shook her head at the welcome news. "Does that mean we can move forward? Does he have an attorney?" she asked.

"To my knowledge he does not. He asked that we draw up the papers and send them to him," Clay said in his professional voice. "I have mixed emotions about it knowing that he should have professional counsel, but also knowing that it would also draw everything out and cost you money in the long run."

"Just treat him fairly, don't take advantage of his ignorance, but let's get the job done," Gaye instructed.

Clay nodded and smiled as she poured them yet another cup of coffee.

"Nothing yet from the company attorneys?" she asked.

"Not yet," he answered. "I expect they'll wait right down to the last minute to see if we panic before they make a counter or accept our offer as written."

For the first time in three weeks, it seemed to Gaye that life was back on course and she could see light at the end of the long dark tunnel. She hoped that she was not being overly optimistic.

He had sat there through the night across the street in the darkness as the storm had beat down on his old sedan and now into the morning as the sun had risen and the dark clouds overhead had been replaced with blue sky. He had catnapped off and on, waking each time a set of headlights made their way down the darkened street.

His diligence had been rewarded just before three o'clock when a dark colored Jaguar had stopped in front of her house and a man had exited it and after several minutes on the front porch had been allowed inside. He noted the license plate number and guessed at the approximate vintage of the blue Jag. Lights had remained on inside the house in what appeared to be the living area and then the kitchen when he was able to observe a woman fussing with a coffee pot.

There had been no sign of the male guest until just after 9:00 a.m. when once again the front door opened and he stepped from the house and made his way back to his car. The woman, his employer's wife he presumed was dressed in a robe and looked as though she'd had a sleepless night as she waved goodbye to her overnight guest.

Mason still had connections at the DMV who, for a promise of a later reward, provided the name and address of the owner of the vehicle. He nearly smirked when he heard the name, Claiborne J. Stevens Jr. and recognized him as her attorney. Game changer, he thought to himself, as he mentally tallied what the information may be worth to his client. A not so smart move for an attorney-at-law to spend the night with his client. This is the stuff that blackmail is made of he thought quickly, while considering who may pay him the most for the information. He decided to not notify his client until he had time to think it through, there'd be enough time later if he did.

Mason had been on the force nearly eight years before his drinking had come to light and he'd been fired for being drunk on the job. In truth he was lucky to have lasted that long as he seldom got through a shift without a little pick-me-up. He suspected it had been his new rookie partner who had made his superiors aware long before the night he ran the cruiser into a parked car while pursuing a car-load of fleeing teens in a hot rod Pontiac. He may have gotten off with just a reprimand even then, had the county sheriff's deputy not been first on the scene. That no love was lost between the two agencies was common knowledge.

If you had connections and knew someone with computer skills, there was little about someone that you could not find out if you had the desire to do so. A person's credit information was about as safe as the lock on your sliding glass door and with it, the right person could do nearly anything they wanted to you. Mason was not above doing a little snooping around when he made the call to a friend in finance and asked for a favor.

"I just need a FICO on a guy who is looking to buy a little real estate from a client," he lied. "He wants my guy to carry the paper until he can get a business loan. Maybe I can steer him your way."

The implied promise of a possible new client was all it took for him to run the credit score illegally. The score came back within minutes at 875.

The loan officer whistled then said, "have you still got plenty of my business cards? This guy is a gold mine."

"I'll do my best," Mason lied again. "I'll talk you up real good."

Mason had his card alright and a dozen like it, he even made notes on them when he used them for his benefit. Once in a while he'd call and ask if the client had contacted them yet, as a cover. Needless to say, Mason used people the way most used motor oil, to keep things running until it needed changed, then threw it away. He'd also been married three times.

"Mr. Stevens, this is Mr. Mason. I have client who has asked me to look out for his affairs in the matter of his pending divorce. I am afraid that you may have breached his trust by spending the night recently with his wife," he said.

In all truth to this point Mason had not made a statement which was untrue and had broken no laws. What he had done however was to put the fear of God in the attorney, who already must have known that he'd made a poor choice by going to his client's house late at night. He let his words sink in while the telephone connection remained silent.

"There was no impropriety...," Clay started to explain, all the while knowing any explanation he may give was useless. "What is it you want Mr. Mason?"

"Of course, what I want is what's best for my client," Mason answered, carefully choosing his words as he spoke. "If possible, I'd like to shelter him from the pain of knowing about your involvement with his wife. What do you suppose this information will cost your client in court when negotiating a settlement? Or you, for that matter, if the bar chooses to look into it?"

Clay's mind was whirling; he had been caught off-base and felt the earth beneath him slipping away. "Call me back tomorrow and we can discuss it," he finally said, then disconnected the phone.

Clay was a smart man who had done a stupid thing. The more he searched for an answer the less he liked the options he found. As it became apparent that no easy solution was to be had, he dialed the telephone and asked Marlene if he could speak to Pastor Tim.

When Clay quickly outlined the situation, Tim invited him to come right over, while encouraging him to trust in God. Marlene nodded but said nothing as he entered the church and made his way to the pastor's office. Tim rose from his seat and moved to an old sofa where he indicated that Clay should join him. As soon as they were seated Tim bowed his head and began to pray, Clay followed suit.

"Father," he began. "Once again we, your children, have relied upon our own wisdom and find ourselves calling out for your guidance and direction. Guide our hearts, minds, and thoughts to your solution. Amen."

Clay raised his head, then told his friend and Pastor the whole story including his feelings for Gaye, how they had spent their time together, and his reluctance to let go of the memory of his wife. In the end he was emotionally exhausted beyond his limits and felt more and more incapable of making good judgments

"God does not fault us for making poor choices," Tim said. "But often our choices have consequences which lead us away from Him toward sin."

Clay could do nothing but nod.

Tim continued, "King David should have known better than invite Bathsheba to the palace, and I am sure he probably did. But up to that juncture he'd not sinned, he'd just put himself in a position to sin. Ultimately, that second choice cost him everything."

"What should I do?" Clay asked.

The old pastor hesitated a moment before laying out his strategy for Clay.

"First and always pray," he said. "Then go to Gaye and tell her what you have told me, make sure she is in full agreement with you. Finally, I'd suggest you and Gaye go to a member of the Bar and retell it to them and see if they will endorse involving the police department.

Clay could see the wisdom in Tim's words.

"Perhaps you should also consider turning Gaye's case over to someone else in your firm to avoid even the appearance of impropriety," he added.

The two friends prayed once more then stood, shook hands, and said their goodbyes. Clay then left without further conversation.

"Gaye, I need to speak with you right away on a very urgent matter, can you come to the office?" Clay asked.

"Of course," she answered. "Is something wrong?"

"Yes and no," he answered. "I'll fill you in as soon as you get here.

When Gaye arrived, Clay and another man were in the foyer waiting for her. Clay introduced the second man as William Spence, a junior partner in the firm, and asked her permission to include him in their conversation. Even as she agreed she felt alarm that a stranger would be included at this stage of the divorce. What had gone wrong she worried, what had happened since last night to prompt such an emergency meeting? They entered Clay's office and closed the door taking seats in an area with comfortable furnishings, away from Clay's desk.

"Let me first just say that everything said here is protected by client-attorney privilege and that I've asked William to join us with a purpose in mind that he may step in and represent you in the future."

The way the meeting was starting did nothing to alleviate the apprehension which Gaye felt. In fact, Clay's formal manner increased her alarm.

"I received a call," Clay began, "from a man who identified himself as Mr. Mason. Mr. Mason indicated that he had been hired by your husband, Doug, to *look out for his best interests*, as he put it. He did not make it quite clear what those interests were or exactly what his standing is. What he did say quite bluntly was that he was aware that I had spent the night at your home."

"Oh my," were the only words which escaped Gaye's lips, but fear and concern filled her eyes.

Clay continued while his protégé listened without interruption. "By innuendo, Mr. Mason intimated that this information could be very damning to your case financially, and may even affect my standing with the Bar if made public."

At this revelation, Mr. Spence nodded but added nothing.

"But," Gaye began, "nothing inappropriate happened. We can tell Doug that."

For the first time since beginning to speak Clay smiled, "that is word for word what I started to tell Mr. Mason until I realized how ridiculous it sounded as a defense."

Mr. Spence finally spoke as though clarification was necessary. "It's kind of like someone in an asylum telling everyone that they are not crazy and they do not belong there. The more they say, the crazier it sounds."

His interjection seemed to lighten the mood somewhat.

"So what do we do? What is our next move if denial will not remedy what is already done?" Gaye asked the counselors.

"Pastor Tim's advice was to begin with prayer, listen to where God guides us, then go to the Bar and confess my inappropriate behavior," Clay answered. "That is," he added, "with your permission."

Spence was nodding again. "Always better to admit our sins rather than to be found out and try and explain them away," he said.

"Poor choice of words," Clay stated, "but I agree with the message."

"It seems so unfair..." Gaye began.

"Life is seldom so," Clay agreed. "That's why I'm still in business."

"What do you think will happen?" Gaye asked naïvely.

Clay hesitated before answering, and then said, "I expect a harsh reprimand from the Board and possibly disciplinary action for my misjudgment and an attempt from Mr. Mason to exhort money to keep quiet."

"Isn't that illegal?" Gay asked, "Isn't that blackmail."

"Yes it is," Clay answered. "But Mr. Mason is smart. He tippy-toes around asking for a pay-off pretty well. I'm guessing he has had some legal training and knows how to do what he's doing without hanging himself."

"You are not considering paying him?" Gaye questioned.

"No," Clay answered firmly. "Once I break it to the Bar, he has no leverage over me, and stands to gain little by telling Doug. I'm hopeful that the prosecuting attorney may try and set up a sting operation and get him for extortion. I doubt that this is the first time he has blackmailed someone."

It was late in the day on day nine when Clay's secretary took the call from the attorneys who represented Gaye's former employer. Before answering, he took the copy of their offer from its folder and placed it where he could easily read it if necessary.

"This is Claiborne Stevens," he said in a tone which made him sound like a pompous, self absorbed, wealthy attorney, exactly like the one who was calling him. He, in fact, was none of those. He was a guy who did his own laundry, washed his own dirty dishes, and looked to match his socks each morning before going to his office. His single indulgence was to take his dress shirts to the shirt laundry once a week and have a housekeeper come in twice a month to find whatever dust bunnies that he had missed when he vacuumed.

The voice on the phone made every effort to emulate what Clay had just said, drawing out each syllable for effect before identifying his purpose for calling. E d w a r d J. B r o w n, as he identified himself, was a senior partner of the firm Brown and Shuster, whose name may have meant something to someone living in New York City where they were headquartered. It meant nothing to Clay as he was tempted to have a little fun with the guy and ask him to spell 'Shyster' just to make sure he had not misunderstood. He did not.

"And... Mr. Brown, just what is it that I can help you with?" Clay asked innocently.

"We represent..." he began, naming Gaye's employer before Clay interrupted him mid-sentence.

"And..." Clay said, "you are calling to what, accept our offer as written or make a counter proposal to prevent litigation?

Brown obviously believed his own press about how powerful and important he was and had expected to dominate the conversation and intimidate the small backwater attorney on the other end of the phone. As he was gathering himself for a reply, Clay took the initiative and spoke again.

"So which is it Brown, get to it, I don't mean to seem rude but I am due in court in a few minutes on a similar case I'm fielding against Wal-Mart," Clay lied.

He hoped that he had not overplayed his hand but knew that playing from strength was far superior than a position of weakness.

"Our offer is $250,000 and not a penny more, and we expect written assurance that the matter is resolved without prejudice," Brown said begrudgingly.

"And the 401k?" Clay asked. "You are prepared in addition to pay the appropriate tax burden created by her dismissal and its necessary liquidation?"

"Chump change," Brown said. "Would you really litigate to save your client a few thousand dollars in taxes?"

"In a minute," Clay said, "but of course the 250K would look like chump change when the jury handed down the verdict of $1.5 million after all was said and done."

"Agreed," Brown said without further discussion. "I'll have the papers drawn and overnight them for signature."

As the line disconnected, Clay raised his eyes heavenward and whispered a sincere "Thank You" to God.

The telephone rang three times before Gaye answered. When the caller ID showed the law firm's name she immediately wondered what new crisis was facing her.

The moment she said a tentative hello, Clay began to speak.

"We should have the papers in the morning," he announced excitedly, "their offer is $250,000 plus the remainder of your 401k, all tax free."

"No strings?" Gaye asked.

"No strings," Clay answered, but it could muddy the water some regarding offering Doug a fair settlement."

"Treat him fairly, but don't give him a free ride at my expense," Gaye responded.

"I'll pass your instructions on to your new attorney Mr. Spence, who I'm sure will offer fair advice to you regarding an equitable settlement." Clay said.

Morning had dawned brightly when Gaye and Clay made their way together up the granite stairs of the courthouse to the chambers of the imposing courtroom where several senior members of the Bar had gathered. In his brief, which had necessitated the meeting, Clay had outlined the circumstances for which the august body may well find reason to punish one of its own.

The proceedings were not completely unlike those of civil court where certain formalities were to be recognized and performed. In his twenty-two years as an attorney, he'd never been a plaintiff and only twice had been requested to sit in judgment of one of his peers. Out of necessity it was a solemn matter, handled with the utmost decorum and reserve.

At Clay's request, William Spence sat in the gallery, available should the court need him for any reason. The only other persons seated were Pastor Tim and Marlene who had chosen to attend to show support for their friend.

The interior arrangement of the room included a podium facing the raised area where the five members of the Bar sat to hear the case. A court reporter was present to take accurate notes of the proceedings. The senior member, a Judge, sat in the middle and presided over the proceedings. It was he who called the meeting to order and asked Claiborne Stevens to address the panel.

"Mr. Stevens, since it was you who admittedly brought your own transgressions of ethical behavior to the court's attention, I would ask that you address the panel and retell the story in detail as you remember it," he said.

Clay approached the podium, looked each of the members directly in their eyes, and began to speak.

"A short background if you will allow me will help set the stage for the current situation in which I find myself mired," he began. "And help you understand how this matter occurred."

The group nodded but said nothing.

"Five years ago my wife was killed in an automobile accident by a drunken driver," Clay began. "I have by choice remained alone and celibate since. Just a month ago I accepted a new client who was wrongly terminated from her long-time employment and on the same day given notice by her husband that he was leaving her with an intent to divorce her for another woman."

Clay gave his words a moment to find their way into the hearts of the panel before continuing.

"As we met initially and began to formulate an effective representation on both accounts, I found that my client's situation brought back memories of the unfairness of the situation which I had personally felt when my wife was taken from me without warning. My empathy for her has lead to a fondness and quite possibly deeper emotional feelings. This feeling of kinship drew me to go to her home when faced with the emotional turmoil of resolving my feelings after my wife's death."

One of the members of the panel raised a question. "So unbidden, you went to her home in the middle of the night, is that correct?"

"Correct," Clay answered.

"And her response was what?" another asked.

"She let me inside out of the rain," Clay said.

"Willingly?" the Judge persisted.

"Hesitantly," Clay answered.

"And you felt what?" the Judge continued.

"Lost, alone, confused..." Clay answered.

"And what did you expect your client to do to help you?" came a question from another member of the panel.

"I don't know, just listen maybe, to understand, to relate to my pain," he answered. "I was looking for something that no one else has been able to give."

"What did you do?" was the panel's next question.

"We sat on her sofa and talked, finally I went to sleep with my head in her lap," Clay admitted.

"Did you have any kind of sexual contact?" the senior Judge asked sternly.

"No, none," Clay answered. "That was the last thing on our minds."

"Is your client in this room?" he asked.

"Yes," Clay said, looking at Gaye.

The Judge looked directly at her as she stood and asked her, "Do you have anything to add or any objection to what has already been said?"

"No," Gaye answered, "except to say that friends should be able to go to their friends when in need without answering to anyone."

"Quite true," the senior Judge admitted, "but that excludes clients and their representative attorneys. Let me ask you, would he have come to your home for help if your husband was still at home?"

Gaye knew she'd been trapped but answered honestly. "I'd never have reason to know Mr. Stevens of my husband was still at home."

Several smiled at her answer.

"What brought you to us?" the senior asked Clay. "Why didn't you just keep quiet and hope you could sweep it under the carpet?"

"First," Clay answered, "I knew it was wrong, and second, when I took it to my pastor he agreed and urged me to come to you, so I made the call."

"Your pastor is a wise man," the senior said. "We also received a call a few days ago from someone who claims to have seen you enter and leave."

"Mr. Mason I'd guess," Clay answered. "I think he was trying to set us up for extortion but must have changed his mind and decided to just stir up trouble."

"Is there anything else we should know?" the senior counsel asked.

"Just that we have settled the wrongful termination suit and Mr. Spence is working to resolve the divorce," Clay answered.

"The Board will discuss your case and advise you of its findings in a few days," the Judge said. "You may go."

True to his word, the Judge called Clay at his office the following week.

"We found that you used poor judgment, put yourself in a compromising position which may have jeopardized your client's divorce case, and opened a door which could impugn the integrity of the legal profession" the old Judge said sternly. "However, we compliment you on your personal integrity, your choice of friends, and your faith in God. You'll have an official letter of reprimand in your permanent file and pay a fine of one thousand dollars to the charity of your choice. He then added with a mirthful voice, "a non tax-deductible contribution."

"G'morning," Clay said to his protégé, Mr. Spence. "How's the case going?"

"Very well I think, Gaye's a wise and generous woman. She's authorized me split the assets and liabilities equally, with the exception of the wrongful termination settlement, right down the middle and she'll pay all of our legal fees from her side," William answered.

"That is generous indeed," Clay said, "given the fact it was he who walked out and into the arms of someone else."

"You could do worse," William said over his shoulder as he turned and walked away, leaving Clay to guess at his meaning.

Clay had trouble concentrating on the day's work with his mind wandering back to William's last statement. His silent prayer was "Lord guide me to Your purpose and to do Your will in all things." He knew that praying into God's will rather than his own was always a safe bet, but left room for God to take him in a completely different direction than he desired.

The $1,000 contribution of course went to his small church with specific instructions to treat it as anonymous. To the fine, he added another $1,000 of his own as a gesture of appreciation for Tim's wise counsel and God's provision.

It had been two weeks since he had seen or made contact with Gaye. He had thought it best to withdraw from her life until the divorce was final. Gaye, however, took his complete absence as a sign that his interest in her had not been personal and with the exception of that one fateful night, only official business.

She filled her days with the tedious chore of trying to find employment, even after her unemployment benefits began. Nothing she found seemed a good fit and nothing that fit was offered to her. She began to feel discouraged and was beginning to think that she'd need to utilize her severance settlement to live on as soon as her benefits ran out.

Healing has a funny way of happening in spite of our propensity to hold on to our misery. Pain and misery is often an anchor which we can count on when life appears uncertain. With no conscious attempt, Clay's heart seemed to be healing and when he thought about his wife the memories became less and less painful. As Gaye had suggested, his memories focused on the good times they had shared and not on the tragedy that ended them. Occasionally now, he'd find himself smiling at an event or circumstance that they had shared as he remembered and relived it in his mind.

The line was long and moving slowly at the bistro near his office, Clay reminded himself to pay closer attention to the time in the future and miss the worst of the lunch hour crowd by leaving his office either earlier or later.

As he neared the front of the line his attention was drawn to the figure of a solitary woman who had just taken a table near the window, it was Gaye.

In spite of himself his heart did a little flip flop. He noted that she had bowed her head and seemed to be asking God's blessing on her food. A few minutes later, his pastrami sandwich in hand, he walked up to her table and asked, "is this seat taken?"

Gaye looked up into familiar eyes and the smiling face that she had tried unsuccessfully to forget. "I was saving it for a friend," she answered coyly. Clay was caught off guard by her reply and looked around to see if there might be someone waiting for the seat.

Gaye couldn't help but laugh at his bewildered look and said, "it seems like I've saved it for a couple of weeks now, good to finally see you." He sat and tried to immediately to try and explain his absence but she waived it away, smiled and said, "I've missed you."

"I've missed you too," Clay said sincerely. "How's the case coming?"

"It is final today," Gaye replied. "I'm a free woman."

Clay couldn't help but catch the implied meaning to the little addendum.

"We should celebrate," he said spontaneously. "That is, of course, unless you already have plans for dinner?" The words seemed to just say themselves without preparation.

"Are you asking me out to dinner?" Gaye queried.

"I am," he answered. "And... inviting you into my life if you are ready to consider that possibility."

– The End –

The Ride

It seemed at first a small thing to give the man walking beside the roadway in the freezing snowstorm a ride. He walked head down, into the fierce storm, his ragged clothes pulled tightly around him, his hooded coat buttoned to his chin. It had been snowing heavily for several hours, and recently the wind had added to the misery which it spelled for those forced to be out-of-doors.

In these current times we are often warned about the dangers associated with something as simple as this gesture of kindness. I ignored the warnings that were playing in my mind and pulled over beside him.

"May I offer you a ride," I asked through the opened window.

He looked up and into the car, his pale grey eyes locked on mine and a slight smile crossed his lips before he answered, "yes, thank you, I was hoping you'd come by."

I pondered the unusual way that he'd accepted my invitation and pushed the button which unlocked the passenger door. Surely he'd meant, "that someone would happen by and stop." As he climbed into the passenger seat, he smiled again with an engaging smile which seemed to alleviate any fears that remained in my mind about being murdered and dumped beside some lonely road. The window closed as I pushed the button and shut out much of the sound of the raging storm.

I leaned toward him, extended my hand and said, "I'm Tim

Reynolds." He took it and said simply, "I'm pleased to meet you Tim," but did not offer his name in return.

The snow had accumulated on the road, quickly filling the tracks my tires had just made and forming a perfectly white blanket across it. My windshield wipers struggled to keep up as I increased the tempo to the fast setting. We sat a moment while the car heater once again brought the interior of the car to a comfortable temperature, then I pulled back onto the pavement behind a semi that'd just passed by. He fastened his seatbelt without ceremony, then put his small bag of belongings across his lap but did not offer conversation.

"Where were you headed?" I asked curiously. "How'd you come to be out in this storm?"

Again he smiled but hesitated before answering. "I sensed that someone needed my help so I've been out searching for them," he said.

"In this storm," I said amazed. "I can't imagine how you'd find them. Is it someone you know well?"

"Since their birth," he said, "but we really haven't stayed in touch lately. I was surprised when I heard their call today."

"If you give me their address, I will drop you by their house," I offered, secretly hoping it wasn't far out of my way.

"Thank you," he answered sincerely, "but I'm not yet sure if I'll be welcome."

I was puzzled and concerned that I may have picked up someone mentally incompetent, as I put the entire conversation into context. The snowstorm filled our tracks as soon as we made them, and the semi truck in front of us seemed to be struggling to hold the road as it became slick and the cross winds played upon its trailer. I stole a glance at my passenger, trying to remember if I'd seen him before, but nothing came to mind.

"Do you live around here?" I asked.

"Sometimes," he answered, leaving me to wonder why his answers seemed to not satisfy me. "This is not my home," he clarified, as if knowing his answer did not fulfill my curious nature. "I just stay where I'm invited for a time, then move on."

I found it odd that the more he said, the more I seemed to want to know, but felt awkward in asking. I noted that nearly an hour had passed and yet no mention of where he might find his friend in need, but I said nothing. Up close, his attire was in a sad state of repair, holes in the fabric and buttons missing, cuffs frayed from use but somehow it seemed to fit exactly the man who wore them.

As we passed a sign nearly covered with snow which indicated the imminent presence of a truck stop, I turned toward him and said, "There's a truck stop about a mile ahead, would you allow me to buy you something to eat and a hot cup of coffee?"

Again I observed the hint of a smile before he answered simply, "if you'd join me, I'd be pleased to share supper with you."

Although when I had made the offer, I had not expected to eat, it seemed that all at once I was famished. "I am looking forward to it," I said sincerely, as the marquee indicated that we'd arrived.

We followed the semi truck into the lot, parked near the building and got out of the car. Instantly, the wind abated and the snow began to fall silently in large majestic flakes as we walked toward the entrance. As the semi driver drew nearer, my companion turned toward him and asked, "would you join us for supper?"

I immediately felt irritation, then anger, at his inappropriate invitation to include a stranger without prior discussion with me, but said nothing.

The old man smiled and seemed to gain energy as he lifted his head and raised his drooping shoulders. "Best offer I've had in a while, I could use some company," he declared. "Herding that rig down the road in a crosswind really takes it out of a guy."

I mentally checked my finances and remembered that I had found a $20 blowing across the parking lot when I had left work before heading home. My anxiety level went down but I still held a little resentment for the stranger's offer.

Inside, we were seated at a table away from the door by a stout young woman whose energy level seemed immutable. She turned over our cups and filled them with coffee without asking. The table was set for four so she asked the obvious, "are you expecting anyone else?"

In my mind I could hear myself saying, "I certainly hope not," when my beleaguered passenger spoke. "One never knows who may come along needing a meal."

I choked off my objection to his statement and made excuse to wash my hands while I tried to retain control of myself. I used the restroom, washed my hands, and regained my sense of propriety, but then lost it immediately as I exited to find that our waitress had gone off shift and was seated with my new friends.

I wanted to walk right past the trio and out the door leaving them to their own resources, but did not. They were laughing and visiting as I joined them, without making an attempt to interject myself into the conversation. It seemed that they hardly noticed as their *meal ticket* took his seat.

The new waitress, who had just begun her shift, approached the table with her order pad at the ready and asked if everyone had had ample opportunity to look over the menus. Of course none had so they turned to our waitress/companion and asked her opinion. By this time I felt like an outsider, out of the loop, almost an interloper at my own party. I proceeded to read the menu, then without waiting for the others, ordered the French Dip with a side of fries.

I couldn't overcome the resentment that had taken hold of me and secretly nourished it as I rehashed in my mind the odd events which had happened since I pulled to the roadside and offered the stranger a ride. As I looked across the table he had finished speaking and I found myself looking into his eyes, which held a kind of sadness that was easy to see but hard to describe. Neither he nor I said anything as we broke eye contact.

Our meal arrived a few minutes later and I noticed that the faire was as varied as those who had ordered it. The waitress had ordered pulled pork with coleslaw, the trucker a ham and eggs breakfast, and my companion a simple bowl of soup with bread. I, of course, had the French Dip to complete the feast. As I looked around immediately I wished I had ordered differently, each of their meals appealed to me more than my own. As I looked up the others had joined hands and were waiting patiently for me to do the same so the food could be blessed. Although no one said a word I felt their rebuke as plainly as if someone had shouted it.

He asked for the Lord's blessing and each of us turned to the task of causing the food to disappear as quickly as possible. We ate for the most part without conversation, each relishing our meal. Two of the four had dessert while my companion and I refrained and enjoyed a final cup of coffee. I found that my resentment and anxiety had nearly abated and resigned myself to the use of plastic after realizing that I lacked the resources to pay cash for our meal.

I stood and walked toward the register, taking note that outside the snow had stopped falling. The cashier had just taken payment from another patron and smiled as I approached and reached for my wallet.

I started to pull out my Visa card when I noticed the new $20 I'd found looked to have been stuck to a second. I took it out, pulled them apart and put the two new crisp twenties on the counter.

"$34.75," the cashier said as she deftly scooped up the twenties, "out of forty."

"Give the change to our waitress," I said, without further consideration.

At the table my three new friends seemed to be enjoying their conversation as they finished their coffee and prepared to resume their lives. The burly truck driver offered his hand and his thanks before recommitting himself back to the icy road that stretched out before him. A few minutes later the young plump waitress with the ready smile which was belied by the worry lines around her eyes stood, gave the stranger a hug, and made excuse that she needed to leave to get home to her children She took her coat from the coat hook near the door and made her way into the snowy night. I could see her car's tail lights before they disappeared as she pulled onto the highway. Right her behind the semi followed suit.

It was snowing harder now, with the wind blowing the snow ahead of it, obscuring everything beyond the nearest of the fuel pumps.

"Are you ready?" I asked the stranger, making reference to continuation of our journey.

"I'll walk from here," he answered. "It's not far now and you've done your part."

Surprisingly, at his declaration I felt a kind of let down, a sense of loss at losing his company and completing whatever "my part" was.

We walked outside together into the falling snow with the wind buffeting us. I noticed that he had gathered his thin worn coat in his hands around him where the buttons were missing, and asked him to accompany me to my car. He followed without speaking. My new LL Bean ski parka lying in the back seat drew me to it and before I could consider the cost, I handed it to him and asked him to accept it. To my surprise he did, smiling as he zipped it and put up the hood. When I offered to dispose of his old one he rejected my offer saying that it still held value. I hugged him awkwardly before watching as he walked toward the roadway and disappeared into the snowy darkness.

The warmth of the diner beckoned me back inside from the numbing cold for a final cup of coffee before continuing my trip. I sat there for several minutes watching the snow fall before forcing myself to leave its sanctuary. I got into the car, buckled my seat belt, and followed my new friends on ward toward my destination.

Thankfully there was little traffic, most others had wisely chosen to stay home and off the slick roadway. My SUV in AWD seemed to handle well but occasionally reminded me that slow and easy got the job done when it slid, then recovered, after catching a tire in a frozen groove in the snow. My lights were ineffective with the high beam catching only the reflection of the snow and the low showing only a few feet before me. I slowed once again and turned on the vehicle's fog lamps which worked much better. I wondered momentarily why I had not passed the hitchhiker, certainly I thought, he could not have came this far this quickly. Perhaps he had caught another ride.

Ahead through the falling snow, I could barely make out the lights of a big rig lying jack-knifed partially across the roadway. I pressed the brake and rejoiced as the anti-lock feature of my new car prevented sliding and slowed me to the equivalent of a fast walk.

Taking the far left lane I was able to avoid the mass of tangled steel which only minutes before had been the old sedan driven by the waitress and the eighteen wheeler piloted by the burly trucker. Both now lay in the snow unmoving, while my passenger friend gently covered their lifeless forms with his worn coat. I knew at once that he had found the friends that had needed his help. Matthew 25:34-40

– The End –

The Keeper

"Fish on!" Jerry exclaimed after he had jerked the stiff boat pole violently backward in an attempt to set the hook.

Tom, who had taken the helm, cut the motor back to a fast idle, which was just enough to give him control of the little twenty-four foot boat's heading in the strong current. He turned in his seat and took satisfaction in his friend's good fortune.

"Keep your tip up," he advised automatically, knowing full well that Jerry already knew the finer points of landing a salmon.

The fish hadn't shown itself yet and had dived deep in a vain attempt to slip the hook. Jerry's rod had a great bow in it, much like an inverted 'C', as he maintained pressure while secretly wondering if the several knots he'd tied had been strong enough. From time to time the fish would run toward the boat, which gave Jerry opportunity to reel in the line as it slackened.

Then after catching its, breath the fish would turn away and peel line off the big Penn reel, seemingly without effort. The steady buzz of the drag however, may have just as well been the hands of a clock counting down the minutes until the fish would lose its strength and vigor. Nearly every true fisherman had felt almost a sorrow for their catch when that time came, knowing that its game's fight had not gained it freedom.

The Chinook finally broke water some fifty yards behind the boat, using its considerable strength and the momentum furnished by the bent pole to arch several feet into the crisp autumn breeze. He shook his mighty head saying "No!" to the forces that restrained him, as he did, the hook turned slightly in his mouth and lost its hold in the hard gristle of his lip.

"Lost him," Jerry said, with a twinge of remorse in his voice. In truth he was not all that unhappy at the loss, as several like him were already in the live well. He joined his friend in the cabin after reeling in the line, with the purpose of replacing the bent hook.

"How many in the boat?" Tom asked, knowing well the answer before he asked.

"Five," Jerry answered, "three Kings and two silvers."

The sun was on the wane and the wind had began to gust as a warning of the impending storm that was already evident farther out in the open sea. The waves were already choppy but still well within the range of safety of their small boat.

"Let's call it a day," Tom said, as he increased the rpm's and changed course toward the coastline.

"Sure," Jerry said smiling. "Call it before I have a chance to hook another and even up the score. You must really need that pitcher of beer to quit while you are ahead."

Tom returned his friends' smile and shrugged his shoulders before saying, "Captain's privilege. 'Sides, no sense of fighting that storm and getting wetter than we already are."

He picked up his cell phone and dialed his wife's number. After several rings he elected to leave a message, "we are on our way in... Jerry's buying the first round, see you at the marina."

Both of their wives had decided to stay behind to visit and shop this trip, although both were seasoned boaters and fisher...women.

Tom and Jerry, as most called them with mirth evident in their voices, were brothers-in-law and best of friends well before Jerry had married Tom's sister.

The marine channel squawked interrupting their light-hearted banter and advised a small craft warning and projected gale force winds and seas in excess of twelve feet by midnight. Already the waves were starting to whitecap as the gusting winds began to affect the boat's steerage.

"Guess you were right," Jerry admitted, as he began to break down the poles and stow them away. "'Tis better safe than sorry they say, to live to fish another day."

Tom had already fastened the life jacket that he'd been wearing when he turned to his friend who was doing the same. "We should make the pier before the worst of it catches us," he said. The waves beside the boat were cresting at four feet and seemed to be gaining momentum as the shoreline came into view.

"Mayday, mayday," came the hurried message over their little marine radio, "we're filling up with water and the motor's dead."

The signal was strong and the message clear indicating that the imperiled craft must be somewhere close by them.

Tom turned to Jerry and handed him the binoculars, "give a look and see if you can see them out there."

Jerry did as he was asked but without result. The waves had increased again which made spotting a small craft riding low in the water nearly impossible.

"Mayday, what is your location?" Tom asked.

After a short pause a voice full of fear and panic answered, "I can't tell, we left Homer this morning and have been moving up and down the coast all day. Our GPS isn't working."

"How far out do you think you are?" Tom asked. "Can you see the coastline?"

"When we ride up on a wave, I can sometimes see some kind of an island south and east of us, just a single big rock I think, with brush and small trees on it," he said.

"Wait one," Tom answered, "I'll try and reach the coast guard for you."

Tom tried all of the open channels more than once and finally received a reply, "This is the US Coast Guard, are you declaring an emergency?"

"We are in contact with a small craft which is dead in the water and taking on water, somewhere east of Eagle Rock out of Homer," Tom said. "Can you send aid?"

"We have nothing in the vicinity – all available craft are north of your location working to evacuate a fishing trawler with a crew of fifteen on board. Our ETA your location is estimated at thirty minutes. Can you render aid?" the Coasty asked.

"Wait one," Tom said, looking at his friend.

"What do you think Jerry?" he asked. "Are you up for a little heavy seas?"

"I don't see that we have much of a choice," Jerry answered smiling. "It could be us out there."

"Coast Guard, this is the King of the Sea #4F29814 answering the distress call, we'll give it a try," Tom said.

"Good luck, King of the Sea," was the reply. "Stay in contact if you will and thank you," said the Coasty with feeling.

"Mayday, this is King of the Sea, hold on brother we're headed your way," Tom said. There was no answer.

Tom gunned the engine as he made a 180º into the wind and

mounting waves, taking care not to dawdle in the trough in the process. Jerry looked at his friend with respect and admiration as he watched helplessly.

"Can I do anything?" he asked.

"If you can get the cover up in the back without falling overboard," he answered, "it will keep some of the wash out of it."

Jerry nodded and moved toward the storage locker where the back cover was kept. As the little boat pitched and rolled, he moved cautiously and slowly. Little by little the snaps found their marks and after several tries the rear was covered and fully waterproof.

"There are some extra jackets up in the nose," Tom said pointing forward. "It may be a good idea to get them out before we need them."

Jerry moved up and opened the small hatch which housed an assortment of extra gear and began to set out the jackets. "How are you doin'?" he asked his friend, "are we gonna make it?"

Tom's eyes left the windshield for a moment and a smile crossed his lined face. "God willin' we'll pick up our fare and be home by supper. You might do well to call the ladies and tell them we are doing alright but have been delayed a mite."

Jerry called the mainland but got no answer, so he left a short message without mentioning their predicament. He bowed his head and silently prayed for God's mercy and direction. When he raised his head, Tom was looking directly at him and said, "never hurts to call on the One who rules the sea and the air."

The little boat was now climbing each wave before breaking into the trough beyond, the bow was often under the crest of the wave for a few seconds before re-emerging. Tom's thoughts turned to a movie he had seen called "The Perfect Storm" and wondered if they'd find themselves in like predicament on a smaller scale.

"King of the Sea, this is Mayday, are you still there?" an anxious voice asked. Tom noted that the craft did not identify itself with name or number which indicated to him it was probably as small as or smaller than his own.

"We are on our way," Tom answered. "How are you doing? Can you see our running lights? When you do, you'll have to guide us since it is unlikely we will see you."

"Our boat is awash," he answered, "but the radio and lights are still working. There's enough flotation to keep us from going down unless it breaks apart."

"Keep prayin'," Tom responded. "We'll find you yet. How many do you have on board?"

"Four," the voice said. "My wife, myself, and our two sons."

"What kind of boat do you have?" Tom continued, trying to keep the man on the radio and his mind occupied.

"Some kind of 'whaler' I think," he answered. "Mostly open with a small windshield and sun top. I rented it at the pier."

Tom pictured an eighteen foot Boston Whaler with an outboard with hardly any freeboard and no protection from the breaking waves.

"I'm surprised you have a marine radio on board," Tom answered.

"They gave us a portable in case we broke down or needed help," Mayday replied. "Wait," he said excitedly, "I thought I saw your light."

Both Tom and Jerry felt a wash of relief at the prospect but were skeptical until they got another call.

"I see your starboard running light and your stern light," Mayday said jubilantly. "You are on our left side about a hundred yards south of us."

"Jerry," Tom said. "I hate to ask you to do this but you'll need to open the front window and stick your head out and see if you can get a look at them. Watch the waves and try and time it so you don't get buried in a roller."

Tom guessed that the waves were regularly in excess of ten feet now and the wind blowing straight at them at something over forty knots as he fought to keep his heading.

"I… I see them," Jerry said, pulling his head inside just as a wave broke over the boat. "How are we going to get then aboard without swamping ourselves?"

"Thinking I can bear a little to the right while keeping our nose into the waves and let the current take us over closer," Tom answered. "I have no idea how we can get four safely on board once we get closer."

"I'm going to unzip the rear cover down the middle but leave the sides snapped," Jerry offered. "I'll tie off a line to our throw ring and try and pull them toward the stern one at a time."

"Sounds like a plan," Tom said as he picked up the mic. "We are making our way over to you now," he advised. "I'm going to run past your boat but keep our nose into the wind and let you get behind us. Do you all have life vests on?"

"Both boys are in vests," came the answer. "The other two were lost over the side in the panic when we began to sink."

"Okay, listen up. We have extras which we'll send over with the life ring once we get into position. Put them on, then let us know when you are ready to send the boys over one at a time," Tom said.

"Please hurry," said a woman's voice. "We are freezing to death over here."

"Yes, ma'am," Tom answered. "We know that and are hurrying the best we can. Are any of you injured?"

"No," the woman answered, "but my husband is diabetic and will need his insulin soon or he'll be in bad shape."

Tom shook his head but said nothing aloud. 'God, please be merciful' he prayed silently, as yet another wave burst over them.

"How're you doing back there Jerry," he asked. "I've almost worked my way into position. Can you tie a couple of jackets onto the ring and begin letting out line when I tell you?"

"Can do," Jerry said as he knotted a short piece of line around the ring and through the armholes of two jackets. "I'm afraid they are doing to drag something fierce," he added. "Not sure I'll be able to hold them."

The little boat pitched violently and threw him against the gunwale. He hit hard and wondered what condition his ribs were in but maintained his hold on the line while the float trailed a few feet behind the boat's stern.

"Take a turn around that big cleat on the rail," Tom instructed. "It'll help you play out the line a little at a time without fighting it too much. Won't help on the retrieve though, you are just going to have to horse them in."

With their boat fifty feet or so in front of the swamped whaler Tom fought to find a speed which would hold them status, while Jerry played out the line with its lifesaving cargo floating toward them.

"When they have the ring and one of the kids ready," Tom told Jerry, "I'll try and drop back a bit while you take up the slack, then when we get as close as we can you'll have to start hauling him in."

"Roger," Jerry answered.

Tom picked up the mic once again. "Let us know when you have the ring and the first boy ready, and make sure that his jacket is tied securely to the ring from the back. We'll need to have him facing away from us to keep his head above water as we try and retrieve him."

"We are tying his jacket to the ring now," Bill told him. "Let me know when you are ready to bring him to you."

Tom looked at Jerry, Jerry nodded.

"We're ready Mayday, ask your son to lay back into the jacket and trail his feet behind him as we pull him to us, try and relax as much as he can and let us do the work," Tom advised.

Jerry felt an instant strain on the line as the boy went from the boat into the open water and began bringing in the line hand over hand, stopping only occasionally to use the cleat to take a short rest. The distance between the boats was only thirty feet now but it felt like thirty yards as the current worked to pull the boy away.

How are you doin'?" Tom asked over his shoulder without taking his eyes off the waves in front of him.

"Ten feet," Jerry answered tiredly, "then I'll haul him up on the platform and help him in."

"You doin' okay old buddy?" Tom asked. "You sound like you are landing a six hundred pound marlin."

Jerry laughed. "It feels like it too," he answered.

Ten minutes later a scared, wet, cold twelve-year-old boy named Billy sat shivering in the chair across from Tom. Jerry handed him a dry sweat shirt and a bottle of water. "How old is your brother?" he asked.

"He's ten but he's big for his age," he answered. Both men thought how odd the mention of his size sounded but said nothing.

"Mayday, your son is safely on board, please get your other boy ready to go as soon as you get the ring," Tom said.

Jerry began playing out the line just as he had before while hoping for the same good result. "God help us," he pleaded quietly under his breath.

"King of the Sea, this is US Coast Guard Kodiak Island, do you read?" the voice asked.

"5 X 5, loud and clear," Tom answered. "We are on location and have retrieved one survivor from the swamped craft, in process now of a second. Are you in a position to render aid?"

"King of the Sea, we have injuries to transport before we can refuel and send air support," the Coasty answered. "Best estimate an hour and forty-five minutes."

"I read you," Tom answered. "Please be advised one victim is diabetic and will require medical attention as soon as possible. Meanwhile, we'll continue our attempt at rescue and will advise progress as able."

"10-4," was the answer.

"Boy is in the water," Jerry said. "I'm beginning retrieval now."

Tom took a quick look over his shoulder and saw Jerry laboring under the strain caused by the drag on the rope, then stole a glance at the boy who was watching silently from his seat. Outside, the rain was now falling in sheets making visibility very difficult in the darkness. The small boat's single spot light was their only illumination.

When the second boy was hauled aboard it was easy to see what the first had meant by his comment. The ten-year-old looked like a husky teen rather than an elementary student. Jerry guessed him at well over a hundred pounds and at least five feet tall. A worried look came over his face as he came forward and leaned down to Tom.

"Depending on their size," he said, "I'm not sure I can do this alone."

Tom knew the impossibility of lending aid while managing the boat in the treacherous seas but could also see that his friend had about run out of gas. "Help us Lord," he pleaded in his heart. "We need You, we cannot do this alone."

The younger boy joined his brother and covered himself up as they shared a woolen blanket. Neither said a word, but both had tears in their eyes.

"The capstan!" Tom said excitedly as he pointed to the small winch mounted on the bow. "Jerry, I think I have an idea. Dig in the foot locker and see if we have an open pulley or two."

A few minutes later Jerry took a seat with several pieces of boat tackle in his hands. "Will this do?" he asked his friend.

"Perfect," Tom said smiling. "We are going to use the electric to give you a hand on the retrieve. It's made to haul in the anchor but I see no reason why it couldn't haul in the two who are left on the boat."

"What do I do," Jerry asked.

"First, secure the snatch block to the side cleat, then open the front window again and take a couple of turns around the capstan with the free end of the line, then through the pulley. It works just like a winch except you need to apply pressure to make it tighten and pull in the payload," he instructed.

Tom watched as Jerry followed his instructions and gave additional information and advice as the task proceeded.

"Mayday, this is King of the Sea, over," he said. "You have some boys here who want to see their momma, is she ready to come aboard?"

"Ready and eager," her voice answered. "Send us the life ring."

"On its way," Tom said looking at his young passengers. "Let us know when you are ready to come aboard."

As soon as she hit the water, Tom flipped a switch and said to Jerry, "put a strain on your line and keep taking up the slack as she comes in."

The little DC motor did just as it had been designed for but lugged down considerably under the additional load, causing Tom to worry if they may burn it out before all were safely aboard.

The tall slim woman needed Jerry's help to climb over the stern and into the boat. She was shaking uncontrollably and was obviously cold and exhausted by the ordeal. Tom took off his down jacket and wrapped it around her, then poured her a cup of coffee from his large thermos. "We're glad to welcome you aboard," he said smiling. "How's your husband doing?"

Jerry was letting the line out one final time when Tom picked up the mic and said, "I've got three here who want to see their daddy and go in and take a hot shower, are you about done fooling around over there?"

For several seconds there was no reply, and then a husky, tired voice answered, "I'm going in now, God bless you."

When he neared the stern it was obvious to Jerry that he was unable to get into the boat without help. Jerry fought to pull his nearly lifeless body into the safety of the boat and may not have had the strength had not both boys and his wife not lent a hand.

"He'll go into a coma without his shot," his wife said. "How long until we can get to shore and get help?"

Tom wanted to reassure her but he knew that the trip back was fraught with peril and that the extra weight of his passengers would necessitate using all of his skill to get them to safety.

"In this weather we'll be lucky to make shore in two hours," he said bleakly. "If we try and hurry we'll find ourselves in the same trouble you just came from."

"Coast guard, this is King of the Sea advising that four survivors are safely aboard and we are headed home. One is likely to go into a coma without insulin, please advise," Tom said.

"Wait one," was the immediate reply.

They waited.

A different voice spoke, "do you have and provisions aboard that are high in natural sugar like orange juice or fruit?"

Jerry was quickly looking in the cooler for anything that may fit the description. He found an apple, several sandwiches, beer and soft drinks, and a six pack of Hershey bars and reported his find to the Coast Guard Medic.

"Is he conscious?" was the first question.

The answer was yes but not alert or coherent.

"Hydrate him with water, as much as he will drink, and give him small chunks of the apple but peel it first to prevent choking. If he improves, let him have a soft drink and monitor his condition," the medic said.

They did as they were advised and then passed the sandwiches to the hungry refugees while Tom fought to keep them afloat. Jerry zipped the rear cover closed making the interior of the boat secure from rain and wind. The boat's heater soon filled the cramped space with much needed warmth. The wind was at their back now making, if possible, steering the boat even harder than before.

Jerry soon recovered his strength and handed Tom a Hershey bar, "do you want to let me spell you for a few minutes while you relax."

Tom smiled wearily then said with a weak smile, "are you kidding me? How could I relax with you driving the boat?"

Both Billy and his brother Tim were sound asleep while Betty sat on the deck leaning back against the foot locker and cradling her husband's head in her lap, a worried look in her eyes. When her head fell forward Tom feared that she had lost consciousness but was then relieved when she raised her head, looked him in the eyes, and mouthed the words "thank you". He nodded but said nothing.

Both the rain and the wind had increased – blowing toward the coast from the open sea, its noise filled the cabin with a clutter of sound making conversation nearly impossible. Jerry found peace and calm inside of himself as he centered his mind on the thankfulness he felt that God had granted them His mercy. He prayed for continued protection and direction as they began to occasionally see a light on the distant shoreline.

"King of the Sea, this is the U S Coastguard, be advised that a rescue response team on shore has you in sight and are awaiting your arrival with medical assistance on hand," the radio relayed, waking the boys from their slumber. All eyes turned to Bill Sr. who still lay on the deck who now opened his eyes wearily and attempted a weak smile.

His wife helped him sit up as he leaned into her body. "So," he asked, "how was fishing, get any keepers?"

Tom smiled and answered. "Nine I think, two silvers, three kings, and four tourists. Jerry caught the most."

– The End –

There But Unaware

I was standing with my friends and coworkers silently reverent while the funeral party continued to arrive. They spoke only in low, muted tones and then only infrequently. The typical weather shade had been positioned over the opened grave and the casket dolly stood beside it supporting its burden as the mourners continued to arrive and nod to one another. I attempted to draw several into conversation without success, so I stood resolutely as the minister began his speech with by reading the obituary from the local newspaper. I had trouble hearing him but noted that many nodded in agreement as the events of the deceased's life were highlighted.

A light spring breeze prevented the warm sunshine from making the temperature uncomfortable and added certain lightness to the event. Early blooming spring flowers in nearby beds seemed to welcome us and invite a measure of happiness to what was, for most, a sad day. As the tribute continued, I noted several family members and neighbors, causing me to wonder at the familiar mix in attendance. Eyes with vacant looks and moist cheeks below them seemed to look right through me as they struggled with their emotions. After what appeared like a long time, the minister's voice seemed to gain strength and power as he brought the short ceremony to a close.

"Ashes to ashes, dust to dust," he pronounced the familiar words, "in the pure and certain hope, we commend Joshua Wayne Thomas to his Maker. May God receive his soul."

My mind seemed to jump as I heard my name clearly pronounced. Confusion filled my mind as I struggled to understand what I had just heard. Certainly, I thought, I must have misheard or the pastor had unintentionally misspoken. I reached out my hand to catch his elbow as he passed by me but felt no fabric when I tried to clutch it. My hands took on a semi-transparent look, I could see right through them to the green grass below. In that instant, I realized that I was not just another guest.

– The End –

A Stand-Up Guy

There were beads of sweat on his brow and a trickle of the same following the creases of his spine as he waited his turn to go on stage. He'd never have dreamed he'd be standing behind the curtain waiting to try his hand at stand-up comedy in a formal setting. For most of his twenty-three years he'd been the life of the party, telling jokes and entertaining his friends as a way to deflect the inadequacy that he felt deep inside. Early on, he'd found that pain was a close cousin to laughter and of the two, laughter was always the more popular. Recalling the words of the song *Tracks of My Tears* from the 60's by Smokey Robinson, "some say I'm the life of the party 'cause I tell a joke or two..." he thought it very appropriate for his circumstance.

He'd always been big and clumsy making it difficult for him to not stand out in a crowd – so he naturally gravitated toward exaggerating in a way that made him fit in where he ordinarily would not have. Who did not love the big teddy bear of a boy with a ready smile and a quick wit, always willing to make fun of himself before anyone else had the opportunity? Superficially, he had a million friends, realistically... only two who cared enough about him as a person to be called the same. But now high school was behind him and most of his class had gone off to college or married, or were working and raising children, while he pursued a lackluster job in the local bakery.

John Candy, he thought to himself, as he continued to wait his turn.

John had made it big while being burdened with both size and weight in a world that seemed to focus only on appearance. The thought gave him confidence that he too may find just the right place which God had prepared for him.

He carefully took the bookmark out of his pocket and re-read the message printed on it. He'd been given it by a local man who wrote books, most likely with the intent that he'd become a customer, which he had not. But still, the message of the bookmark helped him realize that Someone larger than himself valued him. It read, *"You are the proud possession of the Father, the Maker of the universe, and Creator off all things. You are valued and loved by the One who is love. Be humble in spirit but feel valuable and significant as His creation. In your own power you are nothing, less than nothing really, but in Him you are equipped to do wonderful and meaningful things for His kingdom. Recommit yourself daily to the work for which you were created and revel in the fact that you are who you are!"*

It made no difference that he had not come from a religious family or had spent little time reading the Bible, he instinctively knew who God was and believed the message that the slim white piece of paper spoke to him. Ben had never had a girlfriend. Yes, he had had plenty of friends who were girls but never one with whom he'd had a real connection. He'd gone to the senior prom alone and as usual had been part of the backdrop and decorations.

"You're up next," the owner of the restaurant and bar said as he walked by nervously. "Keep 'em laughing!"

The little bar was a favorite hangout of the college crowd and the young marrieds who still liked to get out and dance and drink. Two days a week it had guest comedians and two days karaoke, with the weekend reserved for local bands. As he peeked out around the curtain he recognized several faces from high school and one or two who came into the bakery for donuts on their way to work each morning. He wasn't sure if he should consider them a plus or minus. He elected to call them out by name and try and gauge their response. "Good to see you here Tom, glad to see you back Bill and Mary, etc." and let it go where it would. If they enjoyed the recognition he'd count it a plus, if not, he'd lost nothing.

A sporadic round of applause followed a mousy little housewife-type off the stage. Ben noted there were tears in her eyes as she brushed past him.

"And now, for your entertainment," the DJ turned MC announced, "Mr. Benjamin Stone, a rising local talent."

Ben hitched up his pants, took a deep breath, and walked to center stage as has been said, like a sheep to the slaughter, amid catcalls and clapping. The lights dimmed, a single spot silhouetted his profile onto the white backdrop, a familiar little tune began to play, he dropped his shoulders and moved slowly forward in his imitation of Alfred Hitchcock. When he turned toward his crowd he said simply, "Gooood Eeevening!"

It brought down the house and set the mood just as he'd hoped.

"I see some familiar faces out there tonight," he said as planned, "and I want to recognize them as my former cellmates and AA sponsors. Tom, it's nice to see you are out of jail, and Mary, you and Bill are lookin' fine and drinking 'shine as usual."

As the evening went on, Ben became more comfortable and the laughter more and more spontaneous. When his half hour ended and he was replaced by another hopeful, the crowd nodded and several shouted encouragements after him.

"Nice job," the owner said appraisingly. "Dinner and drinks on the house, anything you want."

Ben thanked him, then walked from the bar into the restaurant and took a table by the wall.

"Sounds like they liked you," a young woman said as she left her table and approached him. "Congratulations. I couldn't remember my lines and they ate me for lunch."

Ben recognized her as the one whose act he had followed. She and he seemed to be the only patrons in the room.

"What's your secret?" she asked, "you seemed so comfortable out there. How do you do it?"

"When you ain't got nuthin', you got nuthin' to lose," he said, quoting another song and smiling.

"No, really," she said as she took a seat at his table without asking, "were do you get the confidence to walk out there like you did? You must have been doing this a while."

Ben was looking at her now, really looking. Not just at the lump that represented a smallish woman in her twenties, short, and a little overweight, with straight brown hair pulled back with a scrunchie. Behind her round gold-rimmed glasses were two very dark blue, intelligent eyes, bordered by smile lines at their corners. It was a little hard to tell in the subdued light, but a hint of freckles seemed to be sprinkled across her snub nose.

He liked the tenor of her voice once the desperation had worked its way out of it. It kind of carried a lilt, as if she had Irish somewhere in her background. All of this in the ten or fifteen seconds before he replied.

"All of my life," he said, "but this is my first night for the big bucks."

They both laughed as the waitress walked to their table and laid down a pair of menus. "Boss says to order whatever you want," she said smiling, "thinks you were pretty good."

She started to rise but Ben caught her arm and asked, "would you stay and have dinner with me?"

"I shouldn't," she began as she settle back into her chair. "I should get home to the kids. The babysitter will be waiting."

"You could call her and tell her you are having dinner with a friend," he said, surprising himself at how it seemed to flow naturally from his lips. "Unless, of course, you are married, in which case I apologize for asking."

"I'm divorced," she declared, and seemed to be watching for his reaction to her statement.

"I'm Ben," he quipped, "do you have another name?"

She laughed a hearty laugh then said, "see what I mean, you are a natural. I'd never thought quickly enough to come right back with that."

"Donna," she said in answer to his question, "Donna Sloan."

Ben was tempted to sing a verse from another song, *Donna the Prima Donna*, but thought he'd stop with the jokes and try and see who this woman was. "Pleased to meet you, Donna," he said instead. "Now, how about our dinner?"

She made a quick call on her cell, nodded at him and smiled, while glancing nervously at her watch. "We're good until 11:00, but she's got school tomorrow so I really need to be there by then."

When the waitress returned, Ben asked what she recommended and she answered without blinking an eye, "the boneless ribeye, the owner loves it and buys the best he can get so he can eat it himself."

He looked over at Donna who nodded. "We'll have two," he said, "medium rare with a nice baked potato if you please." Donna nodded again, this time smiling as she did so.

"Something to drink?" the waitress asked, "some wine maybe?"

This time Donna shook her head, "I don't drink," she said, "maybe just a coke."

"Make that two," Ben added, sounding like he had done this a dozen times before.

They were brought a bread basket with warm rolls, butter, and several types of jams. As Ben buttered his roll and prepared to eat, he observed that Donna was watching him, then bowed her head. He immediately took the hint and asked, "may I bless the food?"

A thin smile crossed her lips, but she didn't reply. He asked God for His blessing on both the food and for their time together. While they waited for their meal, Donna asked him about his job, his dreams for the future and how he came to be a talented comedian. He, in turn, asked about her children, where she worked, and what had brought her here this particular night to try her hand at stand-up. She showed him pictures of her two children, a boy and a girl, ages 10 and 8.

Without hesitation Ben said, "she has beautiful eyes, just like her mother," then began turning red when he realized what he had said.

Donna took off her glasses, smiled and said, "these are just props, I wanted to resemble the character I was playing, an old spinster, but maybe it worked too well."

"I'm just learning not to try and hide who I am," he said seriously. "Hard to hide all of this anyway," he added, looking down at his rotund body. Ben handed her his bookmark and watched as she slowly read the words.

"That's beautiful," she said, "where did you get it?"

"Turn it over," he answered. "It's a bookmark."

She did as he asked and smiled as she read the author's information. "Have you read his work?" she asked.

"Nah," Ben answered. "I don't read much. I just liked how the words made me feel about myself."

Ben watched as she rummaged through her purse and finally found a pen and a paper to write on. "Do you mind if I copy down the information?" she asked. "I love to read and would like to see what this guy has to say."

When their dinner finally came it was already after 10:00, so they went right to work on the juicy steak and fixings without further conversation. A few minutes later, as the last bite found a home, she turned to him and asked, "will you be coming back next week?"

"Yes," he answered. "Well maybe, I'm not sure."

"What do you mean not sure, you were great," she declared.

"I'm not sure if you'll be here," he said. "If you come I'll be here."

"Deal!" she said, "but I'll come to listen to you, not to perform."

"Dinner after?" he asked, kind of shyly.

"You buyin'?" she laughed.

"Sure, unless I can get the owner to buy again," he agreed.

He walked her to her car, it was 10:35 when the awkward moment came and they stood wondering how to say goodnight. Finally, she kissed him on the cheek and before getting into her car said, "until next week then."

Many, many times through the ensuing week Ben's thoughts turned to Donna, wondering, even hoping that there may be the possibility of a real relationship between them. He also had time to worry about her ex-husband and how he'd compare in her mind to the father of her children. Several times he almost tried to talk himself out of going back on Tuesday, but the hope of seeing her again prevailed.

He was scheduled to appear second, giving him time to survey the audience and plan his strategy before going on. He noted that his two acquaintances from the previous week had returned and had brought guests with them, but he saw no sign of Donna. Cheers and jeers filled the bar area spilling into the backstage where he stood waiting his turn. He'd elected not to use the Hitchcock persona again this week but had been inspired to bring props along.

Ben carefully strapped on his fake leg cast and adjusted the crutches until they fit comfortably under his arms, an Ace bandage was prominent on his left forearm, and eye shadow giving the appearance of a black eye. As before, the MC asked for a round of applause for the comedian just leaving the stage before introducing... "and back by popular demand... (drum roll)... Mr. Benjamin Stone!"

Ben took a second to look heavenward and asked a silent prayer before beginning an ungraceful entrance. He knew he looked like a train wreck as he limped to center stage. He took the mic in his good hand and opened with a serious sounding plea, "will all of my well-wishers who told me to *break a leg* last week keep their comments to themselves?"

Again, Ben had captured the audience's attention and gained their good will. The half hour went by quickly, with him falling into a natural kind of banter that hardly seemed rehearsed at all. But try as he might, he could not see Donna at any of the tables.

When the set ended, he went directly into the dining room where two couples had taken tables, and a long-haired woman sat alone with her back to him. There was no sign of Donna.

As he took a table, the owner followed and sat down beside him without invitation.

"Another great night, Ben," he said happily. "I'd like to offer you a paying gig here every week if you are interested. Nothing big in the way of pay, just a little something to help pay the bills and of course all-you-can-eat. What do you say?"

Across the room the solitary woman had stood, turned, and was walking toward them.

"Thank you," Ben stammered. "I'd like that but I really don't know how long I can keep coming up with new material that will keep them coming back."

"Let's just go week to week then," the owner offered. "I'll give you 5% of the gross bar receipts for the night for a half hour's work."

Ben looked at him questioningly.

"That's roughly fifty bucks, but more if you help me increase the size of the crowd or help promote drinks," he answered the unasked question. "It'll also give you a chance to get your name out and who knows, someone may discover you."

Ben looked up and into the familiar blue eyes he'd hope to see. Donna stood respectfully a few feet away from the table where the men were talking, but smiled as their eyes met.

"Donna, please sit down," Ben invited, then to the owner he added, "you remember Donna don't you, she's my business manager. Will you repeat your offer to her?"

With a look of surprise he did as he was asked while Donna, with a half-smile, listened politely without interrupting.

"Are you willing to guarantee the $50 as a minimum, with a percentage in addition as the receipts grow?" she asked through unblinking eyes. "We'd also like to have you consider moving Comedy Night to Friday when the real crowd is out."

The owner was forcing his smile a little when he said, "I can promise the fifty but will need to work out the details on the Friday gig. Can I get back to you later on that?"

Donna looked over at Ben, who smiled broadly and nodded his approval.

They shook hands just as the waitress arrived with menus. The owner left them to visit.

"We are celebrating," Ben announced flamboyantly, "shall we have our usual?"

Both Donna and the waitress laughed and nodded. "Two usuals," she said over her shoulder as she headed toward the kitchen.

"I didn't see you, you look so different, so beautiful with your hair down and without the prop glasses," Ben stammered. "I was afraid you wouldn't come."

He looked at her appraisingly, almost unbelieving, that this beautiful woman would be sitting and having dinner with him.

"We had a deal didn't we," she answered, putting her hand on top of his, "I never lie and never pass up a free meal with a talented man."

"What's the curfew tonight?" Ben asked practically.

"None," Donna answered, "except I have to work tomorrow. The kids are staying the night with grandma and grandpa."

They fell easily into conversation while still holding hands and forgoing the hot rolls that would have interrupted it. She told him about Rob, short for Robert, who had been her husband for two years and had fathered both children before returning to Iraq for his third tour.

They had agreed to divorce before he'd gone back, and made it final just before he'd been killed in an IED explosion a month later. She faulted both herself and him for the divorce, but pointed to a hurried courtship right out of high school as the real problem. They'd been in love with the idea of being in love, but had never really shared more than a bed and a few stolen moments.

"How about you?" she asked. "How come a big, smart, good looking guy like you is still single?"

At first Ben was tempted to think she was making a joke at his expense. It wouldn't have been the first time. Then he realized that she was serious. "I've been saving myself for someone like you," he said with his heart fluttering, like someone going through A Fib.

She gave his hand a little squeeze just as the waitress arrived with their meals.

They ate at a more leisurely pace than the previous time, having no reason to rush home. Gradually, she pulled his story out of him with well placed questions which lacked the effect of interrogation, but gave her the same result.

"Ever been in love?" she asked straightforwardly, then while he was grasping for a suitable answer added, "me neither."

They both smiled and dropped the subject.

"I'd like to see you again," Ben said shakily, "somewhere away from here."

"How about church on Sunday," she responded. "Yours or mine?"

Ben hadn't been to church since his father had passed away, although lately he'd thought several times about giving it another try. He'd been brought up in a Christian home, had received his salvation at church camp when he was thirteen, and been a regular attendee with his parents until his mother became ill and died, and his father followed only two years later.

"Yours," he answered. "Where and when?"

"Great," she said. "I think my children will enjoy meeting you. Can we meet at Denny's about 7:30 for breakfast and ride over together?"

"Denny's on Maple?" Ben asked. "I'll be there at 7:30."

"Now, about my commission?" Donna said seriously. "If I'm going to be your agent we should discuss the financial considerations."

"How's 20% sound?" Ben answered. "And you cover the tip."

They left a few minutes later holding hands on their way to the parking lot, a thousand thoughts running through their minds. When the pregnant moment came this time, he kissed her gently on the offered lips, then backed away quickly as if he may have moved too fast.

"We're getting there," she said affectionately. "See you Sunday."

At home he turned off the television and hunted until he found his Bible. It occurred to him that God's Word was like a good faithful pet dog who waited patiently for you to come home to it. It fell open almost if as answering the question which filled his mind, *how could a beautiful woman like Donna find a guy like me attractive*? He, having spent his life ashamed of who he was and how he looked, had devalued himself to a point which made it difficult for him to understand.

"You're big," said Billy, Donna's oldest, with a sense of awe in his voice. "How big are you?"

Before Donna could correct her son, Ben leaned down and said to the six year old, "that's kind of a hard question to answer, how important is it to you to know?"

"Not that important I guess," he answered. "It's just that you're about the biggest guy I ever seen except on TV."

Ben laughed, then picked the boy up to shoulder level, "this is how big I am," he said pleasantly. "What do you think now?"

"Wow, it's cool. I want to be big like you!" he said with enthusiasm.

Ben put him back down, got down on one knee and looked into Molly's frightened face as she stood frozen in her tracks, squeezing her rag doll. He smiled into her pale blue eyes and said softly, "hello Molly, I'm Ben."

With one arm she held tightly to her mother's leg, with the other she held her doll. Several seconds passed before she answered, "hello Ben, I'm Molly, I'm five."

They had Grand Slams, milk, juice and coffee, with the children sharing back and forth off of each others' plates while giggling wildly.

"Is it always like this?" Ben asked. "Do they always get along?"

"Hardly ever," Donna answered smiling, "but this is Sunday and they are on their good behavior. Do you have any brothers or sisters?"

"Nope, I'm an only child," Ben answered, (wanting to add that his family quit after him because they couldn't feed any more.) "How about you?"

"I had a brother, but he died in a car crash when I was still in high school," she answered. "My mom died with him but Dad is still alive," she added.

"But you said..." he began.

"They are Robert's parents," she clarified. "They live here in town and enjoy taking their grandkids as often as they can. Grandpa is the only male influence they have."

"Finish up, drink your milk, we gotta be going," she admonished her pair in a very motherly way, which Ben admired.

Ben took their ticket to the cashier while the crew finished, then turned just in time to get his big leg hugged by a very small smiling five-year-old. "Thanks Ben," she said brightly. "That was good."

They were just seated in the sanctuary when Molly climbed up into Ben's lap and said, "our daddy was a soldier but he died and he lives with Jesus now. Are you a soldier?"

Ben struggled to say something but finally just answered, "no, I'm a baker."

Just as the first hymn began, a graying couple joined them in the pew. Billy immediately stood on the pew next to the man and gave him a hug. Ben assumed they were Robert's parents.

The sermon was titled appropriately *Through the Eyes of Love*, and spoke to the fact that God is self-identified as being *Love*. Ben listened carefully with both his heart and his ears, intent on receiving the message. Over the next hour, the congregation learned how we as Christians who were created in God's image have the ability to become more and more like Him and to begin to see things as He sees them, *through the eyes of love.*

Following the service, Grandpa and Grandma Sloan invited them all out to lunch where they made an obvious effort to engage Ben and learn more about him. He assumed that they were gathering information in an effort to protect the ones they loved from anyone with evil intentions. Ben liked them and their straight forward way of speaking, although perhaps a little too bluntly, but always with righteous motives.

It was Billy who asked the pointed question in a way that only a child can. "Ben, are you going to be our new daddy?"

After the chin drops recovered and several seconds passed, Ben answered, "Billy, you'll never have a new daddy. Your daddy will always be your daddy and anyone who tries to steal his place in your heart will have to answer to me."

He continued, "any man who comes into your life is lucky to be there and will only be there to help your daddy raise you so that he can be proud of you." He was greeted by smiles all around.

After they finished eating, hugging, and shaking hands, the children, by some prearranged secret mind-meld, went home with their grandparents for the afternoon, without so much as a discussion with their mother.

"See you next Sunday," Gus said over his shoulder as he and his wife walked with the children to their car.

"Guess that just leaves you and me," Donna said to Ben with a twinkle in her eye. "Got any plans for the day?"

"Got to get to bed early," he said without thinking. "I have to be at work at 2:00 a.m."

He immediately reddened and attempted to explain which only made the statement worse and deepened the blush in his cheeks. She let him suffer for several seconds, then said, "how about just a drive then? A quick trip up to the lake where we can watch the water as the night replaces the day?"

Looking down at his clothes he answered, "we'll need to change and I can grab my work clothes in case we run late."

Donna nodded, "good plan. I'll change, then follow you home and we can ride up together from your place."

He followed her to a small townhouse in a neighborhood of the same, with small yards and second story bedrooms. Behind them were small fenced yards and a separate double-car garage backing onto a paved alley. She took less than twenty minutes to peel off her Sunday best and replace them with a casual top and knee length shorts. In her hand was a small beverage cooler. She smiled as she placed the cooler in the back seat, then got into the passenger seat and fastened her seat belt.

"Will I need the seat belt?" she asked in a kidding tone.

"Hope not," he answered, "but it's the law."

As he left the city limits, the road reduced to two wide lanes from four, and the elevation began to change noticeably. In the distance, outlines of evergreen trees dotted the hillsides and as they got closer, the roadway began to feel confined by the steepening hill beside it. Twenty minutes later the road was lined with the colors of dark greens, yellows and reds that represented nature's paint pallet.

The radio played gently in the background when he finally broke the silence. "Who arranged the grandpa and grandma time with the kids?" he asked, not meaning to sound accusing or critical.

"We, we were all in on it," Donna answered. "They asked and I said yes. Does it bother you? Do I seem too pushy?"

"No, of course not," he said smiling, but it had.

"Remember," she said sternly, "I NEVER lie, and I don't tolerate it from others either."

"I'm sorry," he said quickly. "Yes, I guess it did bother me a little or I wouldn't have mentioned it. But, it is not you. It is me that has the problem. This is all new to me and I don't know what to expect."

Donna patted his big shoulder, then said softly, "I'm sorry, I should have asked and not assumed. This is pretty new to me too. My last date was nearly four years ago and that was with the only guy I ever spent time with. It was his lying about small things that finally pushed me away from him. Still friends?"

Friends? he thought. I sure hope not. I hope this is more. But he simply said, "sure, always."

The conversation lagged until they made the last turn which took them down to the parking area by the beach.

"This is beautiful," Ben said, looking out over the blue water. "I haven't been here since my high school graduation party."

"I bring the kids up here sometimes," Donna mused. "It always seems to give me a sense of calm watching the predictability of the waves coming ashore. I imagine the ocean when I sit here and wish I could sit by it forever."

He put out their beach chairs while she rummaged in the cooler and produced snacks and drinks.

They sat quietly, saying nothing, enjoying the moment; finally she said, "I like the way you kiss, you are so gentle and considerate."

Ben didn't know how to respond so he said, "I like how you kiss too."

As the afternoon turned into evening and the sun fell behind the mountains, the shadows darkened the water's surface, changing its color, giving them the sense of loneliness that often accompanies the coming darkness.

"Do you suppose we'll fall in love," Ben said, without meaning to, as his thoughts were converted into a question.

"It's a little frightening, isn't it?" she answered. "How fast things seem to be moving and the powerful feelings already are causing us to ask ourselves such questions."

"It's a *good kind of scary,*" Ben answered, smiling at her reply. "I've never felt so certain and uncertain about anything in my life."

They stayed until the canopy of stars filled the horizon and the sliver of moon added its dimension to the night, then without discussion, picked up their chairs at the same time and headed for the car. The drive home was what one would have called *comfortable silent*, with each lost in their own thoughts and feeling no need for conversation.

Ben did go to bed, trying to get a few scant hours of sleep before his early morning shift, but was unable to shut down his brain long enough for the sandman to catch him. He used his key to let himself in the back door of the bakery and was greeted by Bob, the lead baker.

"Mornin' sunshine, you look like crap. You coming down with something that I don't want to catch?" he asked.

"No, I'm fine," Ben answered. "Just didn't sleep well."

They were a good fit, almost like a father and son team. The older man loved his trade and loved mentoring the younger man who was eager to learn. He was both patient and demanding of his staff, and expected from them the same attention to detail and commitment that he gave.

Ben appraised the situation in the bakery as he tied a clean apron around his ample midsection and washed his hands twice. "Where do you want me to start?" he asked.

"I'm working with the croissants, why don't you begin with the sweet rolls, then move to the raised donuts?" Bob answered.

Ben knew the routine well and nodded without answering.

By 3:30 a.m. he had all of the raised products in the proofing cabinet and had began the cake donuts. Bob was whistling something that had no discernable melody, on the far side of the kitchen.

"Up late?" he said, more as a statement than as a question.

"Yeah, a little," Ben admitted. "I went to church with my friend and ended up at the lake watching the sun go down with her."

"Her," Bob said. "Since when do you have a lady in your life? Come on, tell Uncle Bob all about her."

Ben obligingly shared the whole story with his friend, leaving out only the parts that concerned how deeply he felt about Donna.

Bob was smiling when he said, "well, it's about time that some girl noticed what a great guy you are and snapped you up. Congratulations!"

That simple statement by his friend gave him a surge of energy that carried him through the rest of the shift. The image of her eyes and smile flashed across the screen of his mind frequently. A smile kept finding its way onto his face.

Ben awoke groggily from an almost coma-like sleep several hours after his shift ended, and he had found comfort in his big bed. The cell phone lying on the nightstand was insistent. Finally he reached for it, enabled it, and croaked, "hello."

"Is this Ben?" an unfamiliar voice asked.

Ben nearly disconnected thinking the caller was some solicitor, but heard, "this is Gus, Grandpa Gus. Please don't hang up."

Ben was sitting up now, wondering why Gus would be calling him.

"Donna has been in a car accident," he blurted out. "She's badly injured and she's asking for you."

"Which hosp...?" he began to ask.

"County Memorial," Gus answered. "Hurry!"

Ben was dressed and backing out of the driveway in less than ten minutes, oblivious to the morning sunshine, chirping birds, and smiling children walking down the sidewalk nearby. "Oh please, God," he said without finishing the prayer, unable to consider the possibility of Donna's death.

Gus, his wife Madeline, Billy, and little Molly sat in the ER waiting area. Tears filled their eyes, their tracks leaving marks on their cheeks.

"How? When?" Ben started to ask, but was instead swept into the waiting arms of her anxious family.

"We don't know very much," Gus apologized. "We got the call this morning just before I called you. They were taking her into surgery just as we arrived. She was calling your name when they wheeled her in."

Ben could see the hopeless look on his face and that of his wife and the frightened questioning ones of the children. All of a sudden, his fears were pushed aside and a sense of peace replaced it. "We should pray," he said without consideration.

Pray they did, each in turn and in their own way, tears streaming down their cheeks but hope returning to their eyes.

Hours feeling like days passed before a tall, lean man in scrubs approached them. His demeanor held no clue as to what message he carried. His shoulders were slightly stooped, giving him the appearance of one much older than his years.

His half-hearted smile was grim – his eyes darted to the children questioningly before he spoke. "She's alive and holding her own but I must warn you she's had a great trauma to her brain. We have induced a coma to allow her body to heal without having to worry about anything else. She's in recovery, the nurse will come for you when you can go in."

He drew the three adults aside before adding in a lower voice, "The next 24 hours will determine what happens."

Icy fingers seemed to encircle his heart as Ben mentally considered what he had just heard. She could actually die, he thought to himself. We just found each other and there may never be a happily-ever-after for us.

"Let's go down to the cafeteria and get a snack," he suggested to the group. "We may be waiting here a while before we can see her."

They were reluctant to leave, thinking somehow their presence would change the outcome of what God had planned, but finally Billy stood and took his hand. Molly followed his lead and took the other. Madeline smiled and took Gus by the hand and nodded her approval. Somehow food seems to quiet our fears for a time, as it replenishes the energy that our bodies pour into worry and fear.

Sodas, soft ice cream cones, and coffee seemed the answer to their short-term prayers, as pockets were filled with small snack packages of trail mix, nuts, and candy. Ben looked over once and caught a hint of a smile as Madeline wiped ice cream from Molly's nose. However, the unbearable concern was still in the room as they took a break from the worry and fear of the unknown. Their faces grew long and tear stains appeared on their cheeks as though by magic, as the elevator returned them to the ER waiting area.

"Any news," Gus asked the woman at the nurse's station.

"I'll check," she promised, before leaving her station.

When she returned she was shadowed by another nurse who carried a sense of authority with her.

"She's been stabilized and in ICU," she said. "You'll be able to go in for a few minutes but please try to keep your visit short and quiet. We are keeping her in a coma so that she can rest and recover." She motioned them to follow which they did, with mixed emotions.

The ICU is a scary place for adults as well as children, a foreign place filled with flashing lights and unusual sounds. The children gripped Ben's hands tightly as their eyes first grew big, and then afraid. Donna lay motionless, a tree with several bags of liquids stood by the bedside with long clear tubes running into her arms. The left side of her head was bandaged to the point of hiding her nose and eye and the right showed wear and tear from smaller cuts and scratches that had been treated but not covered.

Her right eye was closed. A kind of hissing sound was made by some machine that aided her respiration – a tube from it ran to the mask that covered her mouth and nose. Lights blinked different colors and readings were shown continuously on the monitor at the head of her bed. Grim images from Ben's youth returned as the scene brought back memories of when he'd stood helplessly by a similar bedside and watched as first his mother and then his father had passed away.

Ben lowered his head and retreated to a place inside where he knew Jesus waited for him. Please Father, he thought, please do not let her die too. Help her to live, for her children, her family, and for me.

Four days, then a week went by without any change except the healing of the minor scrapes visible to the visitors. Doctors and nurses spoke in cautiously optimistic terms which led one to question how much they really knew about the progress that Donna was making. It was not until the twentieth day that there was news, good news.

She was breathing well on her own and a necklace providing oxygen into her nose had replaced the mask. Her head wrap now just included her skull, leaving her still bruised and swollen eye socket open to scrutiny. Occasionally she mumbled something unintelligible or moved her eyes inside their lids. Recent x-rays of her left arm showed that the compound fracture was healing well inside its cast.

Ben was forced to take his paid vacation and then unpaid leave as the many sleepless nights stretched into a month. Still, he stayed by her side, waiting for her to open her eyes and say his name. The children had moved in with their grandparents, where they tried hard to lead more normal lives under the cloud of uncertainty, which hung over all of them.

The morning of the fifty-first day, while Ben was eating an egg muffin and reading the morning paper, Donna opened her eyes and whispered, "'tis fine that thee would await at my bedside. Perhaps we can share sup this eve."

Ben jumped, looking with unbelieving eyes as the familiar voice spoke to him in olde English. When she smiled, the right side of her lips didn't respond as did the left, they drooped slightly. Ben hurried from the room to call the nurse and then called Gus and Madeline. They arrived less than an hour later accompanied by two excited children.

The doctor had already arrived and checked the charts and taken the vitals when they walked in beaming. He quickly took them outside of the room where he spoke to them.

"She's doing well physically but is in what might be called a 'dream state' mentally" he said. "She's living out some fantasy from another time. She thinks she's a princess in the days of King Arthur."

When they returned to the room, Donna raised her head from the pillow, looked at the doctor sternly and asked, "are ye not in league with the Dark Knight who would steal my father's kingdom? Be away with ye at once!"

"No, my Lady," the doctor said, bowing from the waist genteelly. "I serve at your Father's request. I want not but that thou shalt recover your health and return to court."

When Gus stepped forward, she turned to him and asked, "Is this so Father?"

"It is so, my child," he said, playing his part perfectly. "You've been ill, but even now there comes a bloom to your cheeks."

Madeline restrained both children from the bedside which as no easy task by saying, "the medicine which is making her well is causing her not to recognize us yet. Don't try and talk with her, just take her hand and stand there for a minute and see if she knows you."

They did as they were told, standing solemnly, waiting to be noticed. Finally their mother said, "Wye, 'tis Squire Billy Bones and his sister Molly come here to say their hearts, speak up child. What do ye have on yer mind?"

"We're here to see you now that you are getting well," Billy answered.

"Are you going to be alright now?" Molly asked tearfully.

It was evident that both children were spooked by their mother's odd speech and behavior.

When Ben stepped near Donna said, "draw near my love, I would have a word with thee in private."

Gus took the children's hands and withdrew to where his wife stood watching. Both the doctor and nurse had done the same but seemed enwrapped in the conversation.

"I fear," Donna said softly, looking into Ben's eyes, "that I am not fit to wed thee on the 'morrow for I have been sorely wounded. Whilst tho wait for me?"

"I will, my lady," Ben answered smiling, "for as long as it takes."

Donna smiled without speaking, closed her eyes, smiled a second time, and went back to sleep.

"How long will this last?" Gus asked the doctor when they had gathered in the waiting room.

"Impossible to say," the doctor answered, then added, "brain injuries are out of my league. I've called in a neuro-surgeon to evaluate her condition before we move her out of ICU. I'm sure he'll confer with you once he has done some tests."

Two months to the day, after MRI's, scans, and electronic analysis, the new doctor had the family, minus the two children, in for a consult.

"The left hemisphere is still badly bruised – there is indication of minor interruption in the nerves serving the right side of her face. I am amazed that she could be this badly injured and regain consciousness." he said bluntly. "Now, as respects what steps we should take surgically, if we can even remedy the situation, I am reluctant to proceed until we see what healing God has in His plan for recovery."

"Possibilities and likelihoods," Gus said. "We won't hold you to them, just give us your best guesses on what to expect."

The doctor looked doubtful, as though considering if he should answer or not. Finally he said, "there are some therapies that stimulate the brain which have been shown to help in such cases. We will begin them right away, then have this conversation again in two weeks."

Meanwhile, the family had come to expect Donna to speak in her own version of Middle English and refer to the nurses and staff as though they were her attendants, servants, or ladies-in-waiting. Gus was of course her father the King, and Madeline his wife the Queen, with Ben a suitor and knight-apparent. The children she treated not as her own but as 'kids of the court'. When the last of her bandages were finally removed, it was clear that her long hair had been shaved and now stood as though stubble in a harvested grain field.

"My horse," she shouted excitedly one afternoon. "Was he killed or badly injured in the fall?"

The horse, meaning no doubt, the little red Mustang she'd been driving when the accident occurred, had been a total loss and was rusting away in some junk yard.

"Alas, my lady," Ben said shaking his head, "he gave his all. Saved your life no doubt, but was himself unable to be saved."

"A valiant steed, he was," she responded in a subdued voice. "I'll miss him greatly."

Ben had lost nearly forty pounds over the past sixty days due to the stress of the situation and to some part, his absence from the temptations at the bakery. He had little appetite either at work or at home and it showed as his frame took on a different appearance.

"Are you well?" Donna asked one day. "You seem a bit scance in stature."

"Aye, I am my Lady. I'm trying to trim up a bit for our wedding day," he answered.

"My hair," she said wistfully. "'Tis gone and not returning as it should. I cannot bear the thought of marriage in such a state."

"We'll wait then," Ben said comfortingly, "until your tresses have grown out."

It was the most difficult for the children who wanted their mother back the way they had known her. The adults had little trouble, even maybe enjoyed the fantasy a little, as they played their roles in the charade. Physically she healed, the cast came off her arm and she began therapy to regain her strength. She walked the hallways like it was her private castle, and each day a specialist would spend time with her doing mental workouts designed to regain her mental faculties.

One morning she asked a nurse, "why do you people speak so oddly, all those 'thees' and 'thous' and such? You sound like the cast of an old Robin Hood movie".

The nurse did not answer, she just left the room and called the doctor. "She's back," she said simply, "like it never happened."

"Oh Ben," she said. "I'm so glad to see you, but you are so thin, have you been sick?"

"Sick at heart, but I'm over it now," he said smiling. "How are you feeling?"

"Me? Oh I'm fine, just in here resting, waiting to go home," she answered.

She seemed unaware of the reason for her confinement and didn't seem to care enough to even ask about it.

"Billy! Molly!" she exclaimed as her children ran into her room. "Mommy has been missing you. Where have you been?"

Billy looked first at his grandpa then at Ben, both of whom nodded for him to speak. He hugged his mother like there would be no tomorrow, moving aside only as his little sister pushed her way in with grandma's help. It was obviously a reunion of sorts, much the same as to what their loving family may have felt when one returned home after military service.

"We've been staying with Grandpa and Grandma and sometimes with Ben," Billy answered beaming. "But we want to be with you now forever." Molly nodded agreement.

Thirty minutes later the doctor entered smiling, greeted the assembly, and then read the chart carefully. "Are you ready to go home?" he asked Donna. "It looks like your family is ready to have you there."

Donna nodded as if saying 'of course' but did not answer.

"The nurses will get your paperwork ready and I'll write up my instructions and get your release papers signed," he said as he left the room.

Two nurses arrived, removing unnecessary equipment and checking charts to make sure everything was in order. An aid helped Donna into the clothes that Grandma Sloan had brought with them. The atmosphere was about as festive as one could want outside of Disneyland. Even the nursing staff dropped a little of their professionalism and joined in the revelry, snapping pictures and making small talk. Ben stood off to one side, watching with fascination as the miracle unfolded. His heart was full of love and gratitude as he expressed it silently to Jesus.

Seventy-one days after the errant driver had run the red light, Donna walked shakily into her apartment, leaning heavily on Ben's arm. She seemed less alert than she had been in the hospital and still not quite certain why she had been away. Apparently, memories of the wreck and her subsequent struggle for recovery had been mercifully forgotten for the present time.

Madeline fussed in the kitchen straightening up, wiping counters, and putting a teapot full of water on the stove to heat. The children went to their respective rooms to enjoy their security and familiarity. Ben and Gus sat in the living room ineffectually trying to suggest how they may make Donna feel more comfortable or to satisfy her whims while all she seemed to want was to rest. By the time the teapot whistled and Madeline made her way into the living room with a tray full of cups and saucers, Donna had drifted off to sleep. Both men picked up the tiny china cups and following Madi's lead, fumbled to turn the water into hot tea.

After several minutes and with an amused look on her face, she asked, "would you rather I put on a pot of coffee?"

Neither wanted to be ungracious but neither wanted the tea either. Gus spoke first with Ben nodding agreement. "No, this is fine, nice and hot."

In the lounge chair Donna had began to snore, or purr if you like, making a soft relaxing sound somewhere deep in her throat. She was obviously enjoying her nap.

"I'll stay tonight," Madeline said, leaving no room for discussion. "She needs someone to be here while she recovers her strength and to keep the children at arm's length. Ben would have volunteered to take the kids but knew neither of them wanted to be away from their mother.

"I don't have to work until 2:30 a.m.," he said. "I'd be happy to stay here with her until my shift begins."

Gus nodded. "Good plan," he said. "We can run home, put something together for dinner and come back this evening and give you time to go home and get ready, maybe even catch a few winks before work."

It was clearly evident to Ben that he was no longer an outsider, but a valued part of the family. He drew the courage to ask, "I think I love Donna and she loves me, would you object if I asked her to marry me when she's feeling better?"

The 'grands' looked at each other, winked, smiled and answered together, "we have been hoping that you would."

"Donna is home!" Ben declared the moment he walked into the bakery, smiling ear to ear. "I'm going to ask her to marry me."

Bob returned his grin and answered, "'bout time, was worried that you were going to get a job as a baker in a monastery."

Ben spent most of their shift explaining in detail about Donna's remarkable recovery. By the time the shift ended, he was exhausted and had nothing more to say. He slept well that night, and awoke early feeling refreshed and hopeful for the first time in over two months. He showered, shaved, dressed up in his Sunday clothes, packed his work clothes in a bag and left the house. He stopped at a small privately owned jewelry store, took a deep breath, and stepped into the morning air. He looked heavenward for guidance but received none, and went into the shop.

"Good morning," a whiskered and bent old man of indeterminate age said with a smile. "You are up and about early. What may I do for you?"

"I'd like to look at engagement rings," Ben answered nervously.

The kindly old man smiled like he'd never heard those words before and asked, "do you have something in mind?"

"No," he answered. "I really have no idea what she would like, but I want to surprise her rather than have her choose it for herself."

The old man nodded. "I agree," he said. "When they pick it out for themselves I think it always loses some of its specialness. Kind of like giving someone a gift card for Christmas rather than taking the time to invest yourself in the decision."

"But what if she doesn't like it?" Ben asked.

"She'll love it," the old man reassured him. "Besides, it comes with a *happiness guarantee*, if she would rather have something different bring it back and get the full purchase price credited against anything in the store."

Meticulously Ben handled and looked at every engagement ring in the small store before deciding on a solitaire with a white gold band.

"Would you like it sized?" the old man asked.

Ben stood looking like a deer in the headlights for a moment.

"Let's leave it as is until she says yes, then bring her in and we can size it perfectly," he suggested.

Ben nodded.

"How do you want to pay?" the jeweler asked next.

"How much is it?" Ben asked before getting out his checkbook. He swallowed hard when he turned it over and saw the price.

"What does the sticker say?" the old man asked smiling.

"$4995.00," Ben said slowly.

"So five thousand then," the shopkeeper said, rounding the figure up by $5. "And with the Tuesday early-bird discount that comes to $2,500 plus tax. Does that fit your budget?"

Ben glanced quickly at the check register then smiled and said, "Yes, yes it does. I'll take it!"

As they completed the paperwork Ben gave him his name, phone, address, and identification.

"So Benjamin, we are family," he said. "I too am a Benjamin. I trace my heritage back to the days of the Tribe of Benjamin. Are you also of Jewish descent?"

"Stone doesn't sound Jewish," Ben answered, "but I guess we all came from the same line if we go back far enough. I am a Christian," he added proudly.

"I too am a Christian believer and a brother to you, another discount is in order. How about if I pay the sales tax and we call it an even $2,400?"

Ben felt grateful and relieved at his generosity and at how God had guided them to a financial understanding. He wrote the check, took the old man's hand in a firm grip, and left with a velvet ring box which may hold the key to his future.

It was a quarter after ten, and Gus and Madi's brown sedan was parked in the driveway. He parked beside it and walked up the side-walk to the front stoop and rang the doorbell.

Billy opened the door immediately and yelled "Ben is here," at the top of his lungs. Molly stood smiling at him, displaying a jack-o-lantern grin, waiting for him to comment on the recent loss of her front tooth.

"Something is different about Molly," Ben said aloud. "I wonder what it is."

"I losth my tooth, thilly," she said in a semi-disgusted tone of voice. "Grandpa helped me pull it last night."

Ben scooped them both into his arms, then whispered to them in a confidential tone, "I need to speak with you both in private. I need your advice about a secret."

Both looked around as if worrying that someone may be eavesdropping, then giggled and said, "tell us."

As they walked from the living room Gus and Madeline remained seated on the couch, with Donna still as he had left her, sleeping in her longue chair.

"The kids and I are going to have a parley," he said as they proceeded into the downstairs bedroom.

Both Billy and Molly looked up solemnly at Ben who had gotten down on his knees, but still towered over both of them. Neither said a word.

"I love your mother, and both of you," he added impulsively, "and I want to ask your permission to ask her to marry me," Ben said, trying hard not to laugh at their serious faces.

The children looked at each other before scrunching their faces into tiny little masks which he thought indicated they were considering the consequences of the idea. His heart nearly stopped as seconds went by without any sign of their decision. Finally, after what seemed hours to him, they both squealed and jumped into his arms.

"We love you too, we can be a family," Billy said. "And I think Gramps and Grams love you too."

Billy led the solemn procession into the living room, with Molly taking giant steps right behind him doing her imitation of marching. Donna was still sleeping soundly when he announced the news. "Ben is going to ask Mom to marry him."

A week later, after Donna had made nearly a total recovery, Ben stood backstage waiting for his turn to perform. In the audience, occupying the front table, were seven special guests.

"It is my great pleasure to introduce to you, after a long absence, Mr. Benjamin Stone," said the MC.

Ben walked to center stage wearing a full clown suit – top hat with a flower in it, baggy stripped pants, and ridiculous suspenders. An oversized white suit jacket with a red handkerchief hanging carelessly from its pocket completed the ensemble. Cheers and clapping, hoots, and catcalls welcomed him.

"Tonight is a special night..." he said. "Thursday."

Again laughter and clapping.

"No, really, today is Thursday the 13th, my lucky day," he continued.

"Before I get started, I'd like to introduce my very special guests seated up front where I can keep a sharp eye on them. First, my boss and close friend Bob the baker and his wife Claire." They stood and took a little bow.

"Then my good friends Gus and Madeline, and their two grandchildren Billy and Molly." The four stood up and looked at the smiling faces around them.

"And finally, Donna Sloan, who many of you may know as a very funny comedienne in her own right." Donna stood smiling and gave the cheering crowd a little bow. "I'd like to ask Donna to join me here on stage. Please give Donna a warm round of applause."

Donna, obviously surprised and embarrassed, rose slowly and made her way to the stage amid clapping and catcalls, finally stopping and standing beside Ben.

"Donna," he said. "Do you remember when we first met, right here?"

She nodded and smiled, recalling the moment.

"Do you remember telling me that you would never tolerate anyone who lied to you?" he asked.

A hint of fear filled her eyes before she said, "yes, I remember."

"I have a confession to make to you publically," Ben said. "I lied to you about my purpose for asking you here tonight." He then continued without letting her comment. "I am not performing here tonight as I said."

Her jaw took a noticeable set and her eyes hardened but she said nothing.

"Please forgive me," Ben said, while dropping to one knee and fishing the velvet box from his jacket pocket. "I invited you here to ask you to marry me."

He held the opened box toward her, waiting as his words found their way into her mind.

"Donna, will you marry me?" he asked.

The room became silent as the seconds ticked by. She threw herself into his arms and exclaimed "Yes! Oh yes I will!"

The MC, now turned DJ, played the wedding march as the crowd stood clapping and shouting yells of encouragement. Donna's family joined them on stage.

The owner then took the mic and said, "I guess we don't get a show tonight. A round of drinks on the house!"

They were married the following month. One year and seven days later, Ben junior was born to the happy couple.

– The End –

The Black Condor

Upon occasion, my usual genre is interrupted by something less mundane. In this next story, consider that there are powers in both heaven and on earth that are far above what we consider normal. - dc

Mada found himself taken away from what his foster parents called 'his room' to a place which could easily have been right from a movie located in and around the Grand Canyon. At first it was unclear to him if he was dreaming or if somehow, supernaturally, he was standing on a precipice, with a rocky canyon far below. What was disconcerting more than the looming canyon below, was the familiar figure of the *Darkman* who had haunted his dreams since early childhood. His tall, spare frame seemed without clear definition, like an out of focus picture, his dark form tapered away into the backdrop of the fading horizon behind him.

He, however, never failed to recognize the thin hawk-like nose and piercing eyes which, like flaming coals, peered at him from the poorly defined face. Many times he had seen these eyes in his darkened bedroom at night, watching and waiting for him to awaken screaming, before disappearing. His caregivers always kindly told him it was just a bad dream and urged him to return to sleep before leaving and closing the door behind them.

It was as though he was looking at memories of past events

through these two flaming orbs – he relived a horror nearly beyond comprehension. He saw the mother, whom he had never known, chased and taken down by a group of five young black men. He watched helplessly as she was seized, stripped of her ragged clothes, and anchored to the musty smelling earth while the fifth, the *Darkman*, smiled deliciously through pointed teeth. The four looked to him for instruction as she fought and struggled vainly beneath their weight. A laugh, which seemed to fill the earth, issued from his thin lips as he let himself down onto the young niggeress. Her scream rivaled his as she prayed for the death that would be too long in coming.

Only thirteen years old, and yet he understood clearly the events before him, he smelled the sweat, the fear, and the terror that his mother ultimately was forced to accept as the *Darkman* labored over her. The scene changed and was replaced by one utterly outrageous, like one in a scene from an old movie he'd watched called *Inner Space*.

He watched the equivalent of a biology film where a long-tailed spermazoa swam to and joined with an egg, fertilizing it. Quickly, cell division began as each rushed to duplicate themselves. In what seemed seconds, a mass was formed and was quickly followed by another and another which then became a nearly recognizable substance.

Ultimately, a child replaced the mass and rapidly continued to develop recognizable features. Inherently he knew things impossible to know, that the victim of the savagery was his mother, that he was watching his own creation, and that the *Darkman* was his father.

Again the scene changed, much time seemed to have elapsed as he looked down where his mother now lay comatose for nine months in a hospital room. She seemed to have withered and lost all vitality as the child within her stole the life from her. At her bedside, the four and the *Darkman* watched and waited as contractions savaged her in pain, then released her again and again. Medical personnel seemed unaware of the five dark figures which leered gleefully at the ordeal. Torturous minutes turned into hours as the child struggled to free himself.

The doctor conferred with colleagues, then made the decision to deliver by Caesarean section. Just as the scalpel gently broke the skin of the over-ripened stomach, a dark hand from another world grasped the doctor's wrist and pushed the knife deeper and deeper until it severed an artery. As the child took its first breath his mother took her last.

As he watched, time moved rapidly forward chronicling his unfolding life. He relived many events previously forgotten and also some which had left painful memories. Orphan's homes, cruel caregivers, children like himself filled with hate and resentment, and always a sense of loss and a searching emptiness.

He raised his eyes and met those of the *Darkman* standing above him on the rocks that led to the precipice. No words were exchanged between them; however, a *knowing* linked their minds in a nearly telepathic understanding. *You are mine, come to me, give yourself to me,* the awful voice in his mind ordered. *Together we will rule the world.*

At age six, he'd been a tall dark-skinned child who'd weighed less than half of what others his height had weighed. He was, however, strong, active, and not lacking in stamina. His arms, hands, and fingers were long and almost delicate looking when compared with the chubby hands of others. He ran and jumped effortlessly, the envy of others on the grade school track team. It was not unusual that a black boy could jump of course, but how he could at such a young age and with such grace seemed amazing.

Now at thirteen, having moved from foster home to foster home and nearing puberty, he knew inside even before the aforementioned encounter, that he was somehow different than his peers. He was well liked but had no close friends, received well-earned high marks in academics, and easily mastered the high jump and pole vault to earn a letter as an incoming freshman.

The *Darkman* moved toward him, filling his mind with memories and promises for the future. *Come, come to me,* he said, beckoning the boy. Mada moved backward to the very edge of the canyon and looked downward. Hundreds of feet below lay the instruments of his death, large, jagged, unforgiving boulders, waiting there since the beginning of time for just this moment. He turned toward his father resolutely, walked toward the outstretched hands that now appeared as claws... then spun on his heel, ran to the edge, and leaped into the air. As he fell downward, he seemed to find the peace which had always been lacking in his life, a peace he believed only to be found in death.

As fear filled his body, adrenaline coursed through his veins and he felt the skin over his shoulder blades tear for the first time as two wings struggled to unfurl themselves. From the corner of his eyes he could see just the tips of the poorly developed wings which extended only inches past his shoulders. They were ill-suited for the task they attempted to do as he continued to fall at an alarming rate. Far below, a large condor and its mate took flight, making lazy circles below him. They, no doubt, would be the beneficiaries of his broken and mangled body as nature provides for each of its creatures.

At the precise moment that his plummeting body reached the birds in flight, both veered sharply together beneath him. Mada hit them where their wings overlapped like arms around friends' shoulders. His weight bore them downward toward the rocks, and then just a few feet away, the birds parted and resumed flight. Mada dropped the final ten feet and landed hard between two of the largest rocks, falling into the sand and smaller ones. His left ankle was badly sprained, blood was running freely down his back from the two tears in his skin caused by the wings, and his head also bled from a large cut just above his brow. Otherwise, he was unharmed. Red eyes, filled with rage, watched from far above.

Mada's first words upon finding himself alive were, "thank you Jesus." Oddly, he knew almost nothing of the Jesus revered by many as the Redeemer of mankind. He'd seldom entered a church nor opened the cover of a Bible. He mused at from where the unfamiliar words may have come.

Two large black-feathered birds perched on massive rocks just a few feet away eyeing him curiously and making unthreatening noises. These he thought, were his true saviors.

When he awakened and surveyed his bedroom, everything seemed as he had remembered causing him to question whether the events had been just another terrible dream. When he started to stand, his left leg nearly caused him to fall from the pain. When he looked, it was both swollen and discolored. His pajama top stuck to his back when he tried to remove it. It was heavily stained with dried blood, his back however, felt none the worse for wear.

Cautiously, he made his way to the bathroom and checked himself in the mirror before getting into the shower. After showering, he dressed for school and began downstairs to the kitchen from where aromas of frying bacon and pancakes assailed his nostrils. Half-way down, he pretended to slip and fall into the wall, and then down to the landing where he laid until his foster father arrived.

"I'm sorry," he said contritely, "I wasn't paying attention and lost my balance." At the same time he rubbed the large bump on his forehead and complained of pain in his leg.

"We had better get you to the doctor," the man said earnestly, " we need to make sure nothing is broken."

Mada tried to argue but was overruled when his foster mother saw the damaged boy. "Always better safe than sorry," she declared. "I'll take him in right after breakfast on our way to school."

The family doctor had made a special compensation for Mada knowing that he was a foster child and that all injuries must be promptly evaluated and recorded.

"Ninety-four," the nurse announced as he climbed from the scale, "still skinny as a rail but up two pounds since your last visit."

She applied antiseptic to his forehead and closed the cut with two steri-strips before leading him limping into the examination room.

"Let's get an x-ray of that leg," she said smiling at him, "just to make sure it's sprained and not cracked."

The procedure took only a few minutes but when she returned she had both his foster mother and the doctor in tow. She held the x-ray up to the light shaking her head before attaching it to the illuminated screen on the wall. The doctor looked carefully at the film and shook his head also before commenting, "I've never seen anything like it either."

"What's wrong," he asked fearfully, "is it broken?"

"No, it is not broken, only badly sprained," the doctor answered. "But the x-rays show that your leg bones are nearly hollow. They lack the thickness and bone marrow that we would expect."

"Is that bad?" Mada asked anxiously.

"No, no of course not," the doctor answered. "Just unusual. It may be that something in the x-ray machine needs adjusted."

He wrapped the leg, gave Mada instructions to use a crutch for a few days to keep his weight off the injured area, and a prescription for a mild pain killer.

"Call me if you have any problems," he said to Mada and Mrs. Brown, his caregiver. "Use ice of it begins to swell and stay off it as much as possible."

"We need to stop and fill your prescription," she said as they drove away. "How does it feel?"

"It feels fine," he answered. "Don't hurt at all, do you think I really need pain pills?"

"Okay, tell you what, see how it goes at school today, and if need be, we can get them on the way home," she answered.

Mada smiled.

At school he shouldered his crutches and made his way awkwardly toward the office. Mrs. Brown followed carrying his books and the doctor's orders for the school nurse.

By third period he was only using the crutches for the attention they brought him, he had no pain or discomfort at all.

Mrs. Brown was parked in front of the school with a look of concern on her face as she waited for the final bell. She really cared for Mada and prayed that his injuries would not be cause for concern or further treatment. When he walked from the school, he was carrying both crutches in one hand, his books in the other, and visiting with a pretty Latino girl.

"Hi," he said, addressing Mrs. Brown and throwing the crutches into the back seat, "good as new." He smiled at the young girl who walked away with a wave.

"You heard what he said," Mrs. Brown said critically. "Stay off it, and give it time to heal."

"But," he argued, "he also said until it heals, and I think it has."

She shook her head, put the car into gear, and reminded him to put on his seat belt. At home he walked up the drive without a limp, carrying both crutches over his shoulder smiling nonchalantly, with Mrs. Brown struggling to keep up. He bounded upstairs to the bathroom, his books under one arm, where he appraised his head wound. The swelling was gone and only a red line testified of the small cut beneath the strips.

"How's the leg?" the doctor asked Mrs. Brown a week later. "Is he having any trouble with it, pain, or swelling?"

"Not a bit," she answered. "By the end of the first day it was like it had never happened. Can't get him to use the crutches and we didn't even pick up the prescription."

"Kids!" the doctor said. "I wished all of us would heal like they do. Even so, ask him to drop by my office if you will and return my crutches. I'd like to do a follow-up x-ray."

"I'll bring him by tonight," she answered.

"No need," the doctor replied. "Let Mr. Big-Shot walk on over, it's only three blocks and I can evaluate his limp."

"He doesn't limp," Mrs. Brown said, "unless of course he's trying to impress some young girl at school."

Mada entered the doctor's office and was greeted by the doctor himself. It appeared that the office had closed early for the day.

"Come in, come in," said the doctor warmly. "I've been expecting you. Before we begin, I'd like to get to know you better, if that's alright."

Mada nodded but said nothing as he took the offered seat in the empty waiting room.

"Mada, that is an unusual name, do you know where it comes from?" the doctor asked.

"No," he admitted. "It's what I've always been called," he answered honestly.

"Perhaps from your parents then," the old doctor suggested, "a name from their families?

"I never knew my mother or father," Mada said resentfully. "My mother died in childbirth and my father was a man who raped her."

The old doctor nodded solemnly contemplating what he had just heard, then asked, "who told you then of your mother and father? Was it someone who knew them?"

The young man seemed reluctant at first to answer but looked the doctor in his eyes and said, "you would not tell?"

The doctor shook his head and answered, "no, I would not and could not tell. My patients are protected by law from me revealing confidential information unless it involves serious crimes."

Mada began to slowly tell the incredible tale which ended in the injuries he had suffered and of his frequent night time visitor with the red piercing eyes. The old man listened quietly without speaking until he had finished. There were tears in both of their eyes.

"Do you believe me?" Mada asked anxiously.

The doctor looked at him for several seconds without speaking before nodding his head and answering, "I believe you."

"What do I do?" the boy asked him hopefully. "I feel that he will come again and I will be unable to resist him."

"I must pray about this," he answered, "and ask that Jesus provide an answer to both of us."

Together they went into the x-ray room and repeated the procedure on Mada's ankle, and again the film showed unique and strange bone formation.

"I was not always a physician," the doctor revealed. "I once dreamed of being a minister, and went to seminary for several years. Then I tried veterinary medicine and studied it for two years, before settling upon human medicine. What I am seeing in you nearly seems impossible.

What I see in these x-rays is the bone structure of a bird."

"My back," Mada began, having not shared the part about the two wings, "I think I have wings."

Shock was apparent on the doctor's face when he ordered, "Take off your shirt." He then gently and carefully examined Mada's back in detail. He found the small creases where the folds of skin hid and protected the wings underneath.

"Did it hurt?" the doctor asked, referring to the tearing of the flesh which had been necessary to release the wings.

"Maybe a little," Mada admitted, "but I was so frightened I hardly noticed the pain."

"Hymen," the doctor said, mostly to himself as he continued to examine the back. "Tissue designed to be torn at just the proper moment and for the desired reasons. Can you open your wings now?" he asked.

Mada lacked the understanding of what signal to his brain had triggered their opening. "No," he answered, "I can neither feel nor move them as they are now."

Mada's back muscles effectively hid the presence of the two small wings with only a hint that something may lie underneath the tissue by what appeared to be minor swelling.

"Let me try something," the doctor said as he slapped Mada hard across one cheek. Color raised in the boys cheeks and indignation filled his heart. Again and again the doctor slapped him until anger and tears filled his eyes. After the fifth stinging assault, two black wings freed themselves and spread ominously beyond his shoulders and the look in his eyes changed from one of terror to one of fury.

The doctor took the trembling boy in his arms and said, "forgive me son, I needed to find what triggers the wing response. Both anger and fear release adrenaline into your body which in turn gives you the ability to fly."

They clung to one another for several minutes. As his heart beat quieted, the wings began first to sag and finally returned to their secret hiding places. The old doctor smiled and said, "we've now only to find a way for you to control your wings with your mind in a more traditional and less painful way."

Mada put on his shirt and stood to go. "Will you return tomorrow?" the doctor asked, "after I have had time to study and consider what I've seen?"

Mada nodded and left without further conversation, returning home where he notified his family that all was well but did not elaborate further.

That evening at home, Doctor Rogers carefully led his wife Addy into a conversation. "Would you ever consider adoption?" he asked, while enjoying their evening meal.

She stopped eating and looked up abruptly then asked, "what makes you ask?"

"Well," he began. "Our own are raised and we are now financially comfortable and this big house seems way oversized for just the two of us…" he let his voice trail off.

After nearly forty years together she knew there was more to it than what he had said. "Do you have a particular someone in mind?" she asked.

"You know," he continued, "that after they get older the chances of being adopted are slim and none. Most adoptive couples want a baby or small child they can raise as their own without the problems that come with the teenage package."

"Just who is this teenage package that we are not talking about?" she said smiling.

"Oh, just a young black man who is one of my patients," he answered innocently. "His mother is deceased and his father is unknown."

"Where is he now?" Addy asked.

"In foster care at the Browns, his third foster parents in as many years," he replied. "He seems intelligent and honest, just waiting for a chance to grow and become something greater than another black orphan who eventually will live on the streets without education or a chance to get one."

She smiled at her husband knowingly, then said, "I don't suppose I'll have a chance to meet this boy before I give you an answer, will I?"

"If you are open to considering the idea, I thought I might ask the Browns to allow us to take him to dinner some night soon," he said.

"Great timing, how about tomorrow night?" she asked. "I don't have a plan for dinner and I need a break anyway."

"Done," he said. "I'll call the Browns tonight and you pick the place. I'll see him in the office tomorrow and if he agrees, then you can meet him and we can consider it."

The following day was a Friday, Mada had slept poorly and had awakened twice to the red staring eyes of the intruder, they however did not exchange thoughts or travel to some remote location. It seemed he was just being observed.

Once again, when he arrived at Dr. Rogers' office, there was no staff or waiting room full of patients. He relaxed into one of the chairs and looked at the doctor expectantly.

"Some ideas have come to me," the doctor began, "and assuming I am correct, your visitor is either a powerful demon or Satan himself. Neither you nor I are in a position to combat this kind of evil by ourselves and we will surely lose if we try. I'd like to introduce you to the

One who has power over evil and all things, Jesus."

It was nearing 5:00 p.m. when he completed a brief explanation of Who Jesus is. Mada asked few questions, rather, he seemed content to just listen and learn.

"I've asked permission of the Browns to invite you to dinner this evening with my wife and I," Dr. Rogers said hopefully. "Would you be our guest tonight?"

Mada looked uncertain at first, trying, no doubt, to figure why the doctor and his wife would want to buy him dinner.

Finally he smiled and nodded. "Thank you, that would be nice. Have you told her what I told you?"

"No," Dr. Rogers answered. "If you choose to share it with her, it would be by your own choice."

Mada looked relieved as they stood to leave.

"I've been thinking about your name," the doctor said. "I believe it is an anagram for the first man, Adam. If I am correct, Satan himself chose the name for you as his first born creation. He is a liar, deceiver, and impersonator. I think you represent the first of his line of a new creation."

Horror swept over the young man's face, the same horror he'd seen in his mother's eyes.

"In the book of Genesis, about the sixth chapter I believe, it speaks about the Sons of God, or Angels, taking wives of mortal women and creating offspring with undefined powers," he told Mada. "If I am correct, a fallen Angel is your father and thus you are as you are," the doctor said.

They spoke little as the doctor drove them to his home, each no doubt, deep in thought about what had been shared between them.

"Addy, this is Mada," Dr. Rogers said as soon as his wife opened their door. "Mada, this is my wife Adeline whom I call Addy."

They smiled as they appraised each other, then shook hands. "Please come in Mada," Addy said. "We've a few minutes before we have to leave. Our reservations are for 7:00," she added, looking at her husband. They walked through the spacious but unpretentious home, pointing out features which appealed to them personally. Mada listened but said little as he toured the home with them. Each room seemed to have its own personality defined by the variety of items it contained and their arrangement within it.

While the couple lived well and had a good income, they paid their employees well and helped support a long list of worthy charities. The doctor elected to drive his wife's Buick allowing them to all sit in the front seat rather than their smaller car which only seated four.

Middle upper class was how one would have described the restaurant that they had chosen. Good food, a pleasant, comfortable atmosphere, and moderate prices. Mada was surprised when the waiter called his hosts by name and assumed this restaurant must have been one of their favorites. Addy leaned toward Mada and made several menu suggestions but left the final choices for him to decide.

"Do you have family nearby?" Addy asked, obviously wondering why he was not living with them.

"No," he answered quickly, "my mother died in childbirth and I never knew my father." Having said the latter, he winced at the knowledge that he may have indeed met his father after all.

As the evening progressed, Mada relaxed and enjoyed the casual way that both the doctor and Addy spoke with him, in a curious but not overly inquisitive way. The evening ended with a flaming desert of baked Alaska which made the occasion even more special to the young man. It was just after 10:00 when the trio walked to the Brown's front door and rang the bell. Mrs. Brown opened it with a smile and asked them in, however, due to the lateness of the hour they declined, exchanged hugs, and drove home.

"Well, what do you think?" he asked as though they had been in a car lot kicking tires.

"What do you mean?" Addy asked innocently. "I think he's a lovely boy."

"You know darn well what I mean," he said, smiling at her pretense of innocence. "Does he seem like someone you could learn to love and treat as our own?"

"What does he think of the deal?" she countered.

"I haven't asked him or the Browns nor looked seriously into it," he answered. "I needed to get your opinion first."

"Tell me more about him," Addy said, "what do you know that makes him the right fit for you and I?"

"I... I can't tell you," he said. "I wished I could, but I can't. It's a doctor-patient thing."

Addy shook her head, looked at the husband she had know for the better part of a lifetime, then answered softly, "yes, I trust your judgment, and yes I think we could be good parents to him. When do I get to know the big secret?"

"Let me speak to the Browns and their case worker and see if it is even possible, then we can ask him together," he said. "I'll also ask his permission to share his story with you. Meanwhile, please pray for God's protection over him, his soul is in mortal danger."

Late that evening, after the Browns had retired for the day and their house reverberated with the sound of peaceful repose, he returned. Mada awakened with a sense of fear and a sense of something watching him. The red eyes and the black form, blacker than the darkness itself, positioned itself between his bed and the door.

"So," his mind heard, "you did not die as you planned. Did you think you could escape so easily? Do you think you, a skinny child, can challenge your own father?"

Mada felt the grip of cold hands around his heart, terror held him in its grip, he was unable to move, unable to speak. "Jesus, save me" filled his head.

"You cannot call on one you do not know," the form said smugly, his voice filling Mada's ears.

Mada was uncertain if the words came to him in thought or were spoken until the bedroom light illuminated the room. Mr. Brown was standing in his pajamas still holding the light switch staring into the room as the figure dissolved before his eyes.

"You heard him, you saw him!" Mada declared to the sleepy eyed Mr. Brown.

"I heard and saw something," he admitted. "I thought it was you having another one of your bad dreams."

"But, it was not my voice, and you saw him disappear when you turned on the light, didn't you?" he argued.

Brown nodded in resignation and asked, "what was it that I saw?"

"Something evil, something who claims to be my father," Mada declared. "He wants me to go with him."

"Go where?" Mr. Brown asked, "and why?"

"I don't know, I don't know," said Mada, his voice breaking. "Maybe to Hell to do Satan's work."

Bill sat down gently on the side of Mada's bed, the boy leaned into him and they embraced, saying nothing for a few moments. The clock on the night stand showed 12:04 a.m.

"Come on," Mr. Brown said, forcing a half smile, "let's go downstairs and have some milk and cookies."

The barefoot boy followed him, turning on the lights as they went. He remembered the doctor saying that "in Jesus there is no darkness at all."

The following day Dr. Rogers asked his nurse to schedule him out for a half hour and went into his office and closed the door behind him, an unusual event.

"Hello, Mrs. Brown," he began. "This is Dr. Rogers, do you have a minute?"

"Is something wrong with Mada?" she asked anxiously without answering him.

"No, no he seems quite healthy," Rogers answered lightly. "My wife and I are considering a possible adoption and wondered if you and your husband could spend a few minutes with us before we call social services and get into that long line."

"Of course," she answered with a sigh of relief. "There are many ways to approach adoption and we can provide a lot of useful information for you."

"Thank you," the doctor replied. "Could we meet for dinner or coffee soon?"

"We have five fosters now, getting away for us is difficult, perhaps you could come by for coffee some evening," she suggested. "I'll call Bill and see if he has any plans for this evening and call you back."

"Thank you," Dr. Rogers said appreciatively. "Maybe we could bring dessert for all of you to enjoy. I'll be waiting for your call."

Just after lunch the receptionist put Mrs. Brown's call through to the doctor.

"We'd love to see you," she began excitedly. "With five children we seldom get out and rarely have visitors. Is 7:00 too late, some of the younger ones go to bed at 8:00?"

"Seven is fine. We'll be looking forward to a nice visit over cake and ice cream, if that suits you," the good doctor said.

"Addy," he began a few seconds later. "The Browns will see us tonight at 7:00, I promised to bring dessert. Do you have time to whip something up or should I grab something on the way home?"

"I have everything I need for *skillet cake*," she answered, "except the pecan halves. Grab a bag when you pick up the ice cream."

At precisely five minutes to seven the Rogers stood on the front step and rang the door bell. They could hear a cacophony of excited voices and children's screams well before Mrs. Brown opened the door and greeted her guests. It was apparent that they were going to enjoy a special treat this particular evening. Mr. Brown stood back from the door holding a toddler in his arms, Mada stood beside him smiling, flanked by three younger children sporting toothless grins.

Mrs. Brown, Janice to her friends, took the child from Bill and directed Addy into the kitchen where she placed the dessert on the counter. They shared pleasantries before addressing the serving of the large flat *skillet cake* that had become one of Addy's favorite Pampered Chef dessert recipes. In an adjoining room Bill and Tom, with the questionable help of four energetic children, were anxiously setting the table while they visited. Though not well, Tom knew Bill from his church where he was an elder who served on several committees. They had exchanged a guy-nod every Sunday for several years, without really getting to know one another.

The sumptuous cake, baked in a 12" skillet, was decadent with its rich texture – chocolate frosting drizzled with caramel and topped with pecans. Tom was generous as he served the vanilla ice cream, and while none complained, no one had room for seconds either.

It was nearly eight o'clock when Janice put the twins to bed while Addy, Bill, and Tom cleared the table and filled the dishwasher. The older children, including Mada, went to their respective bedrooms without urging, ostensibly to do homework. Addy noted that Mada gave Tom a shy smile and a nod as he left the room. She made a mental note to ask Tom about that on their way home.

With five safely out of sight, the four adults took seats in the comfortable living room and began to visit.

"Janice tells me you are considering adoption," Bill began, "that's quite a step."

To Tom's surprise it was Addy who answered. "It is to us too. Ours are raised and out on their own and I thought we would be looking at grandparenthood rather than parenthood. However, as it is said, God works in mysterious ways."

Tom immediately caught her meaning but to his surprise he heard only sincerity in her voice.

"He does that," Janice agreed. "We never expected to be raising children when we were told that we couldn't have any of our own, and now were are raising the last five of our ten."

They chatted in generalities before Tom finally asked what had been on his mind.

"The older children, I've heard that they are harder to place than the younger ones, is that true?"

"Oh yes," Bill said. "Once they stop being cute and become demanding and selfish, few have the patience or want to take the risk."

"Like kittens," Janice added.

"The agency is always crying for adoptive parents for the ten and over and for multiples," Bill added.

"Multiples?" Addy questioned.

"Children with siblings who want to stay together," Janice clarified, "sometimes we get as many as five with the same birth parents."

"How about Mada?" Tom inquired without elaborating.

"A black teen," Bill said shaking his head sadly. "Unlikely. Why do you ask?"

Tom sighed before speaking. "I have certain privileged information which I am not at liberty to share that I believe may indicate that he is in spiritual danger. I regret I cannot say more."

Tom wondered if he had already shared more than he should have.

"Spiritual how?" Bill asked forthrightly.

Tom shook his head, "I'm sorry I cannot say."

"That's quite a statement to drop on us and leave it hanging," Janice said rather crossly.

Bill spoke slowly and deliberately. "Does it involve the *Darkman*?" he asked.

The three looked at him in shock before Tom answered, "you know about the *Darkman*?"

"I heard and saw him last night," Bill answered. "He was in Mada's room."

The three looked at one another questioningly before anyone spoke.

"May I ask Mada to join us?" Tom asked.

Janice looked up at the clock which read only a quarter to nine and nodded. "I'll go get him," she said as she rose.

"I have to have his permission to share with you what he shared with me in my office," Tom explained.

Janice came down the stairs closely followed by Mada, who was wearing pajamas which were an ill fit for his growing body. Both the sleeves and the bottoms fell far short of covering his forearms or lanky lower legs. He had a puzzled look on his face but smiled as he saw the doctor rise and move toward him.

"Mada and I need to have a word privately," Tom said, "please excuse us for a few moments."

Together they moved into the kitchen where they sat at the table.

"Mada," Tom began, "I'd like to have your permission to share what you and I discussed in my office with your foster parents. I think it is important that they understand what is going on with the *Darkman*."

"He came again last night," Mada said. "Bill saw him."

"I know," Tom answered, "that's why we need to ask them to help us in protecting you."

"The wings too?" Mada asked. "I don't want anyone to know about the wings, they'll think I'm a freak."

Tom nodded, understanding full well the implications of acknowledging that the boy's body structure was part bird and had wings. "Okay, let's keep that part just between you and me for now," he agreed.

Together they walked into the living room, Tom spoke first. "Mada has graciously agreed to share certain events with us tonight but has also asked that this information does not go beyond this room. As you will soon understand, it is both incredible and seems potentially harmful. Let's begin by praying that God will protect and empower us to overcome the evil which threatens Mada."

Tom led them in prayer, which only increased the curiosity of the three who still did not know why they were praying.

Mada spoke quietly and haltingly, looking up frequently at Tom, who nodded each time for him to continue. He painted the picture for them of a threatening presence that had made itself known to him as a small child, and who appeared to him in the middle of the night. Janice nodded, remembering the many times over the years that she'd rushed into his room to find him frightened and crying. Bill, too, was reliving occasions when he'd been called to calm the child who seemingly had been the victim of bad dreams. Addy listened, enwrapped in the story, which was seemingly too incredible to be true.

Mada told of being spirited away to some far off location, (Bill nodded remembering how Satan had done similarly to Jesus), and how he had beckoned to Mada to come to him, or join with him, or follow after him. The inference was that Satan sought a disciple and his son was the perfect one.

Mada told of refusing the command and of hurling himself over the cliff in despair. He did not tell of the appearance of the wings but recounted how the condors caught him and how he had escaped with only minor injuries. When he finished, the room was silent, although the entire audience held back a thousand questions.

Bill spoke first, recounting the events of the previous night in more detail, including the bellowing voice which he heard before opening the bedroom door and of the hulking dark figure which seemed to just dissolve in the light.

"Why haven't I seen it?" Janice asked the group.

Tom answered, "I think with the onset of puberty, it has been more brazen and the need to recruit Mada is more urgent." Bill was nodding.

Finally Addy spoke, "what can we do, what can any of us really do against something supernatural?"

"Nothing, nothing at all," her husband answered. "We have no power, but Jesus has infinite power to control all evil."

"I'd like to consult with the other elders in our church," Bill said. "There's power in numbers."

"How would you do that without telling them the whole story?" Tom asked, before looking at Mada, who was slowly shaking his head.

"Bill," Janice said. "There's power here, in this room right now, we don't need anyone but Jesus and we can speak to Him without anyone's help."

"But," Tom reminded them, "if what we are guessing is true, evil has a stronghold on him, given his family tree."

"Dr. Tom," Mada began. "Is God my Father or is Satan my father? If God is my Father then Satan has no claim on me, but if Satan is my earthly father how do I get away from him?"

Tom looked around the room as though soliciting opinions, no one spoke.

"God is our creator, He created everyone and everything and for that reason He is called our Father. If Satan were truly your earthly father it doesn't change that fact, since He created Satan also. That Satan chose evil does not change the fact that God created him," he answered, stopping to collect his thoughts. "Do you feel drawn to accept Jesus as your Savior?"

"Yes," the boy said solemnly.

"Then your salvation from all sin, including any claim Satan feels he has for you, is in Jesus," Bill announced smiling. "Declare your faith with us now and set him scurrying away like the coward he really is."

The five held hands and with bowed heads, guided the boy into Jesus' arms as he chose eternal life over death.

Even after he accepted Jesus by faith, he looked at them doubtfully. "Are you sure Satan cannot come and steal me away again?" he asked.

Bill picked up the family Bible from its place on the coffee table, turned to John 10 and read verses 27 through 30. "*My sheep listen to my voice; I know them, and they follow me. I give them eternal life, and they shall never die. No one can snatch them away from me. What my Father has given me is greater than everything, and no one can snatch them away from the Father's care. The Father and I are one.*"

"Yes, I am quite sure," he said, smiling broadly.

When it was over they exchanged hugs and smiles, tears flowed freely, then suddenly Bill asked, "you came here tonight to find out about adoption and we have hardly spoken of it, is there something more that we can tell you?"

Addy looked at Tom, put her arms around Mada and said, "I think all of our questions have been answered except one. Mada, would you like to be our son?"

Mada beamed, his eyes wide with surprise when he answered simply, "I'd like that."

It took several weeks, even though the agency expedited their petition, and the Browns eagerly supported the adoption to be approved. During that time their attorney filed a petition for a name change to be concurrent with its approval. When they left the courthouse, they walked hand in hand with their new son Adam Thomas Rogers and drove home.

– The End –

The Black Condor Reborn

Readers of the original Black Condor story will recall that it describes a young, colored, orphan boy whose father was questionably either Satan or one of Satan's fallen angels. I hope that you took note that near the end of the story he is reborn, not only as a child of Jesus, but into an adoptive family, where he gained a new name and a fresh start. New readers should note that while he is now a child of God, regenerated and redeemed, and therefore secure in his salvation, he is not immune to Satan's power. He still lives with the physical marks left by his father. Those include many of the physical attributes of an avian, including wings, and weaknesses inherent to sinful man. - dc

Mada, or Adam, as he is now properly called, has turned sixteen. He has just begun his junior year in senior high school and has been living with Tom and Addy Rogers for nearly three years. Their three grown children have accepted him as a family member and their grandchildren look at him as an older brother rather than an uncle. There has been no reappearance of the *Darkman* in Adam's life.

Adam has started a workout ritual at school which is rapidly changing his thin boyish physique. His shoulders have broadened, his sinewy arms are not bulky but surprisingly strong, and his wings, when opened, are nearly eight feet from tip to tip. His chest and back muscles are sculpted to a thin, almost girl-like waist. At six feet, Tom now looks upward into the dark eyes of his new son, who edges him by four inches.

It took several months before Adam was able to gain mental control of his wings, and several more before he could coordinate their movements effectively. Except when bathing, Adam was never without a shirt and only Tom and Addy were aware of the peculiar addition to his body. In those three years, Addy had never seen but only heard her husband describe Adam's wings. Secretly, she still questioned their existence.

For obvious reasons, opportunities to 'stretch his wings' were severely limited and those few were only in times of darkness at remote locations. His first solo flight was with Tom in attendance, well into the wee hours of the morning, from lovers leap in the foothills miles from the city. Successful? Yes, in that he was not badly hurt or killed, but still he was scratched and bruised and unable to fly back to the point of origin. He'd mostly glided until fatigue had sent him crashing into the low brush and small trees. Tom had picked him up a few minutes later walking in the road far below, where they laughed like school boys all the way home.

Dr. Tom – Adam found it still hard to call him father – prescribed an exercise program for him that included push ups using his wing tips rather than his arms. Gradually, as he was able, they added weights on his back. In just a short time his back muscles grew larger and easily hid the extra bulk of his thin wings, which tucked neatly beneath them. Now when he flapped them, he easily raised himself vertically from flat ground, but not into a horizontal position of flight. Both Tom and Adam were eager for a second attempt from the lovers leap.

Addy, who was not oblivious to their goings-on, made it clear when she said, "next time you two want to sneak out at night and attempt to kill our son, I'm going with you." There was little room left for further discussion.

"How about tonight?" Adam asked smiling. "There's supposed to be good weather and a full moon."

Tom and Addy looked at each other, smiled, and agreed.

At a few minutes after eleven they got into the car, loaded Tom's medical bag, flashlights, snacks, and drinks, a GPS and headed toward the beckoning hills.

"So Adam," Addy asked glibly, "how does this work?"

"We're still trying to find out," the young man answered. "There's more to flying than just having wings, that's for sure."

Tom kept driving and did not join in the conversation. When they reached their destination there was a car, presumably with two teens already there. They parked and enjoyed a soft drink while they discussed their strategy. About a quarter to one the other car and its occupants left the area. Tom moved the Volvo over closer to the precipice and left the parking lights on to discourage others from joining them.

Addy watched amazed as Adam climbed from the car, popped the trunk and removed his shirt. His lean black body was reflected in the red glow of the tail lights as were two huge, nearly transparent wings looming out from behind his shoulders. His face bore a toothy wide mischievous grin.

"Here, put this on," Addy said, pulling a tortoise-shell style bike helmet from her bag, "and before we do this again, I'm going to sew something up for you that will protect you and allows for your wings."

Tom and Adam smiled happily, appreciating that she had joined in their little adventure. After several minutes he stood in the orange glow of the park lights, in black leather motorcycle pants, with a leather belt sporting his GPS and an LED flashlight, naked from the waist to the top of his head that was covered with the black bicycle helmet. Even with his wings down, his six foot four frame looked imposing, with them up and ready for flight he represented some Sci-Fi bird of prey ready to swoop down on its victims.

Below them, far below them and many miles distant, seemingly millions of lights lit the city from which they had just driven. With the vehicle lights now turned off, only the moon and stars illuminated the remote mountain scene. As their eyes became accustomed to the darkness, below them a ribbon of roadway could be seen now and then through the tree lined mountain as it snaked upward from the city to their present location.

"There," Tom said pointing, "between those two large pine trees is a grassy meadow. I noticed it on the way up."

Adam nodded, "yes, I see it too, just across the road and to the left."

Addy strained hard to see what they were describing and as she did, fear filled her. She could picture Adam broken and dying, lying somewhere down below in the darkness.

"Don't do it!" she said, raising her voice. "You'll be hurt and for what, trying to prove some stupid idea that you are some kind of a bird?"

Neither Adam nor Tom considered this anything but a necessary test; to them it was not at all optional.

"I have to," Adam explained. "Don't you see, I have to know."

Tom did not speak.

"Do something," Addy said to her husband. "Stop him before he gets hurt."

"Please understand, it is his right of passage," Tom said patiently. "If he does not do this tonight with us, he'll do it another time when he's alone and we are not around to help him."

"I can't bear to watch," Addy said, sounding very much like the mother she was.

Adam turned on his bicycle head lamp and the LED that hung from his belt down his back, his white teeth showing in the moonlight. "Here I go, say a little prayer for me," he said.

He took a half dozen steps, picking up speed as he did so, and launched himself off the point and into the night. The moonlight caught his shadow and the lights marked his progress as he flew downward under his own power. In the stillness of the night, the steady rhythm of his wings sounded like a flag on a pole snapping in the wind. Far below, as he neared the two tall trees, the marker light seemed to lift, and rather than going between them, he rose over them, disappearing momentarily behind them. A scant four minutes following his takeoff Tom could see Adam through his binoculars standing in the meadow waving his arms. He handed the glasses to his wife triumphantly.

"He made it, can you see him waving?" Tom exclaimed happily.

They drove down to the pickup site where Adam waited for them, stopped the car, and hugged their son joyously as multiple pairs of unseen red eyes watched from the darkness above.

As they drove home, they kept talking over one another in their eagerness to share the events of the previous few minutes, as they had each observed them. Knowing that none of them would find sleep easily, Tom pulled into an all-night truck stop and invited Adam and Addy to have an early breakfast. The meal filled and satisfied them, making the remainder of the trip home a nearly silent one.

Addy began the next day to try and fashion a sort of garment which would protect her son should something happen in flight, but also would allow him to have full use of his wings when necessary. Over two weeks her several attempts fell short of the mark but finally she walked proudly into the living room with her creation in hand, sporting a huge smile.

Satisfied with the protection the motorcycle pants provided, she had worked to match the top with them in a complementary way. The top, also of soft black leather, had long sleeves with reinforced and padded elbows. The back opened with Velcro closures, allowing for his wings to burst free with little effort through the long vertical slits which resembled pleats. She had purchased black kid gloves to complete his ensemble.

The next few days found Tom working late in his shop in the family garage, reworking and modifying the black bicycle helmet. With his wife's help, it was covered with matching black leather which hung loosely down its back and sides, giving the wearer a hooded look, with only his face showing. It fit Adam well and with more Velcro, even allowed for some future growth. Its disadvantage was the lack of ventilation it did not allow in warmer weather. It proved itself on its first daylight flight, after the family satisfied themselves that they had no immediate onlookers high up in the foothills.

The next day the local paper told of two groups of campers who had spotted a 'black condor' in the foothills just miles from the town. Adam immediately adopted the name and Addy stitched the silhouette of the bird on the chest of the suit in white thread.

Over the next few months Adam's faith was tested, first when he found a wallet with a large sum of cash in it, next when his pretty little Latino friend invited him to a party where the guests indulged themselves in sex, drugs and alcohol, and finally when a copy of an upcoming semester test became available as an alternative to studying. With some difficulty, he refused the lure of all three, remembering the promises he had made to Jesus.

As summer yielded to autumn, the days grew shorter and seasonal darkness replaced the long warm summer evenings with shorter cooler ones. Adam found himself leaving school after practice, often needing to use the headlights on the old jalopy that his parents had purchased for him. Twice, he had been startled to see a form standing in the road in front of him, with red eyes peering threateningly at him. Both times he swerved to avoid the apparition but did not lose control of the car. Its appearance was a disquieting reminder that although gone, he was not forgotten. Something seemed to be lurking, watching and waiting for Adam to make a misstep.

He made it through the intersection on a yellow, his mind still preoccupied with the dark presence he'd barely missed hitting with his car. He looked to his right as he passed the row of condemned commercial buildings waiting to be demolished which abutted a poor residential neighborhood. He saw the outlines of three people silhouetted by a single streetlight. It appeared that two men were in the process of robbing and accosting an elderly woman.

He pulled to the side of the roadway a block further and jumped out of his car without hesitation, pulled on his leather coat and put on his helmet, as he ran toward them. As he did, he unfurled his wings on the darkened street and took flight. Just seconds later he landed quietly beside the three, who stood gaping at his towering figure. Without so much as a sound he threw the two men head first into the light pole and helped the shaken woman to her feet. She stared with unbelieving eyes at the smiling youth turned superhero.

"Will you need me to walk you home?" he asked quietly.

"No, no," she answered. "I only live just across the street, I'll be fine."

The two men still lay where they had dropped, unconscious. From a pocket Adam retrieved two zip-ties, joining first their left thumbs and then their right, turning them toward the post, forcing them to embrace the light pole.

Afterward, he removed their clothes and threw them in a nearby dumpster before walking nonchalantly to his waiting car. The old woman watched over her shoulder as she walked, smiling and shaking her head in disbelief. When she got to her tiny apartment she waited until he drove away, then dialed 911 and reported an attempted mugging.

She told them that a Good Samaritan had left them bound naked where the assault had taken place, but neglected to describe her benefactor except that he appeared to be a young black man. Twenty minutes later she heard sirens and saw the flashing lights of two cruisers which stopped across the street. After a few minutes, a knock on the door revealed the face of a smiling policeman.

"Are you the lady who called in an attempted assault?" he asked, continuing to smile.

"I am," she said firmly.

"And, would you like to give a statement and file a complaint?" he asked again.

"I would," she affirmed.

"Thank you," he said. "May I come in?"

"You may," she said, opening the door and backing into the small room.

He asked questions which she answered for the most part in short sentences, without elaboration. She intentionally left out the details when asked about young Adam's appearance or the fact that he flew to her rescue on large black wings. She signed and dated the statement and affirmed that she'd be pleased to appear in court if necessary at some later date.

"We've been after this pair for some time," the young officer said.

"You were their third victim in as many days. One woman is in the hospital now in a coma from the beating they gave her. You've helped get them off the street, thank you."

After he had gone and the cars pulled away, she smiled impishly and poured herself a cup of tea and settled back to relive the events of the evening.

Adam looked in good spirits as he walked in the door, late for dinner.

"You're late," Addy said from her spot at the dinner table. "You should have called."

"Sorry Mom," he said. "I got delayed and time just kind of got away from me, I'll try and do better next time."

Addy found it hard to remain upset at him when he repented and admitted his error.

"No problem, wash your hands and have a seat before it gets colder," she said, regaining her good humor.

Tom noted a special glint in his son's eyes that spoke of something that needed to be shared.

"Anything special happen in school today?" he asked innocently, trying to draw the boy into conversation.

"Nope," Adam answered with a mouthful of broccoli casserole. "'Bout hit old red-eyes with the car on the way home though."

"You saw the *Darkman*?" Addy asked, concern showing in her voice.

"Yup, that's twice this week," he answered, swallowing his milk.

"Why didn't you say something?" Tom asked.

"Was nuthin' to say really," Adam answered. "He was there, standing in the road, and then he was gone, simple as that. I had to swerve to miss hitting him."

"What do you think would have happened if I'd have hit him?" he asked them.

"I don't know and I hope we never find out," Tom answered, not amused by the lightness in his son's voice. "Do not ever think you are a match for him or let him dare you to challenge his power."

Adam went to his bedroom and began his studies, but could not forget how he had saved the old woman. His pride in his accomplishment wouldn't let him rest. He looked forward eagerly to his next opponent, the next opportunity to prove his physical prowess.

When he had finally gotten to sleep, the *Darkman* stood smiling at the foot of his bed. It seems, he thought to himself, that I have found the chink in the boy's armor – pride. That same pride and arrogance was what caused Satan to fall from grace.

Good Samaritan Saves Elderly Woman, Suspects in Custody. Tom's eyes were immediately drawn to the subsequent newspaper story which told the few details which the police knew via the victim of the encounter. Both of the suspects had elected not to speak on advice from counsel. He called Addy and pointed out the short article to her. As she read it and mentally considered the location and time, she got the same thought in her mind as had her husband.

When Adam entered the kitchen smiling broadly and sat down at the table, Tom handed him the paper and said, "tell us what you know about this and why you were late for dinner."

Adam read the article slowly, his mind racing, looking for an acceptable answer, but none came. He decided to minimize his part in the event without directly lying to his parents.

"Wasn't much, he said. "I saw two guys trying to rob an old woman so I stopped and helped her, that's all." Both Tom and Addy noticed he did not look directly at them as he spoke.

"You could have been hurt or killed," Addy said accusingly. "Your new outfit won't stop bullets."

"But they didn't have guns," Adam said defensively.

"And you knew that how?" Tom asked.

Adam had lost all pretense of pride, he sat before his parents embarrassed and repentant, knowing that what they were saying was both true and for his benefit. Several moments passed without further conversation, finally Tom stood and walked over and put his arm around the tall black boy.

"We are both proud of and frightened for you," he said, as Addy joined him to make a trio.

Tears glistened in her blue eyes as she roughly quoted Scripture, "what is meant for evil, God turns to good. I truly believe that God has chosen to use you for His glory. What we need from you is your assurance that you will pray for good judgment before you do what you feel you are called to do."

Tom nodded in agreement, watching Adam's reaction.

"I will, I promise I will next time," he answered. "It just happened so fast I didn't think it through."

"Would she recognize you?" Tom asked, referring to the old woman. "It says nothing here about a boy with wings and a leather suit flying in to rescue her."

"I don't know," Adam answered. "I think she was just grateful and knew it would cause trouble if she started telling some incredible story to the cops."

"How about the thugs?" Addy asked. "Do you think they'll tell?"

"I'm guessing that they won't, who'd believe a couple of dopers who were beating down an old woman to take her purse?" he answered.

"I think we need to add another piece to your costume," Addy said, now smiling. "Some kind of a mask. Maybe something like the Lone

Ranger wore."

"The who?" Adam asked.

"A hero-type from our childhood days," Tom said laughing. "A good guy, ex-Texas Ranger who traveled around doing good and defeating the bad guys. In the days of black and white television the good guys always wore white and the bad ones wore black, it made it easy to know who was who."

"I'll make a stop at a costume shop today while I'm out shopping," Addy said, "and see what they have to offer."

Adam retraced the route of the previous night as he drove to school and saw the old black woman sitting proudly on her front porch in a rocking chair knitting. He couldn't resist smiling as he pictured his own mother doing the same if she'd lived to old age.

He felt a new kind of pride, a healthy one that did not testify of him, but of the love of God. He exchanged nods with other students as he walked from his car to his first class, knowing that he occupied exactly the right space and time that God had created him for.

The air was crisp now, especially in the mornings, when hints of the coming frost crept in, making his breath like something from an old movie about dragons. Adam liked the change and enjoyed the contrast between the sweltering heat and the freezing winter's icy cold. It was dark when he left for school now and dark again on his drive home. Addy worried about their son's lack of experience behind the wheel and the soon-to-be slick roadways.

Traffic was light as he edged his old car out of the subdivision and onto the boulevard; the very *earlies* were already at work and the *laters* were still eating their breakfasts and urging their children to hurry up and get ready for school. Most of the trees looked barren, already having dropped their leaves, giving them the appearance of a soulful witch with her hands raised in the air. A yellow VW bug of mid-70's vintage caught his eye as it pulled in front of him from a side street, without slowing for the stop sign. He sighed and backed off the accelerator, while choking back the urge to use his horn. He knew the car and knew of the tall blond girl driving it, from the parking lot at school. She was far too socially invested to give a dark skinned boy like himself a smile or nod even in passing. Her need to lead rather than wait for him to pass spoke volumes of her general personality.

He followed behind her for several miles, driving a shade over the posted limit with no traffic behind or in front of them. As they approached the high arching bridge that spanned the river below, he instinctively lowered his speed without knowing the reason. The distance between the two cars widened to the point that he could hardly see it in the headlights before it began to slide and spin between the confines of the bridge's railings. He was nearly stopped when it breached the restraining wall and disappeared into the darkness.

With hardly a thought he pulled to the side, took off his jacket, and tucked his tee shirt in his waistband before he leaped off the railing where the car had gone over. His powerful wings freed themselves as he dropped lower and lower until the starlight revealed the silver that was the rushing water. Downstream a hundred yards or more, the yellow bug was already slowly sinking into the cold water.

When he looked inside the car, she was slumped forward, seemingly unconscious and bleeding from her nose. His weight was hardly noticeable as he perched on the front bumper and broke out the windshield with his fist. As one would have expected of her, she wore no seatbelt, which at this particular moment was a plus. Adam was nearly knee deep in the water when he pulled her limp form toward himself and began to rapidly beat his wings. At first it seemed that he'd not be able to rise with the additional weight, but slowly he was able to rise from the water and with great effort, maintain enough altitude to fly to the nearer bank.

Far above them looking down at the scene, several motorists had stopped and lined the rail, trying vainly to spot the car that had caused the breach. Adam lay beside the unconscious girl at the waters edge, gasping for his breath while he tried to regain his strength. In the distance he could hear the sirens of emergency vehicles. As he put on his t-shirt he noted the rise and fall of her chest, the bleeding from her nose had stopped, and her eyes fluttered open, then closed again. Voices, accompanied by lights, were making their way down the long steep embankment from the bridge. He walked toward them yelling as he did, "this way, over here!" As he walked, he formulated the story of how he came to find her.

"I was following her," he said, "when she went off the bridge. When I got down here, her car was floating near the edge so I was able to wade out and bring her to shore."

The EMT's had quickly revived her and pronounced her cold and wet, but not badly injured, when they loaded her into the ambulance and drove off toward the hospital. No one seemed to question Adam's account of the accident, even the police had little to say except that black ice on the bridge and excessive speed had caused it. He left quickly without giving them his name or address. By the time the local news arrived, he'd already returned home to change into dry clothes.

Accounts on the local news were conflicting, some witnesses saying that they'd seen a dark figure hovering over the car before it sank, and others claiming that it was too dark to see anything. Again, the morning paper announced ***Good Samaritan Reappears*** at the scene of an automobile accident and pulled the unconscious young woman to safety before leaving the scene.

"It was you, wasn't it?" Addy said accusingly. "Don't you realize you could have drowned?"

"It was me," he admitted, "but I hardly even got wet. It wasn't like I dived in or something."

Tom didn't join in the discussion. Smiling, he just continued to read the newspaper, pretending not to hear. Later that evening, after Addy had gone to bed, he let himself into Adam's room and asked, "are you still awake?"

"Yeah," he answered.

He sat down gently on the side of the bed and continued. "Sooner or later you know, our secret will be discovered. You know that, don't you?"

"Yes, I guess," Adam admitted.

"And, are you ready to face the consequences when it happens?" he added.

Adam remained silent, considering what some of those consequences would be.

"Like what? What do you think will happen?" the boy asked.

"I think it will ruin your life," Tom said softly. "Change everything you believe in, make you the focus of scientific research, and take away any chance you may have of lasting peace."

"So, what do I do?" Adam asked hopelessly.

"Pray, he answered. "God has a purpose and a plan, ask Him to guide you."

Hopeless as he felt, Adam turned his face toward the wall and, as Tom left the room, he began to pray. Sometime later he must have drifted off to sleep. When he returned home from school, three Netflix movies were on his bed... Superman, Spiderman, and Batman. It did not take a genius to realize who had put them there. He watched all three and noted their similarities, differences, and their common need for anonymity. Of the three, he felt most closely related to Batman, who had only marginal superpowers compared with the other two.

During the school day he passed the blonde who had driven the VW off the bridge, nodded to her and smiled. To his surprise, she nodded and smiled back, causing him to wonder if she may not have been as totally unaware of his presence as he had thought.

"You are right," he said to Tom as they sat at the dinner table. "I've given it a lot of thought and I can see the need to stay in the shadows and out of the limelight. The two opportunities I have had, however, were given to me, I did not seek them. I think God is behind this whole thing."

Both Tom and Addy were smiling as she said, "God is behind everything. Nothing is done of which He is not aware, and without His permission."

"Does He *cause* or *let* things happen?" Adam asked his parents.

"Interesting question," Tom answered. "Both, I think. Although He never causes anything evil. I remember reading Job for the first time and wondering at the way it was worded and how cavalier it seemed God was about letting Satan have his way."

Addy was nodding agreement. "Our Bible study group wondered the same thing, it almost seemed they were a couple of old guys sitting on the front porch in rockers, having their morning coffee together."

All three laughed at the picture it portrayed in their minds.

"And so God allowed Satan to rape my mother and create me for a reason too?" Adam said questioningly.

"So you will bring Him glory," Addy said smiling broadly. "As you are bringing us joy in our lives. All mankind was created to bring glory to God."

As the winter raged, the ground was frozen hard and the snow that had fallen several weeks before showed only the wear and tear of use with no chance of thawing. Some locals declared it the worst winter in recent memory. An oddity in nearby Lake Michigan was the presence of frozen waves, waves that looked as though they were frozen solid while still in motion.

Tom's practice was besieged by injuries caused by slips and falls, broken arms, hips, and even frostbite for the unwary and unprotected. He worked long hours, often coming home late at night exhausted, long after the family had retired, only to rise the next morning and do it all over again. The police, tow truck drivers, ER nurses, and other emergency responders were likewise worn down and more than ready for the spring thaw.

The gray overcast of the short days seemed to blend into the gray of the short twilight before darkness enveloped the night. It was as if God had abandoned the earth and took the light of day with Him. One such day ended with the malfunction of a very old and grossly overworked furnace in an aged high-rise, which blossomed into an inferno while its occupants slept, filling the stairways with fire and deadly smoke. The old building was nine stories high, only the first four of which could be reached by the fire trucks from the ground. In the ensuing confusion to escape, several on the top floors sought safety on the rooftop, where they huddled together, praying for a miracle.

Adam awoke with a sense of urgency, with no idea of why. The bedside clock read 2:47 a.m. He tried to get back to sleep without success and checked the clock again, which now read 2:59 a.m. As he went downstairs to the kitchen, he heard the wail of sirens in the distance. He fixed himself a sandwich and poured a glass of milk before turning on the TV in the family room, with the volume at minimum.

Reporters on the scene were telling of a massive fire, which was out of control, in the low income section of the city, with the possibility of imminent casualties because of frozen water mains which supplied the fire trucks. Without considering his actions, Adam scribbled a quick note to his parents, donned his black leathers, and left quietly by the back door. As he neared, it was evident from the orange hue reflecting off the low clouds, that the fire was massive and out of control. Police cars cordoned off the immediate area to discourage onlookers.

Adam took a deep breath, let it out, bowed his head and asked for God to guide him before slipping on his mask and head gear. In three running steps he was up and gaining altitude over the tree-lined street below. Nearly a hundred feet above him he could see the hopeless faces of several stranded on the roof of the blazing inferno.

Upward he spiraled until he was looking down on the rooftop. A half block away was a shorter, newer office building without all the antennas and guy wires that would have caused him trouble when landing. He said another short prayer and landed gently on the roof among the startled victims. Without speaking, he picked up the smallest and youngest of the children and flew away. Within a minute he returned for a second and then a third.

This time he took a few moments to regain his strength before returning to the burning building. Each time he returned, his burden grew in size, draining his strength. With three adults left, each looking well over two hundred pounds, he knew that a new plan needed to be devised.

When he returned he said, "I'm running out of energy, we are going to need to go down rather than across. I can fly downward much easier than back and forth between the buildings."

When all the children were safe, he walked up to a petite but heavy colored woman. "You're next," he said. She smiled a toothy grin and laid herself back into his waiting arms. He held her tightly and locked his wings as he circled lower and lower toward the pavement where astonished firemen and onlookers backed away. He landed roughly, took three deep breaths and readied himself for the flight back to the top.

"How many are left up there?" a young fireman asked.

"Two," Adam answered. "Two big fellas. I'm not sure I can make it with them."

An older fireman in a white hard hat which spoke of authority moved forward from the crowd and said, "we'll spread the net, if you can get them below the third floor, drop them into it."

Adam smiled and answered, "Roger Chief, I'll give it a try."

The first man did well and released his grip on the boy when Adam told him to, falling safely into the waiting net. However, the last man panicked like a drowning victim and wouldn't release his hold around Adam's chest. Adam glided most of the way down, and then together they fell the last twenty five feet, landing hard in the waiting net.

Exhausted but uninjured, Adam knew he needed to get away from the crowd and the prying eyes of the news cameras, which were pushing their way toward him. The young fireman helped him from the net, handed him a Gatorade and said, "well done Condor, do you need help getting out of here?"

Adam chugged the drink, smiled at his new friend, and answered, "not sure, let's see if I can get airborne and out of sight before I get mobbed."

Limping badly, he took five running steps before angling upward slowly above the cheering crowd. He intentionally went several blocks in the wrong direction before dropping down and circling back to where his old car was parked. He disrobed, put his costume in the trunk of his car and donned a white t-shirt just before a police cruiser turned onto the side street. The spotlight played over the car and its driver before stopping beside him.

"Everything all right here," the officer asked suspiciously. "Do you live here in the neighborhood?"

"No, I mean yes," he answered. "No, I don't live here, but yes everything is alright."

"What are you doing down here?" the officer continued.

"I heard there was a fire and came down to see it," he answered truthfully, "but my car died and I had trouble getting it started again."

"Well, what we don't need is more folks rubber-necking and getting in the way," the officer said with authority. "Why don't you go back home and watch it in the morning on the news?"

"Good idea," Adam agreed. "I'm beat anyway and need my rest." He started the old car, put it into gear and pulled onto the road, giving the officer a smile and small wave as he passed.

The cruiser followed him for several blocks before turning off and leaving him to return home alone. The lights were on when he pulled in, causing his stomach to knot.

"Thank God you are alright," Addy said with a worried frown on her face. Tom stood beside her nodding.

Behind them the small television in the kitchen was showing a continuous feed of the scene of the fire and replaying frequently footage of the mysterious figure in black who seemed to have had wings. The onlookers eagerly took turns telling their versions of seeing the black form ferrying would-be victims from roof top to roof top.

Close-up footage showed Adam as a tall black man in a leather costume, with a mask hiding most of his face. Descriptions varied, putting his height at seven or eight feet, some as high as ten, and estimating his wing span at upwards of twenty feet.

The young among the crowd immediately dubbed him a super hero right out of the pages of a comic book. None of the rescued victims had a great deal to add except their gratitude to whomever or whatever it was that came to their aid. Behind them, the camera clearly showed the fire which still burned out of control, while the several engine companies fought to isolate it from the surrounding buildings. The three of them watched for several minutes without speaking.

Adam felt he must defend his actions to his parents and made his point by saying, "I feel that I was created this way with an evil intent in mind, but that Jesus has plans to use it for good to bring Himself glory. I don't feel it is my place to question His plan for me."

Tom was nodding solemnly. Addy had tears in her eyes as she reluctantly accepted what he had said as true. It is so often difficult to trust completely and not try and maintain some human backup plan in the event God does not perform to our expectations, she thought to herself.

"Maybe you could wake us next time?" Tom said smiling, "so we can get an early start on worrying about you."

The three of them smiled and shared a hug before Addy exclaimed, "get in the shower, you smell like smoke." They laughed again.

The morning paper was filled with pictures and interviews. Headlines read ***Winged-Man Saves Six From a Sure Death***, and speculation ran from some ultra-secret military weapon being field-tested to that of the usual alien encounter folks who of course related everything back to Area 51. When he got to school, it was buzzing as well, with theories and ideas which made Adam a little uncomfortable when his opinion was asked.

"Guy looked a little like you," one of his friends commented, "only taller and better looking of course."

Adam gave him a smack on the shoulder and a friendly shove as an answer.

Judy, the blonde who owned the wrecked Volkswagen bug, looked at him curiously before walking by without adding comment. Later, in the third period class that they shared, she walked near him on her way to her seat and stated, "it was you, wasn't it?"

She continued walking without waiting for his response, seated herself and gave him a knowing smile. As the class ended and the class room emptied, he waited outside of the door. As she passed he said, "what are you doing for lunch?"

"You buyin'?" she answered in reply.

"I'm buying," he answered. "Shall we take my car or yours?"

"Very funny," she said. "I'll meet you out front."

As he walked to the parking lot and was driving around to the prearranged pickup spot, Adam was considering what he might say. Nothing really came to mind. He stopped and opened the passenger door without getting out, she slid into the old Pontiac beside him.

"Nice ride," she said appraisingly, as she looked around.

"Thanks," he answered, while wondering if she meant it as a compliment or as a joke.

"Burgers all right?" Adam asked as he turned onto the street.

"Burgers are fine," she answered sweetly. "Anything but eating another meal in the cafeteria. I miss the freedom of having transportation."

"Was it totaled?" he asked.

"Oh yeah, it took them two days to find it and pull it out," she said glumly. "Cost me $250 just for the wrecker."

"Bummer," he said, as they pulled into the drive-thru at Bob's Burgers.

He ordered for them, paid the bill, and as they sat waiting for their order, she looked into his dark eyes and said simply, “thank you.”

Her meaning was not lost on him – she’d referred to both the meal and her gratitude for what he’d done to save her after the accident.

“It’s just a burger…” he began to answer, but was interrupted.

“You know what I mean,” she said, her clear blue eyes conveying her message. “How do you do it? Fly I mean?”

He thought for a minute about how he should answer or if he should admit what she already suspected. He knew that she knew, so he answered, “can you keep a secret?”

She nodded her head as their order was handed out the window. “I have and I will,” she said softly.

They parked and took their meals from the bag. Adam bent his head as she did likewise, praying silently and asking a blessing upon the food and their time together.

“Wings,” Adam answered her previous question. “I was born with them.”

She giggled like a small child, creating a kind of musical sound. “Can I see them?” she asked quietly.

“Not here, not now,” he said, “but maybe later, somewhere away from prying eyes.”

“Who else knows?” she asked.

“An old woman and the ones from the fire last night,” he answered, and then added, “and I suppose a few dozen firemen, and gawkers who went out to see the fire.”

“But no one but me saw your face?” she said. “No one else knows?”

“My parents,” he said, beginning to feel uncomfortable with the questioning.

She gave his hand a squeeze. “Thank you,” she said. “I’d never tell.”

"You are limping," she said, "were you hurt last night?"

"I twisted my knee somehow when I fell into the net," he answered. "It still hurts like the dickens."

Without a word she laid her hand upon his knee and closed her eyes. He felt a shock in his leg like a bolt of electrical energy, just as she exclaimed, "ouch, that hurt."

His pain was gone. She had tears glistening in the corners of her eyes when she opened them. He looked at her questioningly, wondering what had just happened.

"I'm an *empath*," she said simply. "My abilities are not as visible as yours."

Adam stared at, her wondering what she meant.

"I can often sense pain and sometimes even disease before others know they have it. Sometimes I can take away the pain by assuming it myself," she continued.

"So you felt my injury and took it away by feeling it yourself?" Adam asked. "Why do you do that?"

"I think Jesus gave me this special power so I could know how He feels about us, so that I could act here on earth as He acted when He was among us," she said. "Didn't He experience pain for our sins so that we could experience salvation?"

He fell silent while trying to process what had just happened. He took her hand from his knee, pressed it to his lips and said, "thank you."

The special moment was broken when she exclaimed, "we're going to be late for class!"

They talked very little on the way back to school and had just made it into the parking lot when the bell rang. Both of them grabbed books and hustled to their next class, smiling as they went.

Sleep was a long time coming for Adam that night, not because of the *Darkman* who had been strangely absent for several days, but because of his unusual feelings for Judy. He tried, but was unable to quantify them before finally dozing off well into the wee hours of the morning. However, when he awakened, he was none-the-less well rested and looked forward eagerly to the final day of the school week.

"Morning," he said as he breezed into the kitchen. Tom sat drinking his morning coffee and reading the paper while Addy moved about the stove causing good smells to fill the room.

"Morning Condor," Tom answered laughing. "You've now officially been named The Black Condor."

"Good thing I got you that mask," Addy added, "otherwise we'd have a crowd on our front lawn right now."

Adam smiled and sat at the table where he busied himself with his orange juice.

"How's the knee?" Tom asked. "You seemed to be limping before you lifted off and left the scene of the fire." He, of course, was referring to the film of the event playing over and over on the muted television on the kitchen counter.

"Good as new," Adam answered honestly, while remembering how the healing had been performed.

"I've got to leave early and may be a little late," Adam added. "I'm picking someone up on my way to school."

"Anyone we know?" Addy asked.

Adam struggled with his conscience before answering. "Not yet, but maybe soon. It's the girl who drove off the bridge and into the river."

Tom laughed before saying, "guess she probably needs a lift. I imagine her car is permanently out of order."

"Yeah, she said it is totaled," Adam said, while eating his breakfast.

Judy climbed into his car, fastened her seat belt, flashed him a smile and then said, "be careful going across the bridge, I heard there may be black ice on it this morning."

They both laughed as they pulled away.

"Sleep well?" he asked her, trying to adopt a conversational tone.

"Like a log," she answered. "How about you?"

"Not so good," he admitted. "I kept coming up with questions that have no answers."

"Like?" she asked.

"Like this whole thing, you and I, our special gifts, and where we are supposed to go from here," he answered, surprising himself that he had done so.

"Is there a you and I?" she asked with a teasing voice. "You bought me lunch and now we are a team?"

He fell silent, a little hurt by the truth of her statement.

She picked up on the fact that she'd hurt his feelings and added, "not that we'd make a bad team or anything. Maybe I'll give a little thought about an appropriate costume."

"Like Batman and Robin," he said laughing.

"Yeah, like that," she agreed, "but of course Robin was a guy."

"Do you think that'll be a problem?" Adam asked. "Are super heroes gender specific?"

"Cat Woman and Super Girl were," she continued. "But I suppose it didn't matter to the ones they helped. When do I get to see your wings?"

"That's a little pushy," he said, blushing at the picture it portrayed in his mind.

She pretended to pout, "you promised."

"Okay," he said, pretending to relent. "How about this evening?"

"Where?" she said, with a kind of awe in her voice.

"How about lovers leap?" he said automatically without thinking. He was embarrassed and quickly added, "that's the only place I know where we won't be as likely to be seen."

She was laughing openly at his discomfort. "It's a date then," she said smiling, "but you'll have to pick me up."

During the school day, it occurred to him for the first time that he was black and she was white. The stigma attached to racial differences had never been an issue in his adoptive family but remained a heated one all across the nation. Although America had made strides in the direction of racial equality, it still had a long way to go in finding the same color blindness that God felt for His creation. He wondered if the hurdle may be one too great to for them to overcome

"Maybe we should go with you," Addy mused when Adam told them of his plan to show Judy his wings. "What if you get hurt and need help?"

"I'll be fine," he promised. "If I need help she can bring me back to town just like you would."

"I don't know," Tom said smiling. "Isn't this the same girl who ran off the bridge and into the river?"

"Nothing's gonna happen," Adam repeated. "We'll be home before you know it."

"Take your phone," Addy instructed, "and keep in touch."

On the drive to Judy's house Adam wondered how her parents would view him, a young black man, showing up at their door wanting to take their daughter to lovers leap. Well, of course they didn't know the destination he hoped, but still... He parked, walked up the sidewalk to the front door and rang the bell. After what seemed an eternity the door opened and a 40-something black woman opened the door.

"Yes?" she said questioningly.

"Hi. I'm Adam, Adam Rogers," he said. "I'm here to pick up Judy."

"Please come in Mr. Rogers," the woman said politely, "and have a seat. We've been expecting you."

A tall black man rose from the sofa and extended his hand toward Adam and said, "I'm Ben, Ben Carpenter, and this is my wife Earlene. Please join us while Judy gets ready."

Confusion and surprise must have shown plainly on Adam's face as he stood looking at them without speaking.

"She's adopted," Ben finally said, laughing a deep and hearty laugh.

"I'm sorry," Adam said, finally finding his tongue. "It's just that I was worrying if race may be a problem, and it is obviously not."

"Not here, not with us," Earlene said. "Looks like God provided the answer to your question without you even asking."

Just then Judy breezed into the room, smiling from ear to ear. "Guess you've met my parents," she said, before giving her Mom and Dad a hug. "Have you met Grams?"

Adam stood looking bewildered without answering her question.

"Grams," Judy called out, walking to a nearby room with a closed door. "I've got someone here I'd like you to meet."

The bedroom door opened slowly and a smallish black woman walked into the room with her arm around Judy. When she saw Adam she smiled broadly and said, "seems like I seen that face before some wherez," as she walked right up to him and stuck out a gnarled hand.

"Good to see you again, young man," she said. "We didn't get much of a chance to visit the other night down in the 'hood, did we?"

Ben, Earlene, and Judy stood looking at them wondering what she was talking about.

Adam recognized her as the woman who the two thugs were accosting the night of his first rescue.

"Just visitin'," was the answer to his unasked question. "That's my own place down where we first met."

She turned to her family and explained without adding the detail of how Adam had arrived on the scene, "this here's the young man who put them thieves on the run and saved me from bein' robbed," she said pleasantly.

By the look in their eyes, Adam could see that his stock had gone up in value.

"Nice to see you again," he said, trying hard to hide his surprise. "God sure does work in mysterious ways, doesn't He?"

"That He does, that He does," she said, giving him an impish grin before turning back to her grand-daughter and saying, "I think you'll be safe with him."

A few minutes later they were in the car heading out of the city and into the foothills.

"Did she tell you about me?" Adam asked. "Is that how you knew?"

"Tell me what?" Judy answered. "That you could fly? Heck no, I saw you myself out in the river when you landed on the car, but I thought I was dreaming."

"All she told us was that some young man came to her rescue and saved her from being beaten and robbed," she continued. "Does she know you can fly?"

"I flew in when I saw them beating her," he admitted, "landed right there on the sidewalk. It was my third try at flying and I didn't have my mask yet."

"You should have seen their faces," he added, laughing.

They were both still laughing when they pulled up to lovers leap and turned off the motor. Below them the city lights seemed to stretch out forever, and the canopy of stars overhead twinkled like Christmas lights. The air was crisp as they got out. He opened the trunk and took out his leather shirt, hood, and mask. He was already wearing his black leather pants.

"You want to see the whole enchilada?" he giggled, slipping it on as he did.

"Yup, my super hero at his best," she answered with a special light in her blue eyes.

A minute later he stood in front of her in the light of the headlamps seemingly several feet taller than life, with his black wings extended behind his shoulders on each side. "What do you think?" he asked.

She sucked in her breath and said, "you're beautiful!"

"Want to take a ride?" he asked, trying to ignore her comment.

"Could we?" she asked him in return. "I mean, should we?"

"Why not?" he answered, "what could it hurt? I'll be careful and we can always land if I get too tired and walk back up."

He took her gently in his arms, trying to ignore the feelings she brought with her closeness, and took three steps before launching into the blackness of the night. Three pairs of red eyes followed their progress from behind them as they glided effortlessly away.

It seemed like forever to Judy, but it was only a scant few minutes before they landed on an adjoining hillside, in an opening between old growth yellow pines, which rose like a canopy above them. They kissed, softly and sweetly, almost innocently at first, but then more passionately before stopping. A minute, then two passed before they spoke.

"Maybe that's why Batman and Robin are both guys," she said shakily, "to keep their minds on fighting crime."

He laughed and added, "maybe so."

Reluctantly, they flew together back to where the car waited and retraced their route back to town without substantial conversation.

When Adam checked his watch it was 10:50 p.m. He took his cell phone out and dialed home. Addy picked it up on the first ring.

"Is everything alright?" she asked without saying hello.

"Everything is fine," he answered. "We're back in town and hungry, is it alright if we stop for a bite to eat?"

"Yes," Addy answered for she and Tom, but then added, "we'll be waiting up for you."

"Mom," he said, "I'm sixteen. I'll be careful, get some sleep."

"Like that's going to happen," Judy laughed. "I'll call home too so they know what's going on," she said as she picked up her cell and repeated his words.

Adam pulled into the same truck stop where he and his parents had enjoyed breakfast a few weeks prior. When they walked inside they did not go un-noticed by the few who were sitting drinking coffee and visiting over empty plates. A tall black boy with a young beautiful blonde girl on his arm would always bring attention.

"Mom and Dad and I always get those looks when we go out," Judy said, referring to the several truckers who spoke in subdued tones.

"I've never thought much about it," he answered, "but I expect that my parents get the same reaction when I'm with them."

She looked surprised. "Are you adopted too?" she asked. "And your parents are white?"

"Yup," he said smiling. "They took me when I was thirteen, almost four years ago now."

"And now here we are," she said, taking his arm possessively.

"And here we are," he agreed.

They ate breakfast together and drove the short distance home, each dreading to say goodnight.

"It was the best night of my life," Judy said. "I can't wait to become your Robin."

She kissed his cheek and went inside before he could get out of the car and open her door.

"How did it go?" Tom asked from the living room where he sat pretending to watch television. Addy sat beside him on the sofa struggling to keep her eyes open.

"Great!" Adam said with the enthusiasm of Tony the Tiger. "We had a great time and nothing got bruised or broken."

"Did you meet her parents?" Addy asked.

"Yup, and guess what?" he answered.

"What?" Tom asked, amused by his son's tone.

"They're black, she's adopted, and her grandma is the lady I saved from the thugs the first night I flew," he said in a rush to share all the information with them.

"What?" Tom repeated. "Slow down. You mean she's white with black parents and you are black with white parents, you are both adopted, and her grandma already knew you from the mugging incident?"

"That's what I'm sayin'," Adam answered grinning, "Freaky, isn't it?"

"To say the least," Tom said shaking his head. "Did the old woman recognize you?"

"Oh yeah," Adam answered. "Sure did, but she didn't say a word to anyone about me flying to her rescue."

"I'm headed for bed," he added over his shoulder as he took the stairs two at a time.

An artist's drawing of *The Black Condor* graced the pages of the newspaper the next morning, it looked suspiciously like something adapted from a comic book. Several of the survivors of the fire had been interviewed and, no doubt, handsomely paid for their account of the mysterious birdman. The journalist had also done follow-ups on the previous reports of a condor flying above the canyon west of town and of the witnesses at the scene of Judy's crash who believed they saw a dark-winged form flying over the river the morning of her accident. Interviews with the two would-be robbers who were still in jail gave further credence to the birdman story.

"You're a celebrity," Tom said to Adam while pointing to the picture, "but I think they have the chin all wrong."

"What are you going to do today?" Addy asked Adam.

"I think I'll look for a job," he answered. "I think it's about time to start helping pay my way."

Amazed, both Tom and Addy looked at each other without commenting.

When he returned home late in the afternoon he had a smile on his face. "I got a job! I start work Monday right after school at the car wash. I get my car washed for free, half-price oil changes, 10¢ a gallon off on gas, and nine bucks an hour."

"What are you going to do with all that money?" Tom asked facetiously.

"I'm thinking about a new paint job on the old Pontiac and putting a few bucks away for school," he answered.

His parents smiled thinking it doesn't get any better than this.

Some of the furor concerning the entity known as *The Black Condor* diminished as time went on and no further sightings were verified. Still, it was rumored that the Feds had sent a team of men to the small town to verify or disclaim its validity. No one knew for sure who they represented or even if they existed.

After hard freezes in November and during the Christmas break, the weather warmed and stayed above freezing for a week, causing the snow to melt and the ice on the lake to soften. It was late in the evening on one of these sunshiny days that reports came out on the radio that a trio of school girls had been skating and two had fallen through the decaying ice.

Adam was driving home from his new job when he heard the plea for help. He was only two miles from the reservoir and quickly formulated a plan to try and help. As he arrived, the police, ambulance and EMT's, and a crew of divers from the fire department were cautiously attempting a rescue. He could see that the girls were struggling to stay above water but appeared exhausted and in dire straights.

Changing quickly behind a service building he took to the air without a thought and sailed smoothly to where they were. Even his weight was more than the soft ice could support, forcing him to suspend himself in the air above them. He reached down and grasped a small cold arm in each hand and beat his wings rapidly, lifting both him and them out of the water.

On the shore some hundred yards away a cheer went up from the onlookers as the crews clamored to welcome the hypothermic children with warm clothing and blankets. Only one person had the presence of mind to snap his picture as he lifted off again and flew out of sight behind the buildings where he changed back into his school clothes, before quickly driving away.

The Black Condor Returns read the morning headline, below it was a picture of Adam with his back to the camera leaving the scene of the rescue and taking flight. Eye witness accounts from more than a dozen verified in detail the events that had transpired, also included was a short paragraph of thanks from the parents of the two children he had saved, which completed the article. The Associated Press picked up the article and spread it all across the nation in a single day. Overnight the motels, hotels, restaurants, and bars were filled with reporters and camera crews looking to break the story of the local winged man in black.

Adam was very intelligent and for the past three years had listened and learned a great deal as he had accompanied his parents to church. He'd participated, studied diligently, and questioned his youth pastor at length during youth Bible studies. Because of his suspected heritage, he had a greater than ordinary interest in both Jesus and Satan.

He had a particular interest in the writings of Matthew and in particular Chapter 4:1-10, where Satan had tried to tempt Jesus. It was clear that Satan had been given dominion over the temporal world by God, but what was unclear to him at first was why Satan believed he could offer anything to Jesus which He did not already have. What finally became evident to him was that Jesus, who had been born to become the Savior of the world, did not look forward to such a painful death which heaped the sins of the world on His sinless shoulders, and for a time, even separated Him from His Father.

Adam remembered Jesus crying out to His Father in the garden, asking if there was another possible way to accomplish His will before bowing to God's will. It was obvious to Adam, Jesus wasn't looking forward to His appointed time on the cross, which opened the possibility of another option.

Even so, Adam was ill-prepared when the *Darkman* with the glowing red eyes re-entered his life at the stroke of midnight a month later, and woke him from a sound sleep.

"What do you desire, my son?" the voice asked in muted tones, "what can I give you to fill your heart's desire?"

"Nothing, leave me alone!" Adam said loudly. "You have no claim on me, I belong to Jesus."

"My dear son," Satan cajoled, "surely there is something that you want, something that you have thought about, which I can provide."

A single thing flashed across the screen of his conscious mind, *FAME!* To be admired for his good deeds. He couldn't discount that he'd felt slighted by his need to remain anonymous. His pride was bruised by the lack of recognition he had received.

Satan could clearly see the young man struggling within himself, so he continued to speak, trying to ferret out the cause of his consternation. "You doubtless already know that the promises you've received will not be realized in your lifetime, if indeed they are even true. You should seek your rewards now while you are young and can enjoy them and not spend your whole life waiting for something that may never happen."

"But Jesus' promises are true, as are His eternal rewards," Adam answered, but in a voice that lacked conviction.

"I'm sure He means well, "Satan continued. "But where is He today? Those who believed in Him were still waiting when they died over two thousand years ago. All of His disciples died horrible deaths and where was He when they needed Him most? He allowed His own cousin John to be beheaded, and Moses died a broken man who was not even allowed to lead his people into the so-called promised land after serving his Master his whole lifetime."

"Your God is a God of empty promises, while I, your father, am here with you and can make your dreams come true now, when you can enjoy them," he added. His voice was as sweet as honey, his tone relaxing and non-threatening as it lulled Adam gently away from those Godly promises he had tried so hard to believe.

Outside, the wind had increased, dark clouds had blown into the little valley, and the sound of distant thunder caught Adam's attention.

As he looked out his window a shaft of white light momentarily blinded him when lightening hit the old oak tree beside his house, splitting it in half. The resounding roar of thunder shook the house to its foundations and awakened something in the young man. When he was able to see once again, the red eyes were gone, as was the fear that had held him in its grip.

"Where is God indeed?" Adam mocked. "It appears that He is here with me, alive and well, and with power to do His will in every life."

– The End –

– DANisms –

- Part of winning is recognizing that it is temporary.
- The more I learn, the more I realize how little I really know.
- Self-defensiveness is the reaction to our realization that we have erred.
- Sharing a smile with you has made me a better person.
- Wisdom is often wrapped in unlikely paper.
- Life is like a cat, you can yell at it or accept it as it is, doesn't matter to the cat.
- A major part of learning is understanding that you need to learn.
- Seldom do we know what we know, mostly we continue to search for what we thought we knew.
- If you want to be great, be great – just stop looking for someone else to notice.
- Remember, even our mistakes have value. The one who was "crying over spilt milk" needed it for his cereal, but the dog who cleaned it up was smiling.
- Some things were meant to be walked on... beaches, sidewalks, flip flops... my right of choice of religious beliefs is not one of them.
- When you expect from man what only God can give, you'll live a life of fear and disappointment.
- Yes, you have the right to bare arms, but beware it can lead to skin cancer.
- Knowing what you are not is just as important as knowing what you are.
- It's a good thing that breathing is involuntary, some are too stupid to do it without government aid.

– AVAILABLE NOW –

The Cady Miller Series

SHIELD OF FAITH

"One more thing, Red, then if you want I'll shoot you, okay? Thing is, if you should beat me, I go to Heaven to be with the Lord, but if I beat you, where do you suppose you'll go for all eternity? Have you thought about how long forever in Hell might be?"

Red cursed again. "You don't worry about me miner, you worry about your little family here after I shoot you!"

SHIELD OF HONOR

Amid the explosions and aerial displays that marked our nation's Independence Day, he heard a yell followed by a louder and sharper report that was closely followed by a second and third. Cady, in his blue uniform with Kevlar vest and duty belt, was lifted off his feet by the impact and fell fifteen feet from the pier into the East River.

SHIELD OF JUSTICE

Unknown to others, Cady Miller was a dangerous man, having the physical and technical abilities to inflict mortal injury. His lean stature and rapidly advancing age belied his physical prowess. His pale blue eyes now retained their 20/20 vision by the use of contacts lenses, but more importantly he used that vision to see things others often missed. Skills honed through years of training and discipline allowed him to maintain an edge others frequently lost as the years caught up with them.

These and other offerings available at the Author's website:

www.danneyclark.com / www.danscribepublications.com

– ALSO AVAILABLE –

Chronicles of the WIDESPOT CAFÉ

After college, nine years went by quickly, I moved from job to job, town to town, never having a close relationship or a feeling of belonging. I worked in every industry, every position, in every field garnering small success but feeling alone and empty inside.

To my credit, I lived on my earnings, not touching my investments, but spending all that I made. I drove taxi, waited tables, painted houses, sold shoes, installed computers, cooked, drove truck, did construction, or whatever came along.

Young, healthy, and able to learn quickly, I was easily employable. I have never owned a house, a car, or been married. Like King Solomon, I searched for the meaning of life, and like him, I didn't find it. I had many friends, none close, no ties, few responsibilities, felt no kinship to anyone except possibly the friend and partner I knew in college. But he had now moved on and marched to a different beat.

Then one day I stopped by the Widespot Café intending to just have a meal... that day, it all changed for me. I met Mae and Jib.

ANTIQUES & ANTIQUITIES

Sitting back a distance from the heavily traveled highway linking the northern and southern parts of the state stands a building which looks much like an old barn. The outside is weathered and has been added onto many times by its various owners who were not very discerning in the design.

A large collection of discarded remnants of the past adorn its mottled exterior, adding both a cluttered look and a certain charm.

If only they could talk...

These and other offerings available at the Author's website:

www.danneyclark.com / www.danscribepublications.com

Spoonfuls From Heaven

This little book is much the same as a savory stew, made up of both large and small bites of various ingredients and with a dash of this here and a pinch of that there added for flavor.

Some readers will enjoy the texture and the flavor of the whole stew, while others may enjoy one ingredient more than another. Eaten as a meal, it is my prayer that you will find it both filling and satisfying. ~ Danney Clark

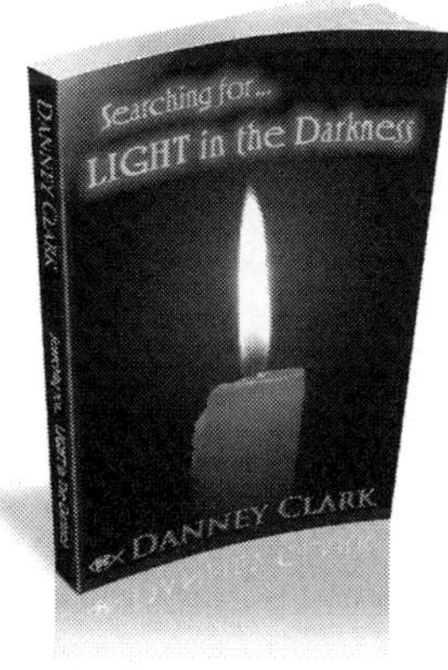

Searching for... LIGHT in the Darkness

Cremains / Dementia / The Birth of a Book
The Conversation / The Means to Murder
The Trigger
The End Game: An American Prophecy

Often we forget how great our God really is, by letting the fallen world overwhelm us and take away our joy. We should recognize that God created the world in the image of Himself, perfect and without sin. Man then, through his disobedience, opened the door to the sin about which these pages tell. Pay special attention to Cremains and recognize that the GOD who is great enough to create mankind is also great enough to forgive mankind and return him once again to perfection.

These and other offerings available at the Author's website:

www.danneyclark.com / www.danscribepublications.com

The EDUCATOR
Six Bright Bulbs

A U.S. History teacher chooses six over-achievers and challenges them to choose a person outside of their family who they feel represents a taste of America's past, then to write a biography of that person for a pass/fail semester grade.

These and other offerings available at the Author's website:

www.danneyclark.com / www.danscribepublications.com

About the Author

Danney Clark is first a practicing Christian, then a husband of nearly 50 years, a father of two daughters, and grandfather of two granddaughters. He is also an Idaho native who values and enjoys the outdoors in all of its varied forms that are so apparent in Idaho.

When he finds a challenge, he is passionate about pursuing it with diligence before moving onward to the next. Questionably an accomplished cook, he devotes much of his time to serving the homeless community and his church home.

His passion for many years has been writing and most recently, God-inspired Christian fiction, or "adventure with a spiritual message" as he calls it. He sees life as an adventure to be enjoyed, appreciated, and shared. Recent retirement has encouraged him to do so.

Made in the USA
San Bernardino, CA
17 October 2015